# THE REMAKE

# THE REMAKE

By Eve Marian

Paige Publishing

September 2022 First Edition



Cover designed by GetCovers

ISBN-eBook: 978-1-7780262-3-2
ISBN-paperback: 978-1-7780262-4-9
ISBN-hardcover: 978-1-7780262-5-6

# Dedication

To anyone who's ever dreamed of a second chance at life and love. This one's for you.

# 1

## Grace

Murmurs of conversation buzzed around me as I fought the urge to swat them away. Sitting at my desk, I held the backspace key and erased the last sentence of my email. Some of my accounting colleagues had pushed the office furniture back earlier, exposing more of the speckled gray vinyl underneath. They now laughed and mingled on that plastic floor, but I frowned as I peered down at my laptop.

*That statement isn't correct, is it? I should check the report again.*

My co-worker and best friend Omar leaned over the side of my cubicle, holding a plateful of cake. "Are you still working?" he asked. The accusation in his voice didn't warrant a response.

"I just need two more minutes," I said, not taking my eyes off my screen, despite the sweet smell of his strawberry and vanilla cake.

He sighed. "Grace, this is a party. Sometimes, you've got to let loose and enjoy the moment."

"Oh, please. It's a retirement party. And for someone whose position I'm after, might I remind you." Instinctively, my eyes flew toward the older man holding two drinks in his hand and the redhead beside him on the makeshift party floor. She laughed and spilled her drink on one of the lawyers from the fifth floor who stood next to her. She might not have looked like it, but Faith Allens was my biggest rival and the only other person qualified enough for the job I pursued. She appeared carefree except when her eyes hit mine, then she reminded me of a viper ready to strike.

Omar must have noticed my gaze wander, so he added, "They can't give her the senior audit manager position. You've been here longer."

I nodded but knew Omar was only trying to make me feel better. Delmar & Tuch didn't have any official policy on promotions, so I wasn't guaranteed to get the position simply because I had more experience than

Faith. Everyone knew she put in extra hours chatting and lunching with the partners while I barely left my office for a bathroom break.

"If I can finish my next project before the end of the week, I know I'll impress the partners. I'll have completed the most audits compared to anyone else in this firm. I don't want there to be any doubt in anyone's mind that I deserve this promotion."

Omar blew out a breath, but it didn't move his perfectly coiffed hair. "I can't believe we're talking about work at a party. You need to relax and have fun. Come have a drink with me."

Raising my fingers off the black keyboard, I listed the reasons why that was a bad idea. "Number one, I'm the designated driver today. Number two, I can't stay late. You know I have to get back home right after this."

"Fine," he huffed, pulling up a chair next to me.

"You don't have to stay with me while I work."

"Oh, I'm not. Because you're not working anymore." He pushed down the screen of my laptop and swiveled my thin black office chair to face him.

"Omar!"

He raised his eyebrow at me and I knew I'd lost this argument based on the sheer determination on his face.

Looking directly at me, Omar smiled. "That's better."

I rolled my eyes and ran my fingers through my hair. Omar had convinced me to cut it into a bob, and I didn't hate it.

"You need a distraction," Omar said, pulling out his phone. "I'm sure I can find some gossip to interest you." When I didn't respond, he looked up and noticed me holding my phone. I couldn't tell if he knew I was typing an email, but he grabbed my phone anyway and turned it face down on my desk. I blew out a frustrated sigh but turned my attention to him.

"Have you seen what the Crawford brothers have been up to? Colton is married, of course, but Luke is all over page six. Look at this." I peeked at the picture on his screen and my stomach churned.

*Oh, god. Of all the people in the world!*

He still had the same tousled light brown hair and green eyes, of course. But it was that smile, that *I-don't-give-a-crap-about-anything* smile that made me want to grab Omar's phone and smash it into a billion pieces underneath my three-inch heel.

"Oh honey, if you bite that lip any harder, you'll make it bleed," Omar said with a grin. "Here, take it."

He pushed the phone toward me, but I held my hands up.

"Don't you dare bring that face any closer to me," I said.

He laughed. "What's gotten into you?"

"That man made my life a living hell back in high school. I couldn't walk any hallway without someone whispering that awful nickname he gave me behind my back."

"A nickname? Well, maybe he liked you?"

I stared at him. "No. He didn't."

"What was the nickname?"

I puckered my lips but didn't say a word. I couldn't get the nickname out.

"Come on, Grace. You can tell me. What kind of nickname did he conjure from a sweet name like Grace Sweeney?" He leaned back and took a bite of his dessert.

I opened and closed my mouth, pressing down on my lips, battling between telling Omar the nickname and realizing it was silly. I gave up and told him. "From my freshman year to graduation, everyone called me *Meany Sweeney*." I'd even pronounced the words in the same taunting voice the kids at school had used.

Omar nearly choked on his cake and gently put his fork down. "I'm sorry," he said. "Did you say 'Meany Sweeny'?"

I narrowed my eyes at him. "I'm telling you this in the utmost confidence. No one has called me that in nearly ten years."

"Ah, honey," crooned Omar, rubbing my arm. "You can't still hate him for that after all these years?"

"You don't understand. It wasn't just the name. Everyone adored Luke. Everyone wanted his approval. If he hated you, then you were like a disease that no one wanted to catch. No one talked to me except for the new students until they realized they had to ditch me or die a social death. You're the first person I've trusted and gotten close to in a long time."

"Well, I'm irresistible and nothing would keep me from you. Not even a horrible nickname like Meany Sweeney."

I groaned. "Please don't say it again. I beg you."

"I won't," he said. "But you can't still be angry with him?"

I wasn't angry at him just because of the name. Luke Crawford had abandoned me when I needed him the most. But I couldn't tell Omar that.

When I didn't respond, Omar grabbed my hand. "Grace, you're a beautiful, successful, intelligent woman who'll be a partner in the largest accounting firm in the city one day. You can't still be mad at some guy from high school."

"Oh, I am," I laughed without humor. "If I ever see Luke Crawford again, he will regret the day he ever met me."

Omar's eyes widened and he looked at me sideways. "I can't tell if you're joking or not."

"I—"

A chime from my phone interrupted me. It was a message from Lorna: Grace, you need to come home quickly.

"I've got to go," I said, pushing back my chair and grabbing my jacket next to Omar.

"What's wrong?" he asked, standing up with me.

"Something happened at home. I'm sorry to cut this short, Omar, but I've got to take you home now."

Omar shook his head. "I'll take a taxi. Go. Don't worry about me."

I reached over and kissed him on the cheek. "Thank you," I whispered. Then, pushing past the crammed bodies next to the elevator, I made it past the entrance and into the parking lot.

Clenching my fist, I tried to calm my fears. Lorna hadn't mentioned what had happened and perhaps I was overreacting.

When I reached the foyer of my condo building, I cursed the slow elevator and the long ride up to the ninth floor. It felt like an hour had gone by instead of fifteen minutes when I finally opened my front door.

"Lorna!" I shouted.

"In here," she called from the bedroom.

Racing through the tiny apartment, I stumbled when I reached her bedroom door. "Mom," I said, breathless.

"Oh, Grace. I told Lorna not to call you." I knew my mother smiled to make me feel better, but it didn't distract me from the bruise forming on her left cheek.

"What happened?" I asked, turning to Lorna.

The petite brunette wrung her hands, but the concern in her eyes comforted me. "She was already in bed when I heard a crash," she said. "I ran into her room and found her on the floor bleeding. I'm so sorry."

"It's not your fault, Lorna," said my mother. "Don't let my daughter's shocked face scare you." She was in bed and the bed sheet covered her frail body.

I shook my head and tried to fix my face. "Mom, what did you do?"

"I was just trying to go to the bathroom. Is that a crime?"

I closed my eyes to maintain my composure because I wanted to scream. "No, of course not," I said instead. "But you know you're supposed to call Lorna whenever you want to get out of bed. You're too weak to make it on your own."

My mother's smile disappeared and her jaw clenched. "I'm not weak," she said. "It was just an accident and you are overreacting."

I sighed. She was as stubborn as I was. "Fine, Mom. Let me just get you some pain meds and I'll be right back."

I wanted her to stop denying what was going on. She was sick and needed a kidney transplant to get better.

I slammed the kitchen cabinet and winced, knowing my mother had probably heard it. Oh well. I didn't care anymore if she heard how upset I was. I *was* mad. It wasn't fair. We never got a break. Ever.

My mother raised me as a single parent. I had to work twice as hard as any other kid to stay in my private high school and maintain my scholarship. Then, in my senior year of college, after the doctors broke the news to us that the cheaper drugs weren't working anymore, I realized I had to land a job at the biggest accounting firm in the city to pay for her medical bills. And now the new meds seemed to no longer be working.

I would scream until my throat hurt if I thought, this time, it would do any good.

Instead, I laid my head on the kitchen table and let the cold surface cool down my nerves. I had to stay positive. I worked at Delmar & Tuch. I was up for the senior audit manager position and would make enough money to pay for better meds and a transplant for my mother one day.

Pep talk over, I stood from the table and walked over to the bedroom. "Here you go, Mom." I handed her the pills, then a glass of water by her bedside.

"Thank you, honey," she said after taking a sip of the water. "How was the party?"

I smiled weakly. "It was great. Lots of fun."

Her smile turned up on the side and she shook her head. "You can't fool me, Grace. You had a terrible time. Didn't you?"

"It wasn't terrible."

"Did you meet anyone?"

"No, Mom." She was constantly trying to set me up on a date. Anytime I didn't make plans on the weekend, her forehead would crease and she would give me these sad, puppy dog eyes. I knew she worried about me, but I had too much to deal with right now to think about dating.

"What about Omar? He's a fine young gentleman," she said, her eyes brightening.

"He's not interested in me, Mom. Our tastes are too similar."

She frowned. "Well, it's still early. Get back to that party and have some fun. You can't stay home with your mother."

"It's fine. I have work to do, anyway. You saved me from a terrible hangover."

"Oh, sweetie. Just one time, I wish you would know what a hangover feels like." She shook her head, as though upset that I wasn't a bigger disappointment to her as a teenager. I snorted at the displeasure on her face.

"Good night, Mom." I switched off her bedside lamp.

"Good night, honey." She closed her eyes and her head fell to the side of her pillow.

Lorna followed me out of the room. "Thank you, Lorna," I said. Hiring her was the best decision I'd made in a long time. I couldn't work knowing my mom would be home alone. "See you on Monday?"

"See you then." She grabbed her purse from the coat rack. "Your mom's right, you know. You should try to work less. I'd be happy to stay with your mom tomorrow night so you can go out. You deserve it, Grace."

"Thanks, Lorna. But I don't really have any place to go."

Her eyes looked sad, but I was fine with it. Sitting at home with a good book, a gallon of ice cream, and a warm espresso was exactly the way I wanted to spend my Saturday night.

After locking the door behind Lorna, I checked on my mom. Her body slumped to the side and she snored softly. Tucking the blanket around her shoulders, I couldn't help but notice how much smaller she had become in the last few months. Time was running out.

Determined, I walked back to the kitchen and fired up my laptop. My assistant should have emailed me my next audit by now. He knew I liked to have it before the weekend. Ah, and there it was, an email from Jackson.

I needed coffee before I settled in to research the company for my next audit. I had one of those fancy espresso machines, but tonight I brewed a pot. It could be a long night.

Setting the coffee to brew, I settled back into my seat and opened the email. Yadda, yadda, yadda, oh, here it is:

"Grace," Jackson's email read. "The next audit will be located downtown. The name of the company is Crawford Corporation."

There was another sentence with an address and something about parking, but my mind was stuck on the company name. Crawford Corporation.

*No. It couldn't be. It had to be some sort of coincidence.*

I frantically typed the name of the company into my browser, and the first hit was the company's website. I scanned it as quickly as I could and read the About Us page. There was a photo of Colton Crawford, the CEO. He looked like the same grumpy boy I remembered from high school. There was also a photo of his brother Ryan. Panicked, I scrolled to the bottom, but there was no photo of Luke. Maybe he didn't work with his brothers. Maybe he just stayed in bed all day and did nothing for a living except travel to Caribbean islands. I could picture that.

My heart slowed down and I breathed in deeply. I hadn't realized how anxious I'd become until the fear had fled. I had jumped to conclusions and overreacted. Luke wouldn't be there on Monday. I had nothing to worry about.

I needed this audit to run smoothly and killing Luke would not please my bosses. But it would make me feel a hell of a lot better. I frowned, feeling a tiny bit disappointed he wouldn't be there and I wouldn't get the chance.

The disappointment had nothing to do with wanting to see Luke again.

# 2

## Luke

*Mmm, this is good, but not spicy enough.*

I reached for the chili powder and carefully tapped a few sprinkles onto the eggs.

*Just a splash of milk—oh and maybe some onion powder, too.*

After adding the extra ingredients, I stirred them all together and took another bite.

*That's it. That's perfection.*

"Oh my god, what are you cooking? I could smell it from the foyer." Erika, the front desk receptionist for the twelfth floor, popped her head into the staff lunchroom, which was located just down the hall from her desk.

"Just some scrambled eggs and bacon. Do you want some?" I plated the eggs onto two dishes and added the bacon I had fried up earlier.

Erika appeared next to me and inhaled a deep breath. "Luke, why do we rarely see you at Crawford Corp? The staff needs you," she teased.

"Because I hate wearing a suit and tie. And then I'd be a miserable asshole just like my brother Colton."

"Well, he isn't so miserable anymore," said Erika, winking at me.

"God bless Frannie," I said. "She's a saint. I don't know how she puts up with him."

"She's amazing and super patient," said Erika. It was obvious Erika was Frances's best friend and still her fiercest supporter, next to my brother.

"So, what are you doing here? Besides, cooking a fine breakfast," she asked, tasting the eggs. She closed her eyes and sighed. I loved the look of a well-satisfied woman. Too bad Erika was already taken. But still, I couldn't help myself.

"What are you doing this weekend?" I asked her, adding more eggs to her plate.

She shook her finger at me. "Oh, don't tempt me, Luke," she said, laughing. "Even though you'd be the only Crawford that could."

"I'm honored," I said, enjoying Erika's good opinion of me.

"Besides, I'm sure you already have plans."

I did. But I would change them for a hard-working girl like Erika.

Putting a hand on her hip, she said, "You still haven't answered my question."

I had forgotten it. I wasn't sure what distracted me more, a beautiful woman standing before me or sharing a meal with one. "What was it again?"

"What are you doing here?"

"Oh that. Yes, most likely my subconscious wanted to forget you had even asked."

She snorted but it was the truth. "I'm here because my brothers guilted me into it. Said they needed my help with business or some bullshit like that."

"You don't sound thrilled about it."

"I'm not the corporate type, in case you haven't noticed." I pointed to my tie that I'd flung onto the chair earlier. "I'm showing up for the meeting and then skipping out for the rest of the afternoon."

"Good luck with that," said Erika. "Colton may be less miserable now that he's with Frannie, but he isn't stupid. You won't get away with it."

I grinned. "I can get away with anything I put my mind to."

Erika looked up with a sly smile. "I bet you could, Luke. I don't doubt it for a minute." She shook her head and left with the plate still in her hands. I chuckled, pleased she was going to finish her breakfast.

"Luke," Colton shouted from his office, which was at the opposite end of the hallway, but his voice carried well enough.

"Erika's wrong. He's still miserable," I muttered on my way to his office, grabbing my tie.

"You bellowed?" Leaning against the door frame, I wrapped the tie around my neck.

He narrowed his eyes and sniffed twice. "Are you cooking?" His dark eyebrows nearly touched his hairline in disbelief.

"Yes."

"We don't have a stove on this floor. How the fuck are you cooking?"

With a shrug, I explained, "I brought a portable countertop burner with me this morning."

"A what?"

"It's like a stovetop—"

"I don't care what it is," he barked. "Why are you cooking? You're here to work."

I rolled my eyes. "I don't work for you, Colton."

"That's why I asked you to join me for this meeting." He pointed to a black leather chair in front of his desk. "Have a seat."

"I'd rather stand."

He stared at me and I stared back. I don't know why I was being stubborn, except that my brothers and I usually made everything a competition.

"Suit yourself," he said and sighed. "Look. Ryan and I have indulged you for several years now."

My eyes widened and I nearly choked on the insult. "You've indulged me? How?"

"We've let you run wild and free and party to your heart's content. It's time to settle down now, Luke."

"What does that even mean, Colton? You want me to get married?"

"No, no. I'm just saying I've watched you bounce around with no purpose. I'd like to give you a seat here at Crawford Corporation."

"I don't want a seat here. Thanks for asking."

He ran a hand through his dark hair, which he inherited from our father. "Our father worked too damn hard to leave us an inheritance and a legacy. You can't live your life with no care, Luke. I'm your family. Let me help you."

"I have no interest in wheeling and dealing. I'm not like you, Colton. And I don't have a law degree like Ryan. I went to college, but nothing grabbed me. You know?"

"No, I don't know. What I do know, however, is what needs to be done. I've always carried that on my shoulders. You've had no responsibilities, and that's going to change."

"What are you talking about?"

"I want you to take over operations."

When my face went blank, he continued. "You will oversee the major building developments and report back to me if there are any setbacks, and we will work through them together. I need someone I trust to tell me exactly what's going on in the field. You'll understand the issues, as you've always been good with your hands."

I winked. "You heard the rumors, too. Have you?"

"Shut up. I'm serious."

I blew out a frustrated breath. "I know little about the company. I'm not your man, Colton. I'm sorry."

He persisted. "We have auditors coming in this week. I want you to help them with anything they need.

It will be a good chance for you to familiarize yourself with our projects and how we run the company."

"And if I don't agree to your stupid game of *Let's teach Luke a lesson*?"

"This isn't a game, Luke. This is business." His jaw did that funny tick thing it always did before he blew up.

I had said no to Colton so many times but he still didn't get it. He never listened to me. Maybe I should show him how terrible I'd be at this job. If I messed this up, Colton would be furious, but he'd finally understand that I wanted nothing to do with the family business and get off my back.

I smiled. "Fine. I'll do it."

"That's the Crawford spirit," he said, returning my smile. Only my lips curled up a little more than his.

*We'll see who's still smiling at the end of this.*

Colton checked his watch. "That must be them," he said, staring down the hallway.

Turning, I saw a pair of suits walking toward us. A man in striped navy pants and a jacket walked next to a woman in a tight black pencil skirt and a white silk blouse. The way she swayed her hips made my palms itch to hold them. Her short black hair framed a heart-shaped face and two dark eyebrows slashed into a straight line as she approached. Her eyes met mine and they narrowed.

That was when I recognized her.

*Meaney Sweeney.*

What *the fuck* was she doing here?

Her white blouse rose and fell with her rapid breaths and her nostrils flared. She looked as pissed off as I felt. Good.

I hadn't seen *Meaney Sweeney* in ten years. That wasn't long enough. I had hoped to never lay eyes on her again.

"Good morning. I'm Colton Crawford and this is my brother Luke." Colton shook hands with the pair. The guy in the suit reached across to shake my hand. I gripped it, perhaps a little bit too long, as I delayed my next move. She hesitantly brought her hand forward and I took it, preparing to intimidate her.

Her small hand squeezed mine harder than I'd expected and her red-painted thumbnail pressed painfully into my skin. My eyes shot up and her smile warned me she'd done it on purpose.

*Oh, game on, Sweeney!*

I caressed my thumb across hers and wiggled my finger inside her palm. She snatched it back. I smiled, glad that I could still unsettle her.

"Why don't we all take a seat in our boardroom? You can set up your laptops and work from there this week." Colton led us down the hallway and into the boardroom. A large mahogany table and twelve white leather chairs filled most of the room.

Sweeney pushed past me to take a seat at the head of the table while the other auditor sat down beside her.

"This room will do nicely, thank you," she said as she opened her laptop. "Have you brought the files we requested earlier? I'd like to get started right away."

She kept her gaze on Colton, but I noticed her eyes shift in my direction before she immediately refocused.

"Luke will grab them for you. He will be your point person for the audit."

"Luke?" she asked, her eyes widening. "I didn't realize he worked here. He wasn't mentioned on the website."

"You looked me up?" I asked, raising my eyebrow.

"I was conducting proper research into my next audit," she snapped back.

Perhaps. But I wasn't convinced. I bet Meany Sweeney still imagined different ways to kill me. She would relish every moment of my torture, judging by the daggers she threw at me every time her eyes met mine.

"Today is his first day, but Luke is familiar with the family business."

"Mr. Crawford, I think it's best if our team works with someone with a bit more experience than..." She looked down at her phone. "Thirty minutes."

"Forty-five," I whispered with a grin in her direction.

"My apologies," she said with a fake smile. "Forty-five minutes."

Colton crossed his arms. "I understand your concern... Miss?"

Her face froze and she darted a look in my direction, daring me to say it. But I held back.

"Sweeney," she said. "And it's *Ms.* Sweeney."

*Huh.* I hadn't thought of it. Was Meany Sweeney married? Did she lay those sharp eyes on some other man every night?

*Poor bastard.*

"Right. Ms. Sweeney," Colton said, correcting himself. "I have the utmost faith in my brother and know he will help you with whatever you need."

"Absolutely," I said. "It will be my pleasure to hamper—I mean help—however I can."

She frowned and her full lips puckered into a sour pout.

"I'm sure your brother will be fine, Mr. Crawford," said the accountant beside her. His eyes bounced between us. I wasn't sure if he was afraid of my brother or Grace. I would bet a little of both and just wanted to move on from this awkward stand-off. I pitied him and what he would endure over the next week.

Grace sighed. "Fine. Let's get started then. Shall we?" She sat back in the leather chair and crossed her legs. I didn't recall Sweeney having long legs. She always wore those baggy jeans and frumpy sweaters.

"Mr. Crawford!"

I wondered if she wore nylons or if those were her bare legs.

Colton nudged me and nodded toward Sweeney. "I think she's talking to you."

Her eyes blazed as I grinned back. "Yes?"

"I will need all your bank statements for the last fiscal year," she said, then smiled. "Now."

Colton narrowed his eyes and whispered. "Do you two know each other?" Then he turned toward me and nudged me to the other side of the room. "Shit. Did you date her? Looks like it didn't end well."

"No. We never dated, but we went to school together."

"Well, you must have done something to her because even I'm impressed with her stare-down approach." He looked over my shoulder at Sweeney and gave a small smile of approval.

"If you like her so much, why don't you take over this audit?" I suggested.

"No, little brother. This time you're going to step up and take responsibility."

I shook my head. Just because I didn't work for Colton didn't make me irresponsible. But he would never see it that way. Not until I showed him how much I didn't belong here.

"Not a problem," I said. "I'll get right on that."

Turning to the auditors, I smiled. "I'll get you those papers right away."

"Thank you," she said and fired up her laptop.

Then I left and walked toward the staff room, thinking which ingredients I could use next to make an omelet, leaving any further thoughts of Meany Sweeney and my task behind.

# 3

## Grace

James looked down at his watch again.

"How long has it been, James?" I asked, not looking up from my laptop.

"One hour," he said. "I'm sure he's just locating everything."

"Crawford Corp knew about this audit months ago. They would've prepared everything before our arrival." I pushed my chair back and removed my blue light glasses. "I'll go find him and see what's taking so long."

Walking down the hallway, I didn't see Luke standing in front of the cubicles, nor was he at the front desk. I walked toward the row of offices to check if he was inside one of them. Colton sat at his desk in the largest office at the far end but no sign of Luke.

Then I heard something.

A soft humming, followed by the low baritone of a man singing a song I didn't recognize but the melody sounded familiar. When I turned the corner, I found Luke in front of some portable burner with a black spatula in his hand and his tie flung over his shoulder. The muscles in his upper back bunched when he flipped something in the skillet and my eyes locked on his bare forearms. He must have rolled up his sleeves before he started cooking. My stomach tightened and I felt sick at my involuntary reaction.

I cleared my throat.

He turned around and his big smile quickly dropped into a frown. "Oh, it's you," he said and turned back to his skillet.

"What are you doing?" I asked through gritted teeth.

"What does it look like I'm doing, *Ms.* Sweeney?"

"It looks like you're not doing your job." I crossed my arms, annoyed that twenty-eight-year-old Luke was no different from the seventeen-year-old boy I remembered. He took nothing seriously. Why should he? He was rich, good-looking, and everyone liked him. He never had to work for anything, including this job. "Why are you even here if you're not helping us?"

"Do you prefer your omelet runny or firm?" he asked as he tossed a pinch of salt into the pan.

"I don't like omelets. I prefer my eggs scrambled," I answered without thinking. I shook my head. "Luke, why are you here?"

He turned off the burner and grabbed a plate. "I'm here because you, *Ms. Sweeney,* will help me prove something to Colton."

The salty scent of the eggs reached me and I hated how much I wanted to taste them. "What's that? That you're terrible at this job?" I snapped.

His eyes shot up to mine and he smiled.

*Seriously*! *Is that why he's in the kitchen instead of helping us with the files?*

Luke Crawford hadn't changed one bit.

"Look, I know this job means little to you, but I take my responsibilities seriously."

"You always took everything too seriously," he said nonchalantly.

If I could scream at him with my eyes, I would. I would tell him what an arrogant jerk he was, but I had to keep my cool in the office. "I need those financials on my desk in ten minutes. Is that clear, Mr. Crawford?"

"Crystal," he said, and his grin reached his eyes.

I turned on my heel and marched out of the staff room.

Arrogant, spoiled, lazy bastard. That's what Luke Crawford was. I couldn't believe fate put him in my path again. I had hoped never to see him again, but now he stood in the way of me wrapping up this audit in record time. I wouldn't let him get away with it. Not this time. No. This time, I wouldn't hide in the hallways or behind my locker door. I would fight back.

A few minutes later, after having settled back down in front of my laptop, Luke walked into the boardroom with a steaming plate in one hand and several paper plates in the other.

"I brought breakfast," he announced, laying the dish in the center of the boardroom table.

"Thank you, but—"

James cut me off when he pushed his chair back and shouted, "All right!"

Luke's eyes met mine across the room and he smirked. I simply shook my head, realizing that not only had Luke not changed, but people still crumbled at his feet whenever he walked into a room. But not me. Not anymore.

"Have you brought the financials?" I asked, tapping my pen on the table.

"Our accountant, Daniel, has emailed them to you. You should have them in your Inbox already."

I checked my email and saw the message from Daniel. "I thought it was your job to provide us with the information?"

"I did. I just got someone else to send it to you. Work smarter, not harder. That's always been my motto."

"I'm surprised you work at all," I mumbled.

"Pardon?"

"Never mind," I said. "We're good for now. You can go back to doing whatever you'd rather be doing right now."

When he didn't reply with a smart comeback, I looked up at him. His eyes roamed over me, then settled on my face. I narrowed my eyes.

"Your hair's shorter," he said, his voice low.

"I'm surprised you noticed." I ran my fingers through my hair and pushed it behind my ear, but a few strands fell over my cheek.

He pulled in his bottom lip then smirked. "Oh, I notice everything about you, Sweeney."

His words unnerved me. We were friends once when we were little. But then we started high school and everything changed. If Luke Crawford had noticed me in high school, it was only to make my life miserable.

"Great. So, you'll see that I'm quite busy right now. I'll call for you if we need anything else." I wanted him gone. I didn't want him looking at me or helping me. Sticking my nose inside my laptop, I prayed he would leave.

Finally, he walked out and I exhaled in relief. I stared at my screen, but instead of the financial report, I saw Luke's fourteen-year-old face.

*

*Fourteen years earlier…*

Luke stood next to me at my locker. He had shaved off his curly brown hair over the summer before high school, making his green eyes and long lashes stand out.

Staring at the color photocopy of The Mona Lisa I taped to my locker, he asked, "Why do you love this painting so much? She looks miserable."

I frowned in confusion. "What do you mean? She's smiling."

He snorted. "No. She's not."

"That's because you're looking at her mouth," I explained.

He shook his head and chuckled. "Grace, sometimes you make no sense at all."

Then he grabbed my backpack and swung it over his shoulder. "Are you still coming to my baseball game tonight?"

I shut the locker door and snapped on the lock. "What time does it start?"

"Four-thirty. You're coming, right?"

"Yeah, I'll be there."

"Okay, because that's what you said last time, but then you didn't show up." His voice trailed off. I nearly missed his words.

"I'm sorry. My mom was helping me with my art project and we both lost track of time. It won't happen again. I'll set an alarm."

He smiled and nudged me on my shoulder. "You better. I really want you there."

I laughed. "I'll be there. Don't worry. This means a lot to you, huh?"

He looked straight ahead and nodded.

"I'll be there," I told him and he walked me to my next class.

I was excited to go to his game. I had every intention of going until I arrived home from school and found my mother lying on the kitchen floor. That night was the first time my mother had passed out. But it wouldn't be the last. Shouting her name, I rushed over to her. As I scooped her head into my arms, I felt a faint pulse beating on her neck. Pulling out my cell phone from my bag, I dialed 911. Shortly after the ambulance rushed us to the emergency room, the doctors told me my mother's kidneys weren't functioning properly and they would have to run some more tests after she was stable. They told me to go home as there was nothing I could do for her right now.

I went home alone, crawled into bed, and cried. I switched my pillow when the cotton became too wet against my cheek. When I soaked that one too, I left it alone, too weak to grab a new one.

I knew my eyes were swollen when I went to school the next day, but I didn't care. My mother was sick and I didn't know if she would get better.

I glimpsed his navy blue and white varsity jacket turning the corner, and I exhaled. Tears brimmed my eyes but I held off the tears. I wasn't sure if I would tell anyone about my mom, but seeing his face, I realized I could trust him with this.

As Luke walked toward me, he kept his gaze straight. I shut my locker and inhaled a deep breath, prepared to go into the awful details of last night. But as he approached, his eyes didn't catch mine and he didn't slow down his pace. He walked right past me as though he hadn't stopped here every morning since we started high school three months ago. I called out his name, but he didn't turn around. Instead, he joined a group of boys laughing and shoving each other. One of them nodded at Luke and they both turned to look at me. Luke's cold stare shocked me. The other guy smiled and patted Luke on the shoulder, pulling him into the group.

Luke didn't speak to me for the rest of the day. He sat next to someone else in the classes we shared and chose a new table for lunch. He didn't even answer his phone when I called him. Finally, that night, I remembered. I had missed his baseball game. Again.

I felt bad for a second but anger quickly replaced that sentiment. How dare he be angry at me for such a small thing when my entire world had gone black last night? I thought he cared about me. I thought he was my friend. Well, I didn't need friends like Luke Crawford. I would take care of my mother. I would take care of myself. I didn't need anyone else. And I definitely didn't need him.

*

"Grace? Are you all right?" James leaned over the boardroom table and waved his hand. "Earth to Grace."

Shaking the memories from my head, I replied, "Yes. Fine."

"You drifted off somewhere else for a while there," he chuckled.

"Just thinking about this report, that's all." I blinked several times to regain my visual bearings.

*Ah, there we are, last year's expenditures report.*

I sank into my chair and lost myself in my work.

The two of us worked for the next few hours, speaking only to answer one another's questions. But when my stomach growled, James looked up and said, "Oh good. You're hungry too?"

I tapped on my phone to check the time. It was 12:30 p.m. "Yeah. Now would be a good time to break for lunch." I shut down my laptop and pushed back my chair. As I turned to unplug my device, the boardroom door opened.

"Looks like my timing is right. I came to offer to take the team out to Ruth's Sports Bar for lunch. The baseball game starts soon."

Of course, it did. Charming and fun, Luke would be the one wanting to take the credit for good timing and an opportune lunch invitation.

"Actually—" I began, but Luke cut me off.

He shrugged. "You can come, too, if you want."

I could come, *too*? Was he kidding? Was he really just inviting me now, as though I weren't part of the original offer? I didn't appreciate him making me look bad in front of my colleague. I was going to decline his offer but not now. Besides, James's face was giddy enough at the prospect of catching some of the game to make him leap onto Luke's back and ride him to the restaurant.

*Ugh, men!*

James turned puppy-dog eyes onto me. "Grace…" he pleaded.

I closed my eyes and sighed. "Let's go."

Luke smiled as though he'd won some standoff, and perhaps he had. But I would not let him get the best of me.

We walked down the hallway and past the front desk receptionist.

"Can I bring you back anything from Ruth's, Erika?" Luke asked as we waited for the elevator.

"I'm good, hun. But thanks for asking."

"I'll never stop asking, darling," he drawled and I rolled my eyes.

Erika smiled even though she shook her head. Why do we all love charmers, even when we see through them? I never understood the appeal, especially knowing that the façade of them caring about us crumbled when we really needed them.

Ruth's Sports Bar was only a block away but I'd worn my three-inch heels today and there was no way I could keep up with the pace Luke set.

I wouldn't let it bother me. I watched as they walked further away. I took my time, staring at the local shops and some of the merchandise set on the sidewalk.

"Try to keep up, Sweeney," Luke said. His voice had the same irritating effect on me, and I nearly growled back at him. Without taking an extra moment to think about it, I removed my heels, one foot at a time.

I marched up behind them and pushed Luke out of the way. "What the…" his voice trailed off when he noticed it was me and not someone else.

"Keep up, did you say? You're the one dragging his feet now."

I heard a sharp intake of breath behind me and perhaps even a low growl, but I didn't turn around. I kept the pace until I walked into the bar and dusted off the soles of my feet before slipping back into my heels. I'd managed to straighten up before the men joined me. Exhaling, I squared my shoulders and pasted a smirk onto my face.

"What took you so long, Crawford? With your long stride, you should've kept up."

He leaned forward, turning his back to James, and whispered in my ear, "So you've noticed the length of me?"

"What?" I sputtered. "No. That's disgusting."

He laughed and winked. "Your face is turning red, Sweeney," he said in a low voice. "I think you're lying."

I wanted to shout, "I'm not, you jerk," but James was too close now, so I said nothing.

James stared at me, though. His eyebrows pulled together. If he suspected that Luke and I knew each other, he kept it to himself.

Luke walked up to the hostess and lowered his head to her. She giggled at something he said and pushed his shoulder with her long, manicured nails. He laughed too and slipped something into her palm.

*Is it his phone number?*

*Who cares… I sure didn't.*

The hostess led us to a table next to the bar where three large screens televised the game. Luke ordered a pitcher of beer and some appetizers for the table, including fried shrimp. I hated beer and fried shrimp, especially together, and Luke knew it. I got sick one night when we were thirteen. Luke brought the beer and I brought the fried shrimp. He was trying to forget something and I was trying to impress him. We didn't get very far into our meal when Luke reached over and held my hair as I puked in a flower pot and swore to never touch the stuff again. I kept that promise. I'm stubborn that way.

It took a while for the food to arrive, but Luke and James didn't seem to mind, their attention focused on the game. I reached for my phone, but as I rummaged through my purse, I realized I'd left it in the boardroom.

*Damn it! Why don't I wear a watch?*

I squinted toward the TV screens, but the time was too small for me to tell. Luke looked over his shoulder at me and smiled. "Are you not having a good time, Sweeney? You haven't touched your drink." He looked pointedly down at the pitcher in front of me.

This felt like some sort of test. Luke dared me to take a sip of that beer with his eyes and I would not back down.

I faked a smile and picked up the pitcher. "Of course, I'm having a good time. I've never had more fun in my life." I poured the foamy brew into a glass and brought it to my lips. The yeasty smell made my stomach roll and I pressed my lips together to hold back a gag. "Mmm smells delicious," I said.

Luke's lips twitched but his eyes gave his amusement away. They danced as though they'd seen nothing as funny as this before.

"Go on, take a sip," he teased.

I inhaled through my mouth and exhaled through my nostrils to push away the smell as I poured the disgusting drink into my mouth. I gulped it quickly before my taste buds could register the vile substance, but I wasn't fast enough. My stomach heaved and I closed my eyes, praying I wouldn't chuck it up in front of James and the entire bar. I fought the smell of beer and fried shrimp in the back of my mind.

When I opened them, Luke's face had changed. His eyes narrowed and he shook his head as though disappointed.

*Ha! Didn't think I could manage that, did you?*

My moment of glory vanished when my stomach curled and a wave of nausea rolled through me.

"Excuse me," I said as I pushed back my seat.

"What's the matter, Sweeney?" asked Luke in a voice that told me he knew exactly what was wrong. I glanced in James's direction, but he hadn't turned his attention away from the TV.

"Oh, shut up," I hissed and ran to the washroom.

I grabbed the sink with both hands and dry heaved a few times, but successfully kept the contents of my stomach in place. I rinsed my mouth to remove any last remnants of the horrible drink. It didn't matter how many years had gone by; my stomach hadn't forgotten that night even though I so desperately wanted to forget it.

By the time I returned to our table, my Cobb Salad waited for me. Too bad, I couldn't say the same for my colleague. With his jacket off, James rolled up his sleeves and dug into his wings with gusto. Luke sat sipping his beer but hadn't touched his burger yet. I would have thought it polite if he hadn't grabbed his beer and slowly sipped his drink when he saw me. I swallowed another wave of sickness at the memory it induced.

"Did you know the Cobb Salad originated in California back in 1937?" asked Luke, holding his beer.

When I gave him a side glare, I thought that would shut him up. But he continued.

"The owner, Robert Cobb, threw some leftovers together, poured some French dressing on top, and Voila!"

"Fascinating," I deadpanned and stabbed a hard-boiled egg with my fork.

Luke winced but didn't say another word, opting to take a bite from his hamburger instead.

"So, James, have you ever been to a game?" asked Luke.

James licked the sauce from his fingers, one by one. "Of course, I have."

I tuned out the rest of their conversation to finish my lunch. After clearing my plate, I wiped my mouth and said, "I think it's time we get back to the office."

James nodded, but Luke interjected. "Don't be silly." He checked his watch. It looked expensive. "We have plenty of time."

"Are you sure?" asked James.

"Of course I am." Luke smiled. "Besides, we haven't even ordered dessert."

"I don't think that's necessary," I said. "We have a lot to do."

"It will still be there when you get back."

"Come on, Grace. Surely, another fifteen minutes won't hurt," pleaded James, but his eyes were glued to the screen. "We didn't take any time during our last project."

I struggled not to roll my eyes at my colleague. Was I the only one who respected work time?

"Fifteen minutes," I warned.

"No problem," said Luke, and he waved the server over. "Please bring us one of everything on your dessert menu."

I groaned. This would take longer than fifteen minutes; I was sure of it.

Two innings later, dessert arrived. I hated to admit my mouth watered at the brownie cheesecake and I may have taken a spoonful of Luke's Crème brûlée when he wasn't looking. Leaning back in my chair, satisfied and replete, I watched the game. The home team was winning and James high-fived Luke when the latest run came in to score.

"That's it for the seventh inning," said Luke.

"Seventh inning?" I asked, trying to remember how long each inning took. I recalled a game lasting nearly three hours and if it were the seventh inning, it would be nearly over. "Oh my god, how long have we been gone?"

Luke checked his watch. "Not long," he said.

"How long, Luke?" I asked, gritting my teeth.

"It's not even three o'clock yet," he muttered.

"Three o'clock?" My voice sounded shrill. "You mean we've been here for over two and a half hours?"

He grinned and sipped his damn beer. "Yep. And I saw you take a bite of my Crème brûlée."

# 4

## Grace

James looked as horrified as I did. "We should get going," he said.

*Do you think?* I wanted to scream but kept my composure.

"Let's go." I grabbed my purse and pulled out my credit card.

Luke waved me off. "I invited you. I will take care of the bill. You go on ahead."

I nodded and rushed out the door, with James right behind me.

"Don't worry, Grace. It's no big deal, really," started James as we walked back. "We'll get the audit done."

"I wanted to get it done by the end of the week."

"Oh," said James. "Well, in that case…"

I groaned. It didn't matter. I would bring work home with me tonight to make up for the extra-long lunch. I was used to it, anyway.

"It's fine. We'll get back on track. But for the rest of the week, we have to keep it simple. When the audit is over, I promise to take you out for a huge lunch. Deal?"

"That's a deal, Grace," said James.

"Good."

My shoulders relaxed and my lungs loosened the closer to the office we got. Heading up the elevator of Crawford Corporation, I even smiled at James when he recounted some of the best plays of the game.

I knew I took work more seriously than others did. While I wasn't sure if that was because of my circumstances or personality, it didn't really matter. I didn't have the luxury to take my time climbing the corporate ladder. I needed to get to the next pay grade fast. Otherwise, the consequences would be too horrible to consider.

Settling back into the boardroom, I'd barely opened my email when Colton Crawford walked into the room.

"Ms. Sweeney," he said, putting his hands in his suit pockets.

I folded my hands underneath my chin, in a semblance of calm, even if the look in his eyes worried me. "Yes, Mr. Crawford?"

"Someone from your office has been calling here for the past couple of hours looking for you. I told him I'd let you know as soon as you returned. The name he left was Steinberg." He nodded, satisfied having delivered his message, and left the room.

On the outside, I sat still, but my insides were screaming. *Oh, shit!*

Glenn Steinberg had called here, looking for me? I checked my phone. He had called it as soon as we'd left for lunch. That was nearly three hours ago.

When I turned toward James, he held his phone in his hands and cringed. He adjusted his glasses. "Four missed calls," he said. "I had the ringer on silent. I'm so sorry, Grace."

"It's okay, James. I'll handle it."

I walked out of the boardroom for privacy and made my way down the hallway. Sticking my head inside the staff lunchroom, I noticed it was empty. I called Glenn's number.

"Hello?"

"Mr. Steinberg? Hi, it's Grace Sweeney returning your call."

There was a pause.

"I guess three hours late is better than never," he said in a gruff voice. "What happened?"

"I'm sorry, sir. We had lunch with the client and lost track of time. It won't happen again." I paced the room. I hated taking the blame for a lunch I didn't even want, but since I was the lead on this audit, being accountable was my responsibility.

"Look, Grace. I hope I don't have to tell you what a big client Crawford Corporation is."

"You don't, sir."

"I put you on this audit because I know you can deliver."

"I can, sir."

"Good. Now, there are a few things I wanted to discuss with you."

I nodded as Steinberg shot off his instructions. I somehow found a pen in the staffroom and scribbled notes on a napkin. After ending the call, I sat at one of the back tables and finished writing my thoughts on the makeshift paper.

Others must have walked in because I heard whispering, but I ignored it until a certain name popped up. "Did you see Luke?"

"I sure did," someone said and giggled.

"I hear he's staying all week," another said.

"Well, I hope he's here longer than a week. Do you see how cute Colton is with Frances? I bet Luke would be just as amazing with his significant other."

*Ha! I doubt it. Luke only cares about one person in this world. Himself.*

"I hear he's great with his hands in the kitchen," said a deeper voice. "I bet he knows how to use them in the bedroom, too." They all laughed.

I stood, not wanting to hear another word about how great Luke would be as a lover. I would probably gag harder than I did with the beer.

"Ladies. Gentleman. How's it going?" a familiar voice crooned into the staffroom.

*Great, the man himself comes to receive his daily dose of adoration.*

I kept my gaze ahead and walked right past him.

"Sweeney, wait," he called after me.

"What do you want, Crawford?" I asked, crossing my arms over my chest.

"I wanted to check in with you. I heard your boss called and sounded upset. Look, if you need me to call him back and save you the scolding, I'll do it."

I smiled, but judging from the confusion on his face, it probably wasn't a friendly one. "I don't need you to *save me,* Luke."

"I—"

"No. I handled it myself. I don't need anyone to save me, except for God to save me from rich, spoiled man-babies."

I turned and walked back to the boardroom. I may have wanted his shoulder to cry on ten years ago. But he had turned it away then. It was too little and too late now.

*

*Fourteen years earlier…*

I hadn't seen or spoken to Luke in two days. He wasn't in homeroom or at the cafeteria after first period. I finally found him at his locker before lunch. "Hey! What's going on?" I asked when I reached him.

He ignored me.

"Luke, why aren't you talking to me? I really need to speak to you. The other night—"

"Let me guess," he interrupted. "You had an art project to finish or a math test to study for or something else more important than my silly baseball game. Because your stuff is always more important than me."

"What? What are you talking about? That's not why I didn't come to your game. And my school work isn't more important than you." He shook his head and shoved books into his bag, not listening to anything I was saying. "Luke!"

He slammed his locker shut and walked away.

"Are you seriously sulking right now?" I couldn't believe him. After I received the worst possible news about my mother, all he cared about was some stupid baseball game.

"Yeah, I'm serious. This is me walking away from you, Grace. I don't need another flake in my life. See you around."

Spoiled, selfish, jerk. I didn't need friends like Luke Crawford. I didn't need anybody.

*

On my way home from work, I drove along the side streets. I needed to clear my head from all the memories that kept roaring back. I hadn't thought of Luke Crawford in so long—except for ways to cause him bodily harm. The memories gave me a headache. I couldn't reconcile the young boy who played with me and brought me ice whenever I hurt myself with the guy that turned his back on me. I guess people change, and sometimes for the worse.

"Mom, I'm home!"

My mother sat on the couch with a pink knit blanket over her lap. "Hi, sweetie. How was your day?"

"It was great, Mom. How are you feeling?"

"Really good. I think we should go out for dinner tonight. How about that Thai restaurant you like? We haven't been there in years."

Despite her smile, creases formed on my mother's forehead and around her mouth. I guessed she was in a lot of pain and probably wouldn't make it on the couch for much longer, let alone a restaurant.

"That's a great idea, Mom. But I'm a little tired from work. How about we order in?"

She huffed. "Fine, if that's what you prefer." She turned back to face the TV but then whipped her head back to me. "Why don't you invite your friend Omar?"

My lips twitched. "Sure, Mom. Omar would love it."

As I removed my blouse, I dialed Omar's number from my bedroom.

"Hey, Grace! What's up, darling?"

"Do you have plans tonight?"

"Um, Richard and I were going to grab some dinner. Do you want to join us?"

"Actually, I was hoping you would come by here for dinner?"

"Are you sure?" he asked.

"Definitely sure. And please bring Richard. I'd love to spend some time with him and my mother needs a dose of reality so she can finally get the idea of you and me together out of her mind."

"Ah, well. If you weren't my best friend, Grace, there may have been a chance for us."

"Richard is a much better partner than I am. I work too much."

"True. And I don't relish the idea of dating another accountant."

We both laughed. "Me neither."

"Is seven o'clock okay?" asked Omar.

"Perfect. See you soon."

I had just thrown away the containers after pouring the food into dishes when the doorbell rang.

"Coming!" I jogged across the small kitchen to reach the front door.

Dressed in a sleek black shirt and brown pants, Omar beamed at me. "Hi!" he said, then leaned in and hugged me.

"Thanks for coming," I reached behind Omar to shake Richard's hand. I'd only met Richard a handful of times before today, and each time had been quick and casual, so I wasn't sure how he felt about hugging. But when he pulled my hand to draw me into his arms for a tight embrace, I knew he was a hugger, too.

"Thanks so much for inviting us. I've been looking forward to spending time with you, Grace."

"Me too, Richard. Please come in."

Omar hung his and Richard's jacket on the coat rack while I went to the living room to check on my mother. Her eyes were closed, but a serene smile played on her face. "Mom. Omar and Richard are here."

Her eyes fluttered and her smile grew. "Oh good. Richard, did you say? Who's he?"

"He's Omar's boyfriend," I said, as I helped her up from the couch and walked with her to the kitchen.

"Oh. I thought Omar was single."

"He isn't. Richard seems nice, though."

"We'll see," she said and I rolled my eyes.

As I settled my mom onto one of the kitchen chairs, Richard bellowed, "My goodness, Grace. This must be your mother. It's obvious where you get your beauty from."

I stared at Omar and pulled my lips into my mouth to stop a giggle from escaping. Omar seemed to fight the same battle.

Richard walked over to us, grabbed my mother's hand, and kissed it. "Richard. Charmed."

"Well, aren't you a gentleman?" she said. "I'm Evelyn." Then she turned to me and whispered. "Grace, you have such wonderful friends."

And just like that, I knew Richard had won my mother over.

But Richard truly was a gentleman. He pulled out a chair for me and Omar before sitting at the table himself.

The conversation flowed as freely as the wine and I even laughed a few times when Richard told the story of when Omar lost the hamster in his apartment and had to lure him back with a piece of tinfoil and peanut butter. Imagining Omar in a suit and tie kneeling on the floor waiting for the furry rodent to come out made me laugh out loud.

"So, how long have you two known each other?" asked Richard as we finished our dinner.

"Too long," teased Omar, and I slapped his shoulder.

"Five years," I said. "Omar and I worked on the same audit and we hit it off right away."

"She got shit done and I liked that," said Omar, standing to clear our plates. I stood as well to help.

I looked back and watched Richard talk to my mom. A satisfied smile stayed on her lips while she folded her hands on her lap. I could tell from her slumped shoulders she was getting tired and I would have to encourage her to go to bed soon.

She seemed to be worsening little by little each day, but I wouldn't panic. I would finish this audit, be promoted to senior audit manager, and get my mother onto the new meds that she needs.

"How's the audit at Crawford Corp going?" asked Omar.

"Terrible. Luke is making the job more difficult than it needs to be."

"Well, you've handled difficult people before. I know you can handle him."

"I can. It's just exhausting that I have to."

"Maybe he's making you work for his attention."

"Oh, it's definitely not that. Trust me. Luke Crawford hates me as much as I hate him."

Omar and Richard stayed a bit longer, listening to my mom tell stories about how I was a stubborn child. They all laughed until Omar whispered something in Richard's ear.

"It's been a pleasure, Evelyn," said Richard.

"Yes, thank you both for having us over," Omar said.

My mother beamed. "The pleasure was ours. It's been too long since we've shared a meal with friends."

"We should definitely do it again sometime," I agreed.

While Richard grabbed their jackets, he smiled and held Omar's hand a little longer than necessary. I smiled, too, happy for them both.

My mother reached over and laced her fingers with mine.

"I wish you had someone in your life like Omar or Richard," she sighed.

I shook my head. "It's fine, Mom. I don't need anybody."

She squeezed my hand. "We all need somebody, baby."

I gulped, unprepared for the emotion that rolled over me. It wasn't sadness… it was more like regret. Or longing, perhaps? I didn't know. But it didn't matter. I couldn't change my situation, so there was no point in dwelling on it.

"I have somebody. I have you, Mom."

"Grace, baby, you'll find someone who'll make you happy one day."

Despite my father having walked out on us when I was a baby, my mother always believed I'd find someone better. I didn't have as much faith as her. Perhaps that was why I preferred working over dating. I would depend on myself, just like my mother did.

# 5

## Luke

While the days were warmer in late May in Syracuse, New York, the nights were still cool. I raised the collar of my black jacket to ward off the chill and stuffed my hands in my pockets as I walked out of Crawford Corporation and into the busy downtown core.

Eric, our family's driver, pulled up to the front of the building. I opened the passenger door and stuck my head in. "Thanks, Eric," I said. "But I'm going to walk home tonight. Say hi to Susan and the kids for me."

"Will do, Mr. Crawford," he said and I closed the car door.

Inhaling a deep breath as I walked down the street, I tried to still the thoughts racing through my head. Colton's face popped up with his tight lips and narrow eyes—his usual look of disappointment. My other brother, Ryan, wasn't in the office today, and I wasn't sure whom to thank for that. Then a heart-shaped face framed with smooth chestnut hair and dark brown eyes drifted into my mind.

I hadn't seen her face in nearly ten years, but it haunted me still. One look from her and I was thirteen again. I didn't want to go back to that time, but I couldn't stop the memories from flooding in.

*

*Fifteen years earlier…*

My shoulder burned from the weight of my bag, which held my baseball bat, balls, glove, and helmet. My dad used to carry it for me, before he, well, before he and mom died in a car accident years ago. Since my uncle became our guardian, I held it. My father coached my little league team, but my uncle hadn't attended a game yet. My best friend Sean's dad would pick me up and drive us to practice and the games. Sean and his dad were away today and I begged my uncle to drive me. He said he would if I'd finally leave him alone. I did. But it was a half-hour past the time we were supposed to leave for my game. The front door opened, and Colton and Ryan walked in.

"What are you still doing here, kid?" asked Colton, looking around the house. Ryan was right behind him.

At seventeen, Colton had been driving Ryan to their after-school jobs.

"Sean and his dad are away. *He* was supposed to drive me." They both knew whom I meant. We rarely spoke his name.

Ryan checked his watch. "Come on, kid. We can take you to practice. But you'll have to walk home after the game or find a ride."

"That's fine," I mumbled, following them into Colton's beat-up sedan. My parents had left us a fortune, but we couldn't touch it until we turned eighteen. And while they gave enough money to my uncle and aunt to support us in luxury, nothing ever trickled down our way. Except for food. They fed us, at least.

"Why would you even ask *him*?" Ryan said when I hopped into the back seat, avoiding the stain in the middle.

"I don't know," I said, annoyed. "I guess I thought..."

"What? That this time would be different?" asked Ryan, turning his body toward the back of the car to look at me.

I shrugged my shoulders, embarrassed to admit it. Ryan shook his head and rolled his eyes. I hated it when he was right, and Ryan was often right.

"You never know. Maybe he might still show up," I said, wanting to prove Ryan wrong for once.

"I wouldn't hold your breath," he said.

"Shut up, Ryan," said Colton. "He's just a kid."

"I'm thirteen," I snapped. "I'm not a kid anymore, so stop calling me one."

"All right, all right, k—" Colton stopped himself just as I curled my fists.

My anger threatened more tears, but I bit my cheek and crossed my arms, holding them back. I was done shedding tears because of my uncle.

When he pulled into the parking lot of the baseball field, Colton whispered, "We're here, Luke. Time to go."

"Thanks," I mumbled, opening the backdoor. "I'll see you later."

I walked toward our team's bench, and a few of the kids nodded at me. But the scowl on my face was warning enough not to talk to me. As furious as I was, I didn't want to release my anger on them. Instead, I channeled it, and hit the ball out of the park three times, including in the bottom of the ninth to win the game. I looked to the stands one last time but saw no familiar faces.

Walking home that night, I remembered all the games I'd shared with my dad. All the hugs when I did well and the pats on the back when I didn't. Despite the crowd cheering for me, I'd never felt so alone in my life. A tear escaped, but I quickly wiped it from my cheek. I would not cry.

I opened the front door to our childhood home. My uncle had moved in with us and my aunt had redecorated. I hated the brown sectional couches, beige walls, and especially that brown leather recliner my uncle always sat in. As I walked up the steps, I spotted my uncle sitting on that very chair in the living room, reading the paper and smoking his pipe. Frozen, I stared at him.

He looked up and his eyes roamed over my uniform. Anger ignited inside of me and my face flushed from the heat. "You forgot."

He shrugged. "Something came up," he said and looked back down at his paper. "But it seems like you got yourself there. You should thank me, boy. I taught you a lesson in resourcefulness." He stuck the pipe back in his mouth and took a puff.

I wanted to stick that pipe up his ass.

I wanted to scream and rage at him, but I knew that wouldn't get me far. It didn't work when Ryan or Colton had done it. It had only gotten them locked in their rooms with no dinner. I would not let him deprive me of the only thing he actually provided for us.

I stomped up to my room and slammed the door. I turned the radio on and the volume up, blasting Nirvana's *Come as you are* from the speakers. I peeled off my uniform and took a shower. When I stepped out, I realized someone had turned off the radio. Walking out of the ensuite and into my room, I found Colton sitting on my bed.

"Come here, Luke," he said.

I sat next to him, rubbing a towel over my wet hair.

"How was your game?" he asked, searching my face.

"It was fine," I said.

When I didn't continue, Colton sighed. "Look, Luke. I'm sorry about tonight. But, when I turn eighteen next year, I promise I'm going to get us out. I'll buy a small place for just the three of us and we'll never have to see them again. We'll have to work hard, but it'll be worth it. We will make something of ourselves despite his attempts to break us down."

I shook my head. "I'm not working hard, Colton. What did working hard get dad? It got them killed. If he didn't take Mom with him to some stupid conference, they'd both still be here!" I shouted.

"If he didn't work hard, he wouldn't have made a fortune to pass down to his kids. Don't be so selfish, Luke."

"I'm not selfish, Colton. I just don't want to be like you. I'm going to enjoy life and screw everyone else. I don't need anybody."

"I think what you need is to cool down. One day, you're going to want someone at your games."

"You're wrong," I shouted as he left my room.

Except that he wasn't.

A year later, I asked Grace to watch two of my games, and both times I looked for her the whole night—but like my uncle, she never showed up for me.

*

Colton lived up to his promise. When he inherited his portion of our parent's wealth on his eighteenth birthday, he purchased a home close to the high school for us to live in. The following year, the three of us, with court-ordered documents in hand, kicked my uncle and aunt from our family home. They didn't leave quietly, shouting about how ungrateful we were and such. It was nearly laughable. I had wanted to move in right away, but Colton didn't want to go back there. He said he wanted to start new memories. But not me. No, I had wanted to fix what my uncle had done. So, three years ago, when I was twenty-five, I bought the home from my brothers, becoming the sole owner, and remodeled the place. The first thing I did was push that brown leather recliner into the backyard and set that sucker on fire. I fucking hated it.

While I didn't tear down any walls, I removed every piece of furniture, appliance, and carpet from the house and filled it with my personal style. I bought a soft cream couch that didn't recline, a huge king-size bed, and, of course, restaurant-quality stainless-steel appliances. Although I didn't cook for many people, only for Ryan and Colton.

When we were kids, Colton would buy us dinner every Friday night until I started cooking. They had agreed my version of the veal sandwiches was better than the store-bought ones and I'd tried a new recipe out on them every week. As we grew older, those weekly meals turned into monthly ones, but we still maintained them even today.

Despite walking in the same direction as my house, I didn't want to go home yet. The scent of sauteed garlic, onions, and something I couldn't quite place awakened my nose. Inhaling deeply, I realized the aroma came from an open window a few feet ahead but down four steps below the main street level. The writing on the glass door read *Mario's Restaurant*. A bell chimed as I opened the door and my eyes adjusted to the darkness within. Dark brown leather booths framed the room and the black carpet and red walls didn't add any brightness.

"Hello," I called when no one greeted me.

Nothing.

I stepped further into the restaurant, then closer to the back room, when I heard someone bang a pot. I pushed the white swinging door open and squinted at the bright lights.

"Who are you?" a voice asked, surprised.

I squinted and rubbed my eyes until a large man with a bald head but a dark, bushy mustache came into focus. "I'm Luke Crawford," I said. "I smelled something delicious and had to come in."

He resumed adding anchovies to a pizza. "And my daughter sent you back here?"

"What daughter?" I asked, looking back over my shoulder.

He huffed. "Is she still on break? I told her to be back in ten minutes. That was thirty minutes ago," he mumbled something else under his breath, but I didn't catch it.

He clapped his hands and flour sprinkled across the counter. "What can I get you? Would you like a personal pizza? We have fettuccine tonight or the sea bass is excellent quality, or—"

"The pizza sounds great," I said, eyeing the various ingredients next to the flattened dough. "Is that pepperoni?"

"Pepperoni?" he repeated, slightly affronted. "No, no, no. This is not pepperoni." He picked it up and offered me a piece. "This is hot soppressata made from my mother's hands. It's a family tradition."

I popped the piece of meat into my mouth and my tongue immediately exploded. I tasted the hot chili pepper flakes first, but then a more subtle flavor started coming through. It was a mix of cured meat, but something oddly sweet. "Is that red pepper I taste?"

He smiled. "Very good," he said. "My mother adds just a hint of red pepper and tomato paste to her recipe."

"It works really well," I said.

"*Perfetto,*" he said. "I'll make you a soppressata and olive pizza. How does that sound?"

"It sounds *perfetto,*" I smiled and watched him as he prepared my meal.

In no time, he shimmied the pizza into a large wood oven, and in less than two minutes it was ready. "That's impressive."

"Ninety seconds," he said. "That's all it takes."

The mozzarella sizzled when he passed me the pizza and oozed when I picked up a slice. I could smell the spice and the hint of garlic he used in the tomato sauce. It all worked really well together. After blowing on the end, I took my first bite. Mmm, all the flavors circled my taste buds at once and made me smile. Delicious.

"This is the best pizza I've ever had," I said before taking another bite.

He smiled. "Grazie."

"What's your name?" I asked, only just realizing I hadn't earlier.

"Mario," he said, then looked over my head and through the small window in the swinging door. "And the girl who just walked in forty minutes late is my daughter, Victoria." He placed both hands on his hips and shook his head.

I laughed at his expression. Despite being angry, he still had a twinkle in his eye as he stared at her.

Finishing the pizza, I said, "I'm sure you guys are going to be a big hit in town. This is really good."

He started kneading a new dough. "Thank you." He tossed some flour onto the dough and punched his fists into it. "We've been open for eight months and it's been, uh, quiet."

"I'm sure business will pick up soon. The first year is the hardest, they say." I looked down at my half-eaten pizza, already full. "I'm going to take the rest of this home." I grabbed a takeout box from the counter and placed my pizza inside. "I'll definitely be back, though." I pulled out my wallet. "What do I owe you for the pizza?"

"Oh, uh, fifteen dollars. You can pay Victoria at the cash register. Come by anytime."

"Will do. Thank you."

I walked back through the swinging door and met with Victoria.

"Who are you?" she asked, her bubble gum bursting over her lips.

I smiled and skimmed through my wallet. "One of your dad's biggest fans." I pulled out a hundred-dollar bill and passed it to Victoria. "Don't be late next time," I said and walked out the door.

Before I reached the third step up toward the street, Victoria called. "Hey, sir, you forgot your change."

"No, I didn't," I said. "That pizza was worth every cent."

As I drove home, I thought about Mario's pizza and how there were probably other restaurants that deserved more attention than they were getting. I wished there was some way I could help them. But when I closed my eyes in bed that night, all I could think about were ways to avoid that heart-shaped face the next day.

# 6

## Grace

The next day, Tuesday, I had stopped by my accounting firm in the morning to help a colleague with one of her client's files, so it was nearly noon when I reached Crawford Corporation.

Stepping off the elevator on the twelfth floor, I didn't think much of it when I noticed the front desk receptionist was missing. I got a little concerned when the boardroom sat empty, even though James had messaged me he would be at the office early today to make up for yesterday's lunch. I hadn't gotten to sleep until nearly midnight, catching up with the lost hours after Omar and Richard had left.

I knew something was up when applause sounded from the staff room at the back. Figuring I would probably find James there, I followed the voices down the hallway.

When I turned the corner, I smelled it. I couldn't put my finger on the flavor, but my stomach growled in anticipation. Behind a crowd of people stood Luke, wearing a white apron over his blue jeans and white-button shirt. "Move back, this is hot, people," he called out, laughing.

He held a large aluminum tray with several pieces of thinly sliced steak steaming inside. Gently placing the tray on one of the staff room tables, he turned to the counter behind him and grabbed two bowls, one filled with grated mozzarella and the other with fresh buns.

"Okay, who's first?" he chuckled.

"Me!" shouted James, and shoved his way to the front. A few others raised their arms as well.

Luke laughed, his palms facing the crowd. "No problem. There's plenty to go around."

*"James,"* I hissed. But my colleague's face was glued to the cheese steak sandwich in front of him. I rolled my eyes. A little louder this time, I called, "James!"

Everyone in the staff room turned around, including Luke. He smiled, obviously pleased to be surrounded by an adoring audience, as usual. When James made eye contact with me, I tilted my head toward the hallway. He followed me.

"Hey! You're back. How did it go?" he asked, taking a bite of his sandwich. My stomach protested that it wanted a bite, too, but I ignored it. I would not ask Luke for anything other than documents for this audit.

"It went fine. How about you? Did you reconcile the bank statements?"

"Yes. All done."

I sighed. "Good. How about the treasurer's reports?"

His mouth opened and closed, and he scrunched up his face again. I crossed my arms.

"Luke was supposed to bring them to me this morning," said James. "But got held up."

"Held up? By what? An oven timer?"

"It's a freaking good steak, Grace. You should have one." He turned the sandwich toward me, offering me a bite.

I held my hand up. "No, thank you. I'm good."

I looked up at Luke, surrounded by his fans, and shook my head. There was no way I could get him out of the kitchen and hand me those reports right now.

"This is getting ridiculous. I'm going to speak to Colton."

I marched down the hallway to Colton's office. He faced his laptop as he pinched the bridge of his nose. He didn't look happy.

Well, neither was I.

I knocked on his door. "Can I come in?"

He looked up, slightly startled. "Ms. Sweeney? Of course, please come in."

"This isn't working with Luke," I said, getting straight to the point.

"What do you mean?"

"I mean, he's not doing his job. He's stalling, distracting my colleague, and downright ignoring my requests."

"I don't think Luke would do this on purpose."

I raised my eyebrow. "Really? How well do you know him, then?"

"Excuse me?"

I shook my head. "Mr. Crawford. I don't want to argue with you about this. We both want the same thing here, and that is to execute a quick, efficient, and thorough audit for you. I'm telling you that the person you assigned to help with the audit is none of those things. I respectfully ask that you assign someone else the role."

Colton steepled his hands under his chin and released a breath. "Let me speak with him." Colton picked up the phone and brought it to his ear. He waited a minute and that crease reappeared between his eyebrows right before he looked up at me.

I smiled. "He's not in his office. He's in the staff room making cheese steak sandwiches."

"He's what?" he asked, getting up from his chair. "Wait here a minute."

He crossed the room and marched down the hallway. "Luke!" he shouted when he reached the staff room. "My office. Right now."

I straightened my lips before Colton returned and stared straight ahead when he resumed his seat.

The scent of fresh sirloin breezed into the room. "You called for me," said Luke. I didn't turn around, but the essence of him made me close my eyes. He smelled delicious.

I felt his eyes on me.

"Has Ms. Sweeney been tattling on me?" he asked.

*Oh, I didn't care how good he smelled, the nerve of that man.*

"I am not tattling, you child. I'm frustrated by your lack of professionalism. This farce has gone on long enough."

"Oh, has it? What do you say, Colton?" asked Luke, crossing his arms and looking at his brother.

Colton's eyes narrowed and bounced between the two of us. "Are you purposely stalling this audit?"

"Of course not," he said, without missing a beat. "I'm just not cut out for office work, Colton. I'm sorry."

Colton closed his eyes and sighed again. "Fine." When he opened them, he focused his attention on me. "What is it you need, Ms. Sweeney?"

"I need the treasurer's reports from last year."

"I asked Daniel for them this morning, but he said they're not in the shared drive," said Luke behind me.

"I'm surprised you even asked," I mumbled.

"Oh, that's right," said Colton, snapping his finger. "I forgot that I saved those reports on my laptop. I hadn't transferred them to the drive. Let me just—"

As he turned toward his laptop, he swore softly, then ran his fingers through his hair.

"What's the matter?" asked Luke.

Colton closed his eyes and said, "I bought a new laptop a couple of months ago. The old one is at Newcastle."

"Newcastle?" I asked. "What's that?"

Colton pursed his lips and rubbed his forehead. "My cabin upstate."

I groaned.

"Don't worry, Ms. Sweeney," said Colton. "I'll drive up this evening after my wife—"

"I'll go," said Luke.

I swiveled my head to stare at him. "You?"

He put his hands on his hips. "I'm in charge of the audit, so it's my responsibility. I'll go. Stay home with your wife, Colton."

I shook my head and put my hands on my hips. "I don't trust you. What if this is another one of your schemes to waste my time?" Luke had let me down before. He would do it again. I was sure of it.

"Everything is always about you. Isn't it, Sweeney?" he sneered.

"In this case, yes, I think it is."

"I don't care what you think." Then, turning to Colton, he said. "Give me your keys to the cabin and text me where to find the laptop. I'll leave in an hour."

Without thinking them over, the words tumbled from my lips, "I'm coming with you."

"You're what?" asked Luke, whipping his head to look back at me. He'd already reached the office door.

"Like I said. I don't trust you. So, I'm coming with you to ensure this rescue mission isn't just a decoy to take more time off of work. Or whatever you do here."

Colton smiled and steepled his fingers underneath his chin again. "I think that's a great idea, Ms. Sweeney."

"Thank you, Mr. Crawford." Then to Luke, "We leave in an hour," I said and pushed past him at the door.

"I just said that. Don't act like you're the one calling the shots," he shouted as I walked down the hallway.

Without turning back, I hollered, "I'm driving."

## Luke

I watched her storm off, her arms swinging, her back straight, and her righteousness resting on her shoulders. Man, she drove me nuts. She was always making assumptions and jumping to the wrong conclusions. What if I was going to take the long way to the cabin? I would still send her precious files by morning. Was she planning to work on them tonight? Probably yes, knowing Grace Sweeney.

When I reached the staff room, there was a steak sandwich left on a plate next to the sink. "I think they saved the last one for you," said Colton, walking in behind me.

I smiled. "That was thoughtful."

"Or just hoping that you'll do it again tomorrow. I heard it was incredible."

I took a bite and chewed slowly. "Not bad. But it's missing something. Maybe some fried onions. I'll ask Mario what he thinks the next time I see him."

"Who?" he asked.

"A guy I met last night. His restaurant is a few blocks from here. *Mario's Restaurant*. Have you heard of it?"

"Nope. But I will check it out now." He crossed his arms and leaned against the wall. "Do you want to be a chef, Luke? Is that what this is all about?"

I had thought about it many times, but I didn't think that I would enjoy cooking if I had to do it every day. I think I would lose my love for cooking if it became my career. "No, I don't think so."

"Then, what's holding you back?"

"I don't know, Colton. I guess… I just don't know which way I want to go."

"You need to figure this shit out, Luke. We're not kids anymore."

"I know that," I said, frustrated with myself. I couldn't help feeling lost every time I thought of the future. If I were honest, it's why I avoided thinking about it most of the time.

"Here's the number to the safe where I store my laptop," he said, passing me a yellow sticky note.

"Drive safe," he said and pat me on the shoulder before walking back to his office.

I looked around the room and started cleaning up the mess. It didn't take too long, most of the stuff I used I placed in the dishwasher. I grabbed my sports jacket and headed downstairs; certain *Meany Sweeney* would be waiting there for me.

Ah, and there she was, sitting in a silver Honda Civic. Reminded me of Colton's first car.

"I like the ride, Sweeney," I said, getting into the vehicle.

"Thanks." Adjusting an ancient GPS device onto her vent, she asked, "What's the address to this cabin?"

"I'll just give you the directions."

"No, I prefer the address."

"Why?"

"Because I'd rather listen to the GPS's voice telling me where to go than yours."

"Oh, Sweeney. There's nothing I'd like more than to tell you where to go."

She narrowed her eyes. "The address, Crawford."

"I don't know the exact address."

"Then what are you doing here?"

"I know how to get there, which roads to take, but I don't actually know the cabin number or anything like that. Trust me. I won't get us lost."

"Why do I have a bad feeling about this?"

"Because you are a generally negative person?"

She sighed and shoved her key in the ignition to start the car.

"Wow, I haven't seen someone start a car with an actual key in a long time."

"Nice you can still slum it with us common folk, huh Crawford?"

"You really should upgrade to something with better safety technology. Like do you even have a rearview camera in this car?"

"No, Crawford. I turn my head, just like every other driver has in the last hundred years."

"I'm just saying, it's about safety not luxury."

"Sometimes, safety is a luxury."

"That doesn't even make sense, Sweeney."

"Shut up, Crawford. And put on your seatbelt."

She pulled out onto the street and turned right. She headed in the right direction at least. "Stay here until you reach the highway, and then just take it north for about an hour."

She nodded and stared straight ahead. I closed my eyes and thought I'd rest awhile. But when I closed my eyes, a light lavender scent piqued my interest. It was fresh, soft, and feminine. It couldn't be Sweeney, could it? I opened my left eye a sliver and glanced at the driver's seat. I glimpsed her legs beneath the steering wheel. Her navy skirt had ridden to her upper thigh and the muscle flexed each time she pressed the gas pedal. I never knew Sweeney had nice legs. I had always liked the shape of Sweeney's mouth but I had never noticed her legs before. *Huh.*

One manicured hand held the lower part of the steering wheel as she drove while her other hand lay on her bare leg. She absently caressed her skin, slowly making circles over her flesh and my gaze shot up to her face to see if she was messing with me.

"What?" she asked, turning her head to look at me.

I narrowed my eyes, but her creased forehead and head tilt seemed genuine.

"Nothing," I said and closed my eyes tightly, trying to forget the image that had flashed in my mind. The image of my hand—instead of hers—laying on her leg, inching up her thigh.

*Fuck that! No way. I can't be so desperate as to want Meany Sweeney. I must be overtired, and not thinking, just reacting to a soft, bare, feminine thigh.*

"I know what you're trying to do," she said.

"Excuse me?" I asked, confused by the insult in her voice. *Did she catch me staring?*

"You're pretending to sleep so that you don't have to talk to me. But you don't have to worry, Crawford. I am perfectly comfortable with silence. You're not making me uncomfortable at all." She pressed on the gas and shifted in her seat, causing the skirt to ride just a little higher.

*Now I'm the uncomfortable one. Is she doing this on purpose?*

"I don't know what you're talking about, Sweeney. I *was* asleep. And I prefer not to hear your voice either. Let's just do ourselves both a favor and not talk for the rest of the way up. Deal?"

She nodded once, but I saw it. Then she turned to stare at me, and raised her eyebrows pointedly. "I thought you were sleeping?"

"You're unbelievable, you know that?" I grumbled. Turning over to my right side, I closed my eyes and shoved Sweeney and her bare thighs out of my mind.

# 7

## Grace

I'd been driving for nearly two hours and Luke had been asleep for most of that time, offering only basic directions before he drifted off. The scenery was consistent but soothing. Large, empty fields surrounded us on either side of the highway.

It was nearly four in the afternoon when I turned off the highway and onto a dirt road. Dark clouds gathered on the horizon, promising rain soon. I wanted to reach the cabin before the downpour.

I leaned over and shoved Luke's shoulder. "Wake up, Richie Rich."

"Ow! Ugh! What's your problem?" he grumbled when I continued to shove him.

"Oh please. You weren't really sleeping. You were too quiet to be asleep."

He narrowed his eyes. "I'll try to snore and mumble next time for you."

"There won't be a 'next time.' You're driving on the way back. I'll be the one taking a nap."

"Fine by me, princess."

"Oh, that's golden, coming from you," I said. "I just turned onto Pine Street from the highway. Where to from here?"

He straightened in his seat and looked out the window. "See that large oak tree up ahead?"

"Yeah."

"Make a right down that street."

"Do you know the name of the street?"

"Nope."

"So, what happens when someone cuts that tree down?"

"No one will cut a tree that size down."

I shook my head and turned as soon as I passed the Oak. His directions led me down a narrow gravel path. Thick, leafy trees lined the path and I couldn't make out any cabins for miles ahead. "Are you sure this is it?"

"Do you always question everyone as much as you question me?" he grumbled.

I thought about that. "No."

Staring at the road, he sat up quickly. "Turn here." He pointed to a dirt road immediately on my left. "Now."

I swerved the car and just missed the ditch. "Um... a little more notice next time. What happened? Did they cut down a tree?"

His lips twitched, but he didn't laugh. Good.

Finally, a red brick house peaked from behind tall branches. A large wooden deck wrapped around the cabin, and a lake jutted up behind it. It was beautiful.

I skidded to a stop in front of the porch, a cloud of dust rising against my window.

Luke got out of the car first as I craned my neck up to look at the two-story cabin.

"Let's just get this over with so you can finish your audit," said Luke. "And we can both be rid of each other sooner rather than later."

"Finally, you're starting to see it my way."

As I walked up the wooden steps onto the porch, the scent of fresh pine and dirt tickled my nose. I wondered if I was allergic to the fresh air. I'd never been to the country, always stuck inside apartment buildings my whole life. There was a time we lived in a small house when my dad was around, but I was too young to remember it. The deck looked as though someone had stained it recently.

A soft curse turned my attention back to the front door, where Luke jingled a set of keys by the lock.

"You've no clue which key works. Do you?" I asked.

"If I did, I wouldn't be trying all of them, would I?" Luke tried a different key and the door unlocked. "There."

Opening the door wider, he motioned for me to go in first. "After you."

I tried to smile, but it probably looked more like a grimace. I wasn't buying Luke's feigned chivalry. The fake smile died on my lips because when I walked in, it felt as though the outside was inside. Tall windows, at least twenty feet high, made up the back of the cabin. You couldn't tell where the trees ended and the kitchen began. The walls were all wood-paneled and the doors themselves looked like tree trunks. It was sort of like living in a tree house, but with water and electricity.

"Wow, this place is amazing," I whispered, mostly to myself, but Luke had heard it.

"It's all right," he said, dropping the keys on the kitchen counter and looking around.

A loud crack of thunder echoed outside and I jumped from the sound. Luke walked to the windows and tilted his head up toward the sky. "Looks like rain."

"I saw the clouds as we were driving in. Let's get those papers and get out of here. Maybe the rain will stay behind us."

Another boom of thunder, and this time the windows creaked under the pressure from a powerful gust of wind. Goosebumps rose on my skin. Those windows weren't looking so safe anymore.

I caught Luke staring at me, creases forming around his eyes. "Are you all right?"

"Yes. Fine. Just want to get going, that's all."

"Okay. The papers are in the study upstairs." He turned back down the hallway and took the stairs two at a time to the second floor. Luke entered the first door to his right. "Here we go," he said and walked toward a high-tech filing cabinet with codes instead of locks.

Looking around the room, I noticed an absence of furniture in this room. There was just a table, two chairs, and a filing cabinet. It surprised me there wasn't much more to it.

"This must be it." Luke pulled out a laptop from the top drawer and placed it under his arm. "Okay let's go."

"Wait," I said. "How do you know it's the right one?"

"Because it was exactly where Colton said it would be."

"But what if the files are missing and he transferred them to a hard drive or something?"

"Why would he do that?"

"I don't know. But we should make sure everything is in that laptop before we leave this place."

"Fine." Luke dropped the laptop on the table and turned it on. As the computer booted up, I couldn't help staring at Luke's hands. His nails were short and clean, but the tips of his fingers had stains on them.

"Do you paint?" I asked, absently.

"Pardon?" he asked, looking up at me, both palms on the table.

I nodded at his fingers. "The stains."

He raised his fingers to inspect them. "Oh, that. No. I chopped some boiled beets last night and I guess some color got into the cracks of my skin."

I was about to respond when another boom of thunder shot through the sky and shook the house. I jumped and let out a small gasp this time. Standing on the second floor, it felt as though the thunder had echoed through me. The lights in the room flickered and then a terrible sound registered. A snap, followed by a creaking in the distance. Then, the loudest crash I'd ever heard. Both Luke and I ran to the front window of the study.

I couldn't believe my eyes. An enormous tree had fallen. The trunk, which was probably as wide as my car, lay across the gravel, blocking the driveway.

"Shit," whispered Luke.

"Oh, my god! That could have hit the car."

"You're worried about the car?"

"Yes. What are you worried about?"

"Sweeney, that tree is blocking our exit. We're stuck here."

# 8

## Grace

This couldn't be happening. I could not be stuck in a cabin in the middle of nowhere with this man. I had to get back home. I had to get back to my mother.

"No, we are not stuck here. Do you hear me?" I said, pointing my finger at him.

He stared at the finger and tilted his head. "That massive tree trunk would say otherwise."

"Well, we'll just go over there and move it."

He rolled his eyes. "Do I look like some sort of Avenger to you? Because unless you have some superpowers I'm unaware of, we're stuck here until someone can cut down that tree."

"Maybe Colton has a chainsaw out back."

He squinted his eyes as though he wondered if I were crazy. "Why would he have a chainsaw?"

I threw my hands up in the air. "I don't know! But at least I'm trying to think of something!" Why wasn't he doing anything? Why was I the only one trying to think of a solution? Typical.

"Fine, I'll do it myself," I said, marching out of the room and racing down the stairs.

"Sweeney!" Luke shouted. "Where the hell are you going?"

"Where do you think I'm going?" I swung open the front door and marched toward the tree. The rain pelted me from the sky but I didn't care. From the second floor, the tree looked big, but the closer I got, the more massive it became. When I reached the fallen giant, the top of its trunk was near my waist. I wiped my eyes and looked around for some sort of leverage. I knew little about physics, but I knew I needed a lever if this thing was going to budge. Other smaller branches were laying on the ground but those would break.

*A jack! I have one in the car.*

I ran to open the driver's side and popped open the trunk.

*There it is!*

I grabbed it and slammed down my trunk before racing back to the tree. Shoving the jack as far underneath the tree as possible, I cranked it.

Footsteps pounded behind me. "What are you doing?" Luke asked when he reached me.

"What does it look like I'm doing?" I shouted above the rain and wind.

"Trying to change a spare tire on a tree?"

"No. I'm trying to move this damn thing!"

"That's not gonna work. Come inside, Sweeney, before you catch pneumonia."

"No," I said and tried again. It would not budge, not even an inch.

"Ahh!" I shouted and smacked the tree. Then I hit it with my other hand and pushed as hard as I could. "Come on, you stupid thing. Move!"

Luke grasped my shoulders and pulled me back. "Come inside," he said. "I've already called someone."

"You did?" I asked, turning around to look at him.

His light gray pants deepened to charcoal from the rain and his white buttoned shirt clung to his chest as he breathed. He wiped his face with his hand and pushed back his long, wet strands of hair. He stared at me. I must have looked like some drenched rat, as his eyes roamed over my body.

"Come inside," his voice was softer now so I agreed. He grabbed my hand and pulled me toward the house, probably afraid I'd make one last attempt to move the tree. I did think about it, but decided it was useless.

I raced up the front steps, and Luke let go of my hand once we were inside. I stood at the entrance dripping wet. "I don't want to ruin Colton's floor. Do you have a towel?"

Luke looked around and opened a door next to the entrance. He pulled out a large black coat with a fur-trimmed hood. "Take off your clothes and put this on."

"Excuse me?"

"It's better if you get out of those wet clothes. Don't worry, I'll turn around."

My teeth started chattering from the cold. "All right," I said, grabbing the jacket. When I raised my eyebrows expectantly, he turned around.

I unbuttoned my blouse and removed my bra, pulling down my pants next. Fortunately, my panties were still dry, so I kept those on.

Picking the coat off the ground, I slipped my hands into the arms. The coat reached just above my knees but covered all the important bits. "Okay, you can turn around now."

Luke swiveled to face me again. Placing his hands on his hips, he examined me. His mouth twitched.

"What?" I asked.

"I can barely see you. It's like you've been buried alive in this coat."

I cracked a smile because seeing Luke soaked to the bone, a grin on his lips and his hair falling over, reminded me of when we were friends. A long time ago. His bulging biceps and chest muscles proved that a lot of time had passed since I was friends with the skinny boy who liked to play baseball.

He reached for the hem of his shirt and pulled it up and over his head. Buttons clinked on the floor, but I couldn't move my eyes away from his bare chest. The shirt had hidden the six ridges of his abdomen and a large tattoo across his upper shoulder. Luke had a tattoo. I squinted to see better, but when he pulled down his zipper, I spun around. "What are you doing?"

"Taking off my wet clothes."

"Well, what are you going to put on?"

"Nothing. But I'll go grab some dry clothes from upstairs. I'm sure Colton has some extra. I'll see if I can find something for you, too"

"Okay, hurry."

He chuckled as he walked away. "This is not funny, Crawford."

"You should see yourself from my angle. It's freaking hilarious. What are you so afraid of, Sweeney? That you might jump me if you saw me with my pants off?"

"Don't be ridiculous," I waved a hand behind me as I kept my back turned. "Just go."

When his footsteps reached the second floor, I turned around. I didn't want to see Luke Crawford naked. I didn't want to think of him as anything other than that selfish, spoiled little boy I remembered. Until now, he'd done nothing to disabuse me of my recollection, so I didn't need a hot body to change that. God, who knew I was so desperate for sex? I had one serious boyfriend after college, a few bad dates in the last couple of years, and that was it. It was quite an embarrassing dry spell. No wonder Luke's fitness-magazine-cover chest made my stomach drop.

"Found something," he called from upstairs.

"Thank god," I mumbled.

Luke jogged down the steps wearing a pair of gray sweatpants and a tight white t-shirt. I groaned internally. Why did this somehow look hotter?

He held out a bundle of clothes. "Here. These are for you."

I grabbed the small heap. "Thanks. I'll go change upstairs."

When I reached the bathroom on the second level, I locked the door and examined the pieces in my hands. A pair of gray sweat socks and shorts fell to the floor as I sized up the pale blue dress shirt. I tilted my head. The shirt could work. I slipped it on and buttoned it to the top. Picking up the socks one at a time, I put those on, too. However, upon closer inspection, I noticed the shorts were actually boxers.

*Oh, no! No freaking way I'm wearing Colton's underwear.*

I stuck my head out of the bathroom. "Hey, Crawford. You made a mistake. You gave me Colton's boxers."

"Not a mistake," he shouted from downstairs.

"There's no way I'm wearing your brother's underwear."

"They're clean. I checked."

"Ugh, gross. Still not happening."

"Suit yourself!"

My panties weren't wet from the rain so I could still wear those, but it would be awfully breezy walking around with just the shirt on. I looked down at the shorts and shuddered. Nope, still not wearing Colton's boxers. I picked them up and placed them on the large white counter.

Walking down the steps, I heard the crackle before I felt the heat from the fire. Luke had started one while I was upstairs. He had also placed a towel next to the fireplace and laid our wet clothes on top.

"Thank you," I said, walking to the living room to stand behind him. He turned and whatever he was going to say died on his lips because he choked. His mouth opened and his eyes widened. It was a bit funny to see him that way. Of course, he'd never seen me in anything like this. It felt good knowing I had that brief effect on him. He recovered quickly and cleared his throat.

"The shirt fits nicely. I mean, it looks good on you. I don't mean—"

I fought back a smile. "I know what you mean, Crawford."

He nodded but kept staring at me funny. "Um, you said something about calling for help earlier."

He snapped his fingers, "Yes. I called a lumber company. They said they're backed up, but they should be here by morning."

"Morning!" I gasped.

"Yes. There are a lot of fallen trees, and some are on major roadways. We're not exactly a priority right now."

"But, but… aren't you rich or something? Can't you pay someone to come tow the tree away?"

"Yes, but they'd get blocked by the other fallen trees on the road trying to get to us. I'm sorry, Sweeney, but it looks like we're going to be here for a while."

I smacked my forehead and went in search of my purse. I found it where I'd left it in the hallway earlier.

"Where are you going?"

"I need to make a phone call."

"To your husband?" asked Luke, his voice a little high-pitched.

"My what?" I said, coming back to the living room.

"You corrected Colton the other day when he called you 'Miss'. So, I'm assuming you're—"

"Independent? Not attached to any other person or inclined to disclose my marital status? Yes, that's correct. My personal life is just that. My business. So, if you'll excuse me. I have a personal call to make."

I jogged back upstairs to the bathroom and closed the door. It wasn't all that private of a conversation, but I didn't want to give Luke the satisfaction of knowing that I was still single, not even close to being in a relationship. The only thing I snuggled up to at night was my laptop.

"Hi, Lorna. It's me. How are you?"

"Fine, Grace. Is everything all right?"

"Not exactly. Can you spend the night at my place with my mother? I know it's a lot to ask and I will pay you time and half, but I'm stuck in a cabin up north and I have no way of getting back home tonight."

"Oh, my gosh. Are you all by yourself?"

"No. I'm here with Luke Crawford."

"Luke Crawford. Do you mean one of the Crawford brothers? Wow, I didn't know you two were dating."

"We're not. It's a long story. Can you do it?"

"Yes, of course."

I sighed with relief. "Thank you, Lorna. Can I speak to my mom?"

There was silence on the other end. "Hello? Lorna?"

"I'm here. I just checked her room and your mom is still sleeping."

"It's five-thirty."

"She's been resting since four. Should I wake her up?"

"No, that's fine. Let her sleep. I'll have to call the doctor and let him know that she's been really tired lately."

Lorna must have heard the stress in my voice. "Don't worry, Grace. I'm here tonight. Try to relax."

"I will. Thanks again."

After ending the call, I went downstairs to sit next to the fire, but Luke wasn't there.

"Crawford," I called.

"I'm in the kitchen."

I walked to the back of the house and turned to my left. I found Luke filling a pot from the kitchen faucet.

"What are you doing?"

He raised his eyebrows. "What does it look like I'm doing?"

"About to boil water?"

"You always were the smart one, Sweeney." He placed the pot on top of the stove and turned the burner on. "I found some pasta in the cupboard. No fresh tomatoes to make a sauce, but I found some garlic. I can do a traditional *aglio olio*."

I pursed my lips and cocked my head, thinking I hadn't heard him. "Ai-what?"

He smirked. "*Aglio olio.* It's a traditional Italian sauce. It's just garlic and olive oil with some spices. But it tastes pretty good. Are you okay with that?"

Considering I had planned to starve until morning, I thought his idea sounded brilliant. "Sure, that works."

"Great. Can you grab me a head of garlic over there in the pantry?"

I opened the first door to my right but found nothing except cereal boxes and cans of vegetables. I tried the next door and found the garlic. "Ha! Gotcha!"

"Do you greet all your vegetables in the same manner?"

"Yes. I find I like them better than people."

He barked out a laugh. "I bet you do."

"People demand things. Or they misconstrue my words or feel they are owed something when they've done nothing to earn it. Vegetables, numbers, and books are a lot easier to understand than people."

"You really are strange. You know that, right?"

"You see? You just misconstrued my words."

"No, I didn't. I understood what you said. I just found it strange."

"Whatever, Crawford. Just because you have a way with people doesn't mean you understand them."

"Look, Sweeney. It's obvious we are both still..." He trailed off as he chopped the garlic.

"Still what?"

"How do I put this? Sensitive about what happened in the past."

I scoffed. "I'm not sensitive, Crawford. I'm mad."

"Fine. You're still mad at me. And frankly, I'm still mad at you. But we're stuck here for at least another twelve hours. Why don't we try to forget the past for just one night and pretend we are two strangers getting to know one another?"

"I wouldn't be spending the night with a stranger."

He sighed. "You know what I mean."

"Fine. One night. I'll pretend that I never knew you in high school. Is that what you want?"

His face scrunched up. "Not exactly. But I think you get what I'm trying to say."

"Fine. I agree."

I grabbed myself a bottle of water from the fridge. "Do you want one?" I asked Luke.

"No, I'm good."

I took a large sip of water and wondered about the last time I spent time with someone I found attractive.

"Do you like it hard?"

I choked on the water and wiped the dribble over my mouth. "What?!"

He stared at me like I'd lost my mind. "Do you like your spaghetti firm or soft?"

"Oh." I cleaned a few drops of water from the floor with a napkin. "Ah, firm."

"Me, too."

I gulped. I had to stop thinking about sex before I said something that would embarrass me. But I couldn't resist. "The firmer the better," I croaked. When Luke glanced up with a puzzled look on his face, I spun around and rushed out of the room before he could hear me laugh.

# 9

## Luke

Grace was acting very strange. Well, stranger than usual. She kept biting her lower lip in the kitchen and pulling at the collar of her pale blue shirt. While I would usually take those as signs of sexual interest, in this case, I highly doubted it. Grace Sweeney hated me, and I wasn't too crazy about her either.

She only cared about work and never bothered to understand those around her. Just like when we were in school—it was all about the work—and never about just having fun and being with the people you supposedly cared about. She chose her work that day and didn't come to my game and while I knew it sounded petty, I had needed her there.

My phone ringing jerked me from the memory. But the name on the caller ID was someone from my past: Jared Michaels. He was one of my best friends back in high school and owned a tow truck company. I called him yesterday to help me with this tree situation.

"Hey Jared, what's going on?"

"I spoke to the people up in your county. Looks like they're gonna wait 'til mornin' to clear up the roads. So, I'll be up there by noon."

"Sounds good. Don't forget to bring your biggest haul and a chainsaw. This tree is huge."

"Looking forward to it, bud. You're lucky you still have electricity up there, so you can watch TV. Too bad you don't have company to spend the night with."

"I do. You'll see her tomorrow. But it's not like that."

"Wait, you do? It's not like you to miss out on an opportunity," he laughed and I felt uncomfortable knowing he would be right if it were anyone else but her. I would have thought the same thing.

"I'm here with Grace Sweeney. So, nothing will happen."

"Wait! What? You're at the cabin with *Meany Sweeney*?"

I hadn't heard the nickname out loud in nearly ten years. When Jared had asked why I wasn't having lunch with Grace in the cafeteria, I said because she was mean and selfish and I was done with her. I admit, it was a douche thing to say, but I was mad. He called her Meany Sweeney that day and kept up the nickname for the rest of the four years. I don't know if it ever bothered her though, she never seemed to react to the name.

"Her name is Grace, Jared. We're not kids anymore."

He laughed on the other end of the phone. "Come on now, I was just having a little fun. How does she look?"

"What?" For some inexplicable reason, I didn't want Jared picturing Grace in his dirty mind.

"You know, does she still walk with her nose up in the air or stuck in a book?"

"No, Jared. She doesn't. I'll see you tomorrow, okay?"

"Yeah, tomorrow."

I hung up the phone, feeling somewhat annoyed with Jared and myself if I was honest. Did I sound just like him in high school?

"Was that Jared Michaels you were speaking to?" Her voice made me catch my breath, as I wasn't expecting her. She held a glass of amber liquid in her hand, swirling it before taking a swig.

When she caught me staring at her hand, she gave a wry smile. "I hope you don't mind that I found the bar and poured myself a drink."

Her hair fell forward and she tucked it behind her ear. She crossed her arms under her breasts, exposing a few inches of soft skin just above the straining button. I swallowed, but my throat felt tight.

"I don't mind at all," I said hoarsely. I cleared my throat. "Yeah. It was him."

Her eyes narrowed and she brought her glass back to her mouth, taking a longer sip this time.

"What's wrong?" I asked.

"Nothing. I just can't stand the guy, that's all."

"He's not so bad."

"Easy for you to say. He didn't make fun of you for four years."

"He didn't do that. Did he?" I looked up and her lips formed a straight line as she watched me.

"He called me…" She waved her hand in front of her face. "That stupid name… every chance he got. He even…"

"He even?"

"Nothing. It was a long time ago."

"No. Say it. What did he do?"

If he had touched her, I would hurt him back. I mean… I would do that if he had touched any woman inappropriately. Right? My hands weren't shaking just because it was Sweeney.

"He..."

I inhaled, waiting for her next words.

"He ruined it." My mind raced, wondering what her words meant.

"Ruined what?"

"The painting," she whispered.

I exhaled loudly. *Thank God*. "What painting?"

"Just forget it," she said and put her drink down. "How can I help?"

"No," I said, setting down the knife. "What painting?"

She rolled her eyes. "It's stupid."

"Obviously not to you."

She sighed. "Remember the art project we had in first year? The one I worked all night on with my mother?" Her eyes softened and she looked away as though lost in thought. "I decided to paint my version of The Mona Lisa. She went to every craft store to find the right shade of brown for me."

"Who did?"

She smiled. "My mom." Her voice cracked and she cleared her throat. I didn't know Sweeney could get this sentimental about paint. Or maybe she could since it had to do with a school project.

"Anyway, Ms. Reynolds, the art teacher, displayed it at the front of the school next to the basketball trophies. But the next day someone had written… you know… across it." She looked away. "It was ruined," she breathed. "Jared teased me about it in the cafeteria later."

Of course, he did. What an idiot. I would call him back after dinner and tell him I'd gone with another towing company.

"I took the painting down and told Mrs. Reynolds to get rid of it."

Her lips trembled and I couldn't understand why an art project made this stone-cold woman so emotional. But my heart ached for her. I put my hand on top of hers over her drink and squeezed.

"I'm sorry, Sweeney," I said and meant it. It was important to her, even if I didn't understand why. I should have been there for her. And I would have been if she'd been there for me.

I snatched my hand back and continued chopping the garlic. "Dinner will be ready in a few minutes."

She stared at my hands and then up at me before taking one last gulp to finish her drink. She walked out into the hallway. "Does your brother have a bottle of wine we can open for dinner?"

"White or red?" I called out.

"I don't care."

"There's a wine fridge on the other side of this island."

She walked back toward me, pushing her hair out of her face, and bent over the fridge, tapping a finger to her lips. The pale blue shirt rode up the back of her thighs and I couldn't tear my eyes away.

The frying pan sizzled and water overflowed from the pot, causing the burner to flame up. "Shit," I murmured, turning down the heat.

Sweeney rushed over with a dish towel and wiped down the mess next to me. "Thanks," I said.

She turned too quickly and bumped her chest into mine. "Oof!" She placed her hands on my chest to push herself back, but they remained there until she slid them down to my waist.

I froze, unsure if this was the alcohol or Sweeney. I watched her closely as she stared at my shirt and then her hands as she inched them across my stomach. My muscles flinched at her touch and she snatched her hands away.

*What the hell just happened?*

"Sweeney?" I asked.

The oven timer beeped and she jumped. "Ah, dinner's ready."

I nodded but continued to stare at her. She rubbed her arms and sat down at the table, gazing out the window. I drained the pasta, then poured the garlic and olive oil inside the pot and mixed it with the spaghetti. Scooping out two platefuls, I placed the dishes on the wood table in front of her.

"*Bon appétit,*" I said and passed her the Parmesan cheese.

"Thank you for making dinner," she said and poured some wine for the both of us.

I raised my glass. "To the future."

She smirked and clinked her glass with mine. "To the future."

We dug into our pasta.

"Mmm, this is amazing," she said. She groaned a little too and the sound vibrated through my body.

"It would have been better with a bit of parsley," I said, focusing on the flavor of the dish rather than wondering what she would taste like underneath that shirt.

"Pardon?" she asked.

*Shit. Did I say that out loud?*

"Parsley. I said it needs parsley."

She squinted and then looked down at her wine. "I think this should be my last glass."

I nodded and wiped the bead of sweat from my brow. I didn't speak for the rest of the meal, worried something stupid would come out of my mouth and she seemed content with the silence.

When I placed my fork on the table, she picked it up along with my plate. "You cooked, so I get cleaning duty."

"We can do it together," I suggested.

"Nope. I didn't help you cook, so it's only fair. Besides, I find cleaning relaxing."

I shook my head. "You really are strange, Sweeney."

She laughed and pushed me out of the kitchen. I raised my hands. "Okay, I'm going. I'll check on the fire in the living room."

By the time she joined me, I'd revived the fire to a sizable blaze. Colton taught me to make one when I was ten. There weren't many opportunities to practice since we stopped camping after my parents died. My uncle wouldn't take us, and Colton focused on his career once he turned eighteen.

Spotting the full glass of wine in her hand, I grinned. "I see you changed your mind about another glass."

"You only live once. Isn't that your motto, Crawford?"

"Yeah. Something like that." The motto was, we don't live forever, but she was pretty close. It surprised me she even remembered.

She sat on the couch, her back against the armrest, and raised her knees to her chest. The long shirt slid down her thighs, leaving the back of her thighs exposed. Her smooth skin gleamed in the dim light and shadows crept in secret places. Sweat gathered at my neck, so I joined Sweeney on the couch, away from the fire. But I felt no relief, having moved away from the heat and closer to her. Out of the pot and into the frying pan, as they say.

She took a sip of her drink and stared at me. "Are you still mad at me, Luke? Because I'm still quite pissed off at you."

I laughed because she didn't sound drunk, but I knew the whiskey and now the wine had loosened her tongue a bit.

"Yeah, I'm still mad, Sweeney. But we called a truce for the night. Remember?"

Her eyes narrowed, but instead of responding, she took another sip of her wine.

"What did you do after high school, Luke?"

I rubbed the back of my neck and stared at the fire. "I went to Business School at Oxford. I graduated, but I spent most of my time at restaurants or traveling around Italy, France, and Spain, learning recipes from the locals."

Then I smiled at a memory. "One time, I hopped on the back of some girl's motorcycle and she drove us to a secluded field. I thought I'd made a bad decision, but it was just her family's home. They baked fresh bread and pizza from a stone oven that was centuries old. It was pretty wild."

"That kind of stuff happens to people like you," she said.

"People like me?"

"Yeah. The take-life-as-it-comes type. No plan, no worries. Just live. Sometimes I wish I was like that, you know. Carefree."

I wasn't sure if that was a compliment. I didn't think it was. It sounded quite similar to Colton's speech about me finally taking on responsibilities.

"Why? What did you do after high school?"

She raised her eyes and held her glass from the rim as she spoke. "I went to the local college. Worked all summer to earn enough to pay for whatever the scholarship didn't cover and then got my Master's in Accounting. Applied for an internship at Delmar & Tuch and I've been there ever since."

"I'm glad it was all worth it," I mumbled. A part of me was happy she got what she'd always wanted, but it still stung that she had put her work before our friendship.

She narrowed her eyes. "Maybe I've had too much to drink, but I don't follow. What do you mean, you're glad it was worth it? Worth what?"

"Nothing," I said. I'd promised a truce. I wouldn't bring up the past.

"Spill it, Crawford."

"It doesn't matter. You got what you wanted, even if you had to sacrifice people on the way. We all make choices. Looks like yours paid off the way you wanted it to."

Her lips pursed and she put the glass down on the side table next to the couch. "What choice did I make?"

"Forget it, Sweeney. We agreed to leave the past behind us tonight."

"No. I agreed to not hate you for one night. So, tell me, what decision did I make?"

Fine. She wanted to play this out. If I was the irresponsible one, then she was the self-absorbed one. "You chose your work instead of our friendship. But I'm over it, Sweeney. So don't sweat it."

"What the *hell* are you talking about?" She straightened herself up from the couch.

I rubbed my forehead, truly not wanting to get into this. But now that I started it, I had to finish. "Remember my baseball game? You promised you would come, but you stood me up—again. I didn't know which assignment took priority this time, but it didn't matter. I was done with you choosing your work over me."

Her eyes bulged and she opened her mouth, but nothing came out. She stayed like that for a few seconds until she fell forward, laughing. "You're incredible, you know that?"

I shook my head, confused. "What?"

"You think I didn't come to your game because I was working on an assignment?"

"Yeah. Just like the last time. That art project you're so fond of."

She shook her head. "You selfish, self-centered bastard."

"Now wait a minute—"

"No, you wait. You never asked me why I didn't come—"

"I didn't have to."

"You never allowed me to explain."

"I didn't want to hear it," I mumbled. When she didn't continue, I looked up. Tears filled her eyes and her face scrunched up as though she were in pain.

"What is it?"

"Forget it. It doesn't even matter anymore." She folded her arms and rocked on the couch.

"Grace," I whispered.

Her head snapped up and her eyes searched mine. I realized I'd called her by her first name for the first time since that day. "Tell me what happened."

Her eyes brimmed with tears and one finally escaped, but she shook her head while she wiped it away.

"Please," I whispered. "I feel like there's more to this story."

A wry smile played on her lips, but she didn't seem amused. I leaned forward and placed my hand on top of hers and rubbed my thumb along her soft skin.

She bit her lip and looked up, trying to stop the other tears from falling. "That night, my mom—" her voice cracked and I squeezed her hand. "I found her in the kitchen. She had passed out. I couldn't wake her, so I called the ambulance."

For a second, fear gripped my heart, but scattered as I reassured myself that Grace's mother was fine. I'd seen her at graduation. "Go on. What happened next?"

"I rode in the ambulance with her. She was so pale and I was terrified as the paramedics put an oxygen mask on her and tried to wake her up. She didn't open her eyes until we reached the hospital. I was so scared."

"Of course you were." Noticing she fought back tears as her face scrunched up, I tried to reassure her. "But she's okay now."

"That's just it," she said, a tear escaping, but she wiped it with her palm. "That night, they told me my mother's kidneys aren't functioning properly. She requires special medication and will one day need a transplant. I was old enough to know we didn't have the money for a transplant." She dropped her head and I tried to pull her into my arms. She pushed me back and glared at me. "When I tried to tell you about it the next day, all I got was some nonsense about a baseball game. I couldn't believe you were upset about me missing a game when I thought I would lose my mother."

I knew what losing a mother and a father felt like, but I didn't want to dismiss her pain. She was just a child when she found out and she was all alone. I had my brothers. She was supposed to have me, but my head was too far up my ass to see anything but my own problems.

"I'm so sorry, Grace."

I leaned forward to gather her into my arms. I wanted to hold her and tell her everything would be all right, the words I should have said years ago. But she put her hands up and sniffed. "I'm fine. My mother will be fine, and I don't need you to comfort me anymore, Luke."

She was right. That time had passed and I'd missed it.

*God, how did I miss it?*

"Grace—"

"It's getting late," she said and stood from the couch. "I'm going to bed."

I nodded and rubbed my neck, holding myself back from calling out to her.

*But what would I even say now?*

So many emotions ran through my body. I felt guilty for not being there for Grace; shame for realizing how self-absorbed I'd been…*maybe still am*. And I felt regret for letting my pride hold me back from asking her why she didn't come to my game all those years ago. I sat on the couch with my head in my hands when Grace's voice pulled me from my thoughts.

"Luke?" she called. Her voice sounded hesitant.

"Yes," I said, rising from the couch.

But her words stopped me when I reached the top of the stairs.

"Why is there only one bed?"

*Oh, fuck. I forgot about that.*

# 10

## Grace

Watching Luke's eyes change from cold to compassionate unnerved me. In his softened features, I recognized the boy I once knew and cared about. But he didn't exist, and maybe he never did. Just because he felt regret now having discovered the circumstances of that night, didn't mean he wouldn't do something like that again. Luke Crawford hadn't changed. I saw how he didn't care about his responsibilities at work. He only cared about attention. No. Luke may have felt guilty, but he was still the same guy. He put himself first.

At the top of the stairs, I counted four doors—two on either side of the hallway. I tried the first door to my right, but that was Colton's study. The one beside that was a bathroom. Crossing the parquet floor of the hallway, I tried the third door. Inside, a stuffed giraffe stood proudly next to an ivory crib. *That's strange.* I didn't think any of the Crawford brothers had babies.

Shrugging my shoulders, I walked out and into the last room. I spotted a king-size bed with a black leather headboard covered with a white duvet beside a black dresser and an ornate mirror on the wall. It looked as though Colton had bought the furniture, but his wife had added some accessories to brighten it up. For a second, I thought to check the next room as Luke would surely expect to sleep in the Main bedroom, then realized this was the last room. Which meant…

"Luke,"

"Yes?"

"Why is there only one bed?"

Heavy footfalls pounded up the wooden steps. Then Luke appeared in the bedroom doorway. He looked around the room and rubbed his neck. "Shit, I forgot. Colton had mentioned something about wanting to turn the second bedroom into a nursery. Didn't realize he had done it."

"That's great. I'm happy for your brother and sister-in-law. But why didn't you tell me?"

He scoffed and put his hand on his hip. "I didn't know this was going to be an overnight trip."

"Well, it certainly is now," I said in a sarcastic tone.

His eyes glanced over to the king-size bed and then back to mine. They held my gaze and my body felt them rake over my lips, my neck, my entire body. I shuddered.

"I could—"

"No." I couldn't sleep in the same bed as him. I just couldn't.

"I was going to say I could take the couch and you take the bed."

"Oh." A twang of disappointment rang in my voice that he hadn't thought to sleep in the same bed as me. I cleared my throat. "Thank you. That's kind of you." I looked around the room, but the wood floors didn't seem like a better alternative to the couch. There was a large chair in the corner of the room. "Maybe," I started.

He caught the direction of my eyes and shook his head. "It's better if I'm not in the same room," he said. "Good night, Grace."

"Good night, Luke," I said and waited as he inhaled a deep breath and walked away. He was right. It was better he wasn't in the same room. I may… uh, I might, I don't know… strangle him in the middle of the night.

When he left, I exhaled the breath and dropped onto the bed. Staring at the ceiling, I tapped a finger on my arm.

He infuriated me. One minute he was this self-centered man-child, the next he looked into my eyes like some lost boy wanting to find his way home. *Ugh!*

I closed my eyes, hoping that would make the image of Luke go away, but it didn't. His green eyes and light brown hair materialized in the darkness.

Why did it matter that he now knew about my mother? And why did sharing the truth about her make me feel closer to him? Was I that desperate for someone to hear me out? Was I that lonely?

The silence in the quiet, dark, empty room was deafening.

I rolled to my side—overcome with emotions I couldn't comprehend—and tried to sleep.

The clock next to the bed glared at me: 11:16 p.m.

I puffed up my pillow. 11:47 p.m.

I pushed my hair off my neck. 12:24 p.m.

Giving up, I snapped the covers off me and got out of bed. Since I didn't have an overnight bag, I slept in my panties and the shirt Luke had given me, but now even these seemed stifling. I unbuttoned a couple more buttons of the shirt and fanned myself. A glass of cold water would probably help me sleep.

I tread lightly down the steps, not wanting to wake Luke, but I didn't have to worry. As I turned the corner toward the kitchen, I saw him standing over the island with a glass in his hand and a bottle of whiskey beside him.

His eyes squinted and looked confused, as though I were a ghost or some apparition. Then they widened as I neared. "What are you doing?" he asked, his voice hoarse in the dim light.

"I couldn't sleep."

He watched me as I walked toward him. Slowly, he raised the glass to his lips but didn't take his eyes off of me. The pale blue shirt clung to me and I pulled it away to cool down my skin. As I approached, I noticed Luke's skin was flushed, too. A bead of sweat lay at the base of his collar.

"Would you like a drink?" he asked.

"Definitely."

He turned to the cupboard to grab a glass.

"Are you hungry?"

My stomach growled on cue. I smirked; I couldn't help it.

"Sure. What have you got?"

"I can scramble some eggs for you. I saw a carton of egg whites in the fridge that hasn't expired."

"Mmm," I walked over to the fridge and pulled out the freezer drawer. Bingo! Rocky Road ice cream. "Do you think Colton has any chocolate sauce?" I asked.

Luke swallowed, his Adam's apple jutting up and down. "God, I hope so." He rummaged through the pantry and grabbed a squeeze bottle.

I clapped my hands together, then reached for two bowls and a large spoon. After filling up the bowls with three scoops of ice cream, I passed them to Luke to sauce them up.

Squeezing slowly, he looked up at me expectantly. "Say when."

I shook my head and grinned. Reaching over, I put my hand over his and squeezed harder, releasing a downpour of chocolate sauce.

"Perfect," I said.

He laughed. "Still have that sweet tooth."

We took our bowls to the couch and feasted.

"So, what else have you been up to? Have you been to any of the art galleries in New York City? I recall you saying something about them." He snapped his fingers.

"Wait. It was breakfast in New York, then dinner in Paris. Wasn't that the dream?"

I always did dream big. I couldn't believe he remembered.

"Nope. You're looking at it. The dream I mean," I said with a mouthful of ice cream. "This is the most time off I've had in years. What about you?" I wanted to change the subject.

"I've traveled some," he said sheepishly. The gesture was so out of character I stared at him for a moment.

"Don't hold back on my account. Tell me about all the adventures you've been on."

He raised his eyebrows.

I laughed. "Okay, sounds like that would take all night," I playfully nudged him with my foot against his thigh on the couch. He stared down at my toes. Thank goodness I'd given myself a pedicure last week. My mom had insisted on a spa day, so I'd relented and painted our nails.

"All right. There was this one time, a friend and I decided to drive to New York and take a cruise to Bermuda. Colton refused to lend me the yacht, so I found a way to go, anyway."

"Oh, the yacht was unavailable, so you had to slum it with the common folk, did you?"

He tilted his head and tried to look annoyed, but his brown hair fell forward and covered his eye, making him look roguish instead. "As I was saying, we took a cruise to Bermuda and didn't realize when we disembarked for an excursion to reset our watches. The island is one hour ahead. We spent the day at the beach and as we walked along the pier toward the ship, we noticed hundreds of passengers waving at us. My friend thought they had recognized me, but as we got closer, I heard someone shout, 'Run! The ship's gonna leave without you!'"

"Oh my gosh, that's right. Cruise ships warn you to be on time, otherwise, they'll leave you at the port and you'll have to find your way back to the next port."

"Exactly. And the next port was New York and since our passports were still on the ship, we would be stuck on the island and I knew Colton would kill me. So, we jumped."

"Wait, what? You jumped?"

He shrugged his shoulders. "We hightailed it and dove into the water just as the ship took off without us."

"No, you didn't?"

He laughed, taking a spoonful of ice cream. "Sure did. Swam along the ship until they lowered a small boat to collect us."

I sat back and stared at him. "I don't believe it."

"Trust me. I wouldn't make that up. It's pretty embarrassing. For the rest of the trip, everyone on the ship called us The Castaways. But not in a good way, you know." He laughed and collected my bowl when I scraped the last of the Rocky Road onto my spoon and licked it. Placing the bowls on the side table, he pulled the fabric ottoman up against the couch so we could raise our legs and lean back. It was quite comfortable. "Thank you," I said and yawned. The ice cream had hit the spot and cooled me down at the same time. I felt satiated and relaxed.

"I can't swim," I admitted. "I'm terrified of water."

"I'll have to teach you sometime."

"I don't think so. I'd probably drown you trying."

"I'm tougher than you think. And so are you."

I stared at him sideways. "You're right. I am."

He yawned this time and leaned his head back. My eyes drooped, and I snuggled deeper into the couch. Luke said something, but I didn't hear him. His voice sounded far away, and then I heard nothing.

A little while later, I felt cold. I opened my eyes to find Luke asleep beside me. I considered going upstairs to bed but worried I'd wake up completely if I tried to navigate the stairs now. It was better if I stayed here. I grabbed a soft wool blanket from the opposite couch and laid it over Luke's body, then I slid inside and fell asleep.

# *11*

## Luke

The scent of vanilla surrounded me, and something so distinctly feminine that it made my mouth water. A warm weight lay on top of my thigh. When I reached down and felt the soft curve of a woman's leg only inches away from my groin, my body reacted. I jackknifed off the couch, throwing a blanket I hadn't noticed before onto the floor.

Grace braced herself with both hands on the couch, her eyes bulging out, and her chest heaving. "Oh my gosh, what's wrong? What's happening?"

"Uh… nothing." I had no idea why I reacted that way, except my next move was to pull her leg closer to me, then run my hand up her thigh… and that definitely wouldn't be a good idea so I launched myself as far away from her as possible.

"I think I heard some trucks outside. I'll go check it out."

"Okay," she said slowly as I walked out the front door.

The morning sun's rays blazed through the leaves, blinding me momentarily. As I squinted past the fallen tree, I noticed a white van down the road. Huh, maybe there was someone here after all. I jogged down the gravel driveway and spotted two men with their hands on their hips surveying the road.

"Hey," I called out to them.

They both turned in unison, looking me up and down. I wore a white t-shirt and gray shorts. I didn't look like another worker. "Are you the guys from the tow truck company I called?"

"Mr. Crawford?" one man asked.

"Yes. That's me."

"Yes, sir. We underestimated the size of the tree, so we're just waiting on a second truck to arrive to help us out. But it looks like it will be another couple of hours or so."

I didn't mind, but I had a feeling Grace wouldn't welcome the news. "Thanks. I appreciate the update and you coming on short notice." I had called them after firing Jared.

I jogged back to the cabin and spotted Grace's silhouette holding a mug and peering through the screen door. She still had the pale blue shirt on and seeing her wait for me in that shirt pulled on some unrecognizable heartstring. I'd never thought of getting married before, but picturing my wife with her hair tousled, wearing nothing but my shirt, had an appeal I'd never realized before. It definitely had nothing to do with Grace in particular. Absolutely not.

"Will we be leaving soon?" she asked as I walked up the front steps.

"It'll be another couple of hours, at least."

She sighed and ran her fingers through her hair. Despite the early hour, sweat gathered at the nape of my neck and the July air was stifling. Looking over Grace's head, past the cabin's windows, an idea popped into my head.

I smiled. "Come with me."

"Where are you going?" she asked, her eyes narrowing.

I chuckled at her annoyance. "You'll see."

"I don't like surprises, Luke." She crossed her arms.

"I don't think you'll like this one, either. But you'll thank me for it."

She grimaced. "Egotistical much?"

"Come on, Sweeney. We don't have all day."

"I've got work to do. And—" I grabbed her hand and pulled her toward the back of the house.

"What do you think you're doing?" she sputtered.

She wrenched her arm back and I stopped to look at her before asking, "Are you chicken, Grace?"

I tried not to smile when I saw her face contort. Oh, I knew how much she hated it when I called her chicken. Gritting her teeth, she said slowly, "Let me just put my mug down."

Gently, she placed it on the kitchen counter. "Fine. What is it we need to do?"

"We need to begin your lessons." I winked and walked out the back door. Hesitantly, she followed.

Standing in front of the lake, I removed my socks and shoes. I placed them on the grass before walking onto the sandy shore. Looking over my shoulder at Grace, her fingers pressed tightly into her arms. I pushed anyway. "Are you coming?"

She scanned the lake. "I don't see a motorboat, a paddleboat, not even a life jacket anywhere. What are we doing?"

"You're not going on any boat, Grace. I'm going to give you your first swimming lesson."

She scoffed. "Well, sorry to disappoint you. But you're not my first. I had swimming lessons when I was ten, and if you recall they went horribly wrong."

I frowned. "I don't recall you taking swimming lessons."

"That's because it was only one lesson and I kicked the instructor in the nuts when he tried to push me into the water. My mom took me home after he was incapacitated and couldn't continue the lesson."

My eyes widened, and for a moment, I regretted my spontaneous decision. She smiled at the look on my face. Oh, no. Grace Sweeney would not get out of this that easily. I jogged a few feet deeper into the dark lake, raised my arms above my head, and dove in—white t-shirt, gray shorts, and all. The splash was the last thing I heard before the rush of the water.

I broke through the surface and shook out my wet hair before slicking it back.

She stared at me, then cleared her throat. "That was a nice dive. Are we done yet?"

"No. We're not. Come on in. The water's warm."

"It's not the temperature of the water I'm worried about. It's the depth and likeliness of losing my air supply."

"You're not going to drown."

She threw her hands up in the air. "That's it. You put it into the universe. I'm done. I'm definitely not getting into the water now."

"You're not superstitious, are you?"

"No. I'm practical. I don't need to know how to swim."

"What if one day you're thrown overboard?"

"I promise you, that won't ever happen."

Silence. Then I began…

"Bock, bock, bock."

"Are you making chicken noises?"

I could see the indignation steam from her ears. She would throttle me if she could. Maybe it would spur her into the water. "Bock," I said, more quietly this time.

"I don't have a swimsuit."

"Neither do I. I don't think the fish will care."

Her eyes grew twice as big. "There are fish?"

I thought it best to avoid answering that question. "That's not even your shirt. You can change into your regular clothes once the lesson is over."

"Are you even certified to give lessons?"

I shook my head. Grace Sweeney only did things by the book. "Why don't you live a little and get a swimming lesson from an uncertified instructor? The thrill is unbelievable," I deadpanned.

"This really—" she started and I threw my best bait.

"I get it. You suck at this and you won't do something unless you're perfect at it. Afraid someone may judge you for it."

She fell for it hook, line and sinker. Maybe because it was the truth. She marched down the grass and onto the sand, her arms swinging at her sides. Her mouth formed a straight line, and her face was as gray as the lake. When her toes splashed the water, she froze. And the angry woman became a terrified little girl. Her eyes rounded and her chest started heaving. "I can't do this," she whispered.

Something pounded within my chest, and I moved quickly to grasp her hands. "It's all right. I'm right here. You can do this."

When her hands began to tremble, I interlaced them with my fingers. "We don't have to move much further than this if you don't want to."

She nodded but stared at her legs. The water reached her ankles and I could see her pink toenail polish peeking out between the sand. When she looked up, she nodded again and took another step forward.

"That's it," I coaxed.

Her hands trembled again and she bit her lip. I wanted to take her fear away. "Look at me." When she kept her head down, I brought my finger to her chin and raised her head. "Look at my eyes." Her eyes were a deep brown shade. I could lose myself inside them if this wasn't Grace Sweeney.

She took another step and the ground dropped about a foot and a half; the water sluicing against the top of her thighs. "Oh, god," she cried out.

Grabbing onto her forearms, I squeezed. "I've got you."

She nodded more emphatically this time.

"You're doing great." Looking at the ground behind me, I knew there would be another significant drop. "The next one will probably sink you to above your waist. Are you ready for that?"

"Sink me?"

*I'm so stupid.*

"Okay, poor choice of words. I mean, it will reach your waist. I'll be right here. I won't let you fall."

Looking back behind her shoulder, I wondered if Grace was determining if she could make a run back to shore without falling. "Grace, I'm here for you. Let me help you."

She turned her face back to look at me. Her eyes watered and her face contorted. I wasn't sure what sort of emotions were playing out in her head right now, but I knew I had to be patient. I stepped closer to her, pressing my body next to hers. She gasped and so did I. But I wasn't the one afraid of drowning.

I wrapped my hands around her waist and waited. I held her for what felt like an eternity, as I held my breath, not wanting to rush her with an impatient sigh. Finally, she placed her hands on my arms and stepped forward, pushing me further into the water. I caught her when the ground dropped and pulled her tighter against me. Her whole body trembled, and so did mine.

She looked down at the water sloshing below her breasts, and she smiled. "I did it."

It was like when the sun came out after the rain. I smiled. "You did it."

She laughed this time. A full and joyful laugh that shook her whole body and mine. She rocked me to my core. Looking down at her smiling face, I remembered all the things I had once loved about her.

"Grace," I whispered as I lowered my head. She closed her eyes and my heart pounded like a jackhammer against my chest.

"Luke! Hey! Luke!" I snapped my head up and watched a figure approach from the driveway out front. As he came closer, my stomach sank and I lost my grip on Grace. She held me tighter as she turned around. "Oh, my god!" she said on an exhale. "Is that Jared Michaels?"

"I'll get rid of him." I bent down and picked Grace up to carry her back to shore.

"What are you doing?" she shouted and pushed her body away from me.

"I thought this would be faster." It only took five steps to reach the sandy shore and I gently put Grace down. She straightened the pale blue shirt, but it still clung to her in all the right places.

"Looks like Meany Sweeney just got a little sweeter," said Jared with a wink.

"Oh my god," said Grace, once again. "I've got to get out of here."

"Grace, wait!" I called, but she was already halfway to the house.

My footsteps ate the ground as I walked toward Jared. "What are you doing here?"

"Well, I got your message pretty late. You didn't give me much notice to call my tow truck driver, so I came up, anyway."

"Well, you wasted your time, Jared. Now go home."

"What's gotten into you, man?"

"Did you spray paint Meany Sweeney on Grace's artwork?"

"What?" he asked, looking around as though he would find the answer behind a tree.

"Was that you? You said back then you didn't know who did, but Grace said she heard you admit it. So, tell me the truth."

"It was just a joke, Luke."

I shook my head at his words and how they disgusted me. I disgusted myself. "Get out, Jared."

"This was like ten years ago. Why does it matter now?"

"Because it always mattered. I just didn't understand how much until now."

I walked back to the house, leaving Jared behind me.

"Grace?" Moving around the house, I couldn't find her, but I heard the shower running. Racing up the stairs, I knocked on the door. "Grace?"

"The road is clear. I want to go home now."

She wasn't in the shower. Her voice was next to the door.

"Can I come in?"

She turned off the water and opened the door. She had changed into her work clothes and her face was the same blank look I'd met in the boardroom. It was as though the newfound connection we'd made was left back at the bottom of the lake. Even if I held my breath, I knew I wouldn't have enough air to retrieve what we'd lost in the water. I was drowning. And I was afraid I would never get the chance to hold her like that again. *But what could I say?*

I couldn't find the words.

Instead, I heard myself mutter, "Yeah. I'll take you home."

# 12

## Luke

Even though I kicked Jared out, it was too late. Grace's face kept its cool demeanor back to town. Sure, her conversation was polite, but she held me at a distance with her short replies or simple murmurs.

I felt like I was fourteen again, wanting to ask her why she was shutting me out or feeling like I should apologize. But I had done nothing wrong. I had told Jared not to come. I kicked him out when he showed up. What more could I do?

After driving Grace home, I drove to the office but didn't go in. I walked around the neighborhood instead. My feet knew where they were going, even if my mind was distracted.

"Mr. Crawford, great to see you," boomed a voice from the kitchen.

"You too, Mario. And please call me Luke." I leaned against the counter that separated the dining room from the kitchen. "What are you making?"

"I'm trying a new recipe. It's rapini and sausage on pizza. What do you think?"

"I think that sounds delicious."

He laughed. "I plan to blend the rapini until the mixture becomes a sauce for my pizza, then crumble the sausage meat on top and add some hot peppers."

"You're making me hungry, Mario."

"I've got one cooling down right now that you can try."

"I knew coming here would cheer me up." I rubbed my hands together before taking a bite of Mario's latest creation. "Mmm, this really is fantastic. You're a genius, Mario."

"Aw, thank you very much."

"How well do these pizzas freeze? Have you ever thought about selling them prepared for the freezer?"

He stopped kneading the dough and looked up at me. His lips pursed. "I never thought of that. But, yes, that could work. You would just have to put them in the oven for twenty minutes."

"Oh, I know a ton of people that would buy them for the convenience. Whether you're coming back from a long day at work or hosting a dinner party."

I grabbed my phone and jotted down some notes. "I'll put some ideas together and send them to you and Victoria."

"Thank you, Mr.--, I mean, Luke."

I took another bite of the pizza. "Oh, it's my pleasure. Besides, I want to take my mind off of things right now."

"Oh? Is something bothering you?"

"Yeah."

"Anything I can do to help?"

"No. Not unless you can turn back time."

He chuckled. "No. I don't have that kind of power. But wouldn't it be nice if we could erase the past or remake our lives like pizza dough? Oh, I would—"

"What did you say, Mario?"

He pressed his lips and looked up at the ceiling. "I said it would be nice to start over—"

"No, the part about erasing the past." I grinned at him. "That's it."

"What's it?"

"Thanks, Mario. You're the best." I stood from the table, stuffing my phone in my back pocket.

"Oh, anytime," he said and poured some green sauce all over his dough. "My wife always says she doesn't know what she'd do without me. Of course, she rolls her eyes when she says it. But I think she means it." He laughed and his belly bounced with each chuckle.

"I'll see you later," I called as I rushed out of the kitchen. My heart raced as an idea formed in my head. I wondered if it could work.

As I climbed into my car, my phone rang.

"Hey, Colton. What's up?" I turned the car away from the curb and merged into traffic.

"Why aren't you at work?" he growled.

"I'm going to be out for the rest of the day. Grace has the files she needs and Daniel is on top of anything else that may come up. I'll be back in the office tomorrow."

"Luke! I swear—"

"I know, I know. And I'm not trying to be an asshole right now. There's just something really important I have to do right away."

"It better be worth it."

"She is."

"She?"

"Uh, I meant, 'it'. It's worth it. Okay, talk to you tomorrow." I ended the call and drove toward a street I hadn't been to in nearly ten years.

My knee bounced impatiently as I approached the building. The marquee with the school insignia was still the same and the grass looked better than I remembered. The custodian, Old Jerry, must have retired.

As I walked up to the front doors of my old high school, I wondered what excuse I would use to persuade the admins to let me in. Alumni meeting, no. Picking up a student, but I didn't know anyone here.

"Can I help you?" a voice asked through the video camera at the door.

"Yes. Um… my name is Luke Crawford… and—"

"Crawford, did you say? As in the Crawford brothers?"

"Um, yes." I wasn't sure if this was a good or a bad thing to admit. My brothers and I didn't have the best reputation in the media.

"Oh my gosh, Melanie. Luke Crawford is at our door."

"Then let him in," a monotone voice said through the speaker.

A loud buzz sounded at the door and I walked inside. A woman, bouncing up and down behind a large desk with her hands clasped together waited for me.

"Mr. Crawford, it is such a pleasure to have you visit our school. We appreciate all the donations Crawford Corporation has made over the years. The students…"

she droned on as I began to piece her excitement together. She was impressed by the money.

"Thank you, Ms.—"

"Principal Cunningham. But you can call me Maggie."

"Thanks, Maggie. I was hoping to speak to the art teacher, Mrs. Reynolds. Is she still here?"

"She sure is. Let me get her for you."

Maggie walked—correction—skipped to the back of the office, where she picked up a microphone. "Attention. Can Mrs. Reynolds please come to the office? It's very important." The way she whispered the last part, made me feel a bit uncomfortable.

"Um, thanks again, Maggie."

A few minutes later, a tall woman with vibrant red hair and a white apron completely splattered in paint walked into the office.

"What the heck was that all about?" she asked, wiping her hands with a towel. "Did Van Gogh come back from the dead or something?"

"Mrs. Reynolds? I don't know if you remember me, but I'm—"

"Luke Crawford," she said, putting the towel down on the desk. "I thought you were some rich playboy now. What are you doing back here?"

"Colton was more… Never mind. I came to see you about a painting."

"Are you looking to invest in a new artist? I have some recommendations I could give you."

"No. It was an art assignment you gave out in my first year."

She stared at me, her eyes blinking behind purple glasses. "You're inquiring about something you painted almost ten years ago?"

"Yes. And it wasn't my painting. It was Grace Sweeney's."

She shook her head. "And they call me the eccentric one," she murmured as she opened the door for me to exit the office. "Well, if we still have it, it would be in one of the storage rooms. I'm a little busy, but you're more than welcome to take a look."

As I followed Mrs. Reynolds down the familiar hallways, a feeling of nostalgia ran through my body. I walked past Grace's first-year locker, remembering how I would wait for her every morning there, eventually avoiding it like a bad rash.

There was the gymnasium that led to the field where we won the state championship. I had looked for Grace that night, but she wasn't there. Walking with my eyes downcast, I wondered if she was at home taking care of her mother that night. The thought made me sick to my stomach.

Mrs. Reynolds led me to her old classroom. There weren't any desks, only easels, and a few pottery stations. "Knock yourself out." Following her outstretched hand toward a door near the back, I walked into the storage room.

There were piles and piles of white canvases all over the room. There were some piled on top of steel shelves, while others leaned up against the walls. Scanning the room, I didn't see any signs or notes indicating the pieces were in any particular order.

*I should turn around and go home.*

But then I remembered Grace's face when she saw Jared and I crouched down to the pile closest to me and flicked through the canvases.

I recalled the painting was of The Mona Lisa, but I wasn't sure how many other students would have tried to paint her over the years. I'd gotten through nearly a third of the art pieces when one caught my attention. Pulling it from the pile, I held it in front of me.

It looked like the right painting, but there was nothing written over it and the signature in the right corner clearly stated the artist's name was Miles. I put it back down and flipped over the next piece.

"How are you doing there?" Mrs. Reynolds popped her head into the room as she adjusted her purple glasses.

"I haven't found it yet." I didn't turn around but continued to search instead.

"Well, if you—"

"Wait! I think I found something." My heart sped up as my eyes scanned a painting stuck between two shelves. I noticed it because it was the only one I'd seen placed in this position. "Can you give me a hand?"

Mrs. Reynolds stood beside me as I pushed the shelf away from the wall. "Are you able to shimmy the canvas free?" I grunted.

Mrs. Reynolds used both hands to pull on the piece of art, but it didn't move.

I pulled a bunch of canvases off the shelf to lighten the load and tried again. "When I say go, I need you to pull as hard as you can. Ready?"

"Ready."

I gripped the steel shelf and pulled it toward me as hard as I could. Groaning from the strain on my muscles, sweat trickled from my forehead. The shelf didn't feel as heavy as before, but I still couldn't get it to move more than a sliver. "Come on, dammit. Move!" I grunted.

"It's moving!" shouted Mrs. Reynolds. "Just a little more."

Planting my feet and imagining a second chance with Grace, I pulled on that shelf as though my life depended on it. My muscles burned, but the sound of metal grinding against concrete was music to my ears.

"I've got it!" yelled Mrs. Reynolds just before she fell backward, landing on her rump. "Oof!"

I ran toward her. "Are you all right?" I asked, extending my hand to help her up.

"Yes. Yes. Fine. This rump can withstand a lot more than a fall."

I cleared my throat and banished any thought of Mrs. Reynold's rump from my mind.

"Here you go," she said. Then, "Oh, no!"

"What's wrong?"

She frowned and bit her lip. "I'm sorry, Luke. But the portrait is ruined."

She turned it over for me. Written in black spray paint were the words: Meany Sweeney. I sighed. "I know, Mrs. Reynolds. That's why I'm here. I want to restore it. Do you know how I can fix it?"

Crossing her arms and tapping a finger to her lips, she stared at the painting. "It's going to take a lot of work and even more patience, and I still don't know if it'll work."

"I'll try anything. Just tell me what to do."

"First, soak only the spray paint with olive oil to loosen it up. Let it sit for a few hours. Then try to scrape it off. This probably won't remove all the spray paint except for the thickest parts. Then, using a paint thinner—or maybe acetone may be better—pat the rest and be careful to only remove the spray paint and not the oil paint underneath. Did you get all that?"

I nodded, making a list of supplies in my head when a sense of excitement that maybe this would work came over me. Turning to my old school teacher, I rushed to hug her and wound up swinging her half a turn in my excitement. "Thank you, Mrs. Reynolds," I said.

She patted her hair when I put her down. "Well, that was quite exciting." She put her hand on my wrist. "I hope it works out for you, Luke. I can see that painting is very special to you."

"It is," I said and meant it deep in my heart. "I've got to go. Thanks again, Mrs. Reynolds."

"Anytime," she said, waving me off. "I haven't had this much fun since that seance with my late husband."

*Seance?* I was ready to ask her about it but thought better of it. "I'll see you later," I said instead and strode back to my car with a three-foot canvas in my hands. I drove back to my home and started on the restoration.

I grabbed the bottle of extra virgin olive oil from my pantry and brushed the oil onto the thickest parts of the spray paint. While I left that soaking, I went in search of acetone. I didn't have any, but I remembered some turpentine I kept in the garage. However, I worried using it would remove some of Grace's work. So, I got back into my car and drove to the nearest pharmacy.

"Where would I find acetone?" I asked the cashier.

She stopped clicking her gum long enough to stare down at my bare fingernails. I rolled my eyes. "It's not for me."

She blew a bubble. "Do you want pure acetone or just a basic nail polish remover?"

"What's the difference?"

"Well, one takes off acrylic nails and the other takes off regular nail polish."

The first one sounded stronger. "The acrylic one."

"Do you want the berry or lemon scent?"

"I don't care," I growled, impatient now.

"You're the one that asked for my help, you know."

"I know. I'm sorry. I'm just in a bit of a rush."

"Nail emergency?"

"Yeah. Something like that."

Fortunately, she rang me up quickly and I was back home in less than thirty minutes. But when I checked on the progress, the spray paint still looked quite dry. So, I brushed on a bit more oil and started preparing beef wellington, distracting myself from the time.

# 13

## Grace

Sometimes, sitting next to my mom, snuggled up alongside her on the couch, I felt like I was ten again. The movie, *The Notebook,* played on the TV. It was one of her favorite movies, and this scene in the rain always gave me the chills. So, I stood to grab a drink, not wanting to see anything remotely romantic right now. I was so confused about Luke. One minute I hated him, the next he was sweet and reminded me of the person he once was, then bam! Jared appeared and I was *Meany Sweeney* again.

"Can I get you a drink?"

"Shh. This is the best part," she said, always the hopeless romantic. I didn't understand how she continued to be, even after my father left. I didn't even remember what he looked like since he just up and left soon after I was born. *So, forgive me if I don't believe in happily ever after.*

"All right, all right," I said, walking toward the kitchen.

As usual, my laptop sat open on the counter and I clicked the mouse to refresh my email. No new messages. After returning from the cabin, I worked non-stop to catch up on the lost time, and fortunately, James kicked himself into high gear with me. Tomorrow was Friday, and if I worked hard, I would get it all done by the end of the day.

A knock at the door caught me by surprise. It was 8:30 p.m. on a weeknight. Lorna had left hours ago. *Omar?* Sometimes he called me to chat, but he never showed up unannounced at my door.

"Was that the door, sweetheart?" my mother asked.

"Yeah," I said, cautiously.

"Well, don't answer it, in case it's an intruder."

"It's not an intruder, Mom," I called back, but would check the peephole, anyway.

"Who is it?" I called, walking toward the door. I knew whomever it was could hear me as the walls and doors in this building were so thin.

"It's me," said a voice from the other side.

*Luke? What's he doing here?*

"I know it's late. But can we talk?"

"Who is it, Grace?" My mom called out.

"It's just someone from work, Mom. I'll take the conversation outside."

"Don't be silly. Whomever it is can come in."

"It's better that they don't," I muttered to myself, unlocking the door.

When I opened it, Luke stood in a white t-shirt and blue jeans. His light brown hair looked tousled and a five o'clock shadow darkened his face. He looked fantastic.

"What are you doing here?" I asked, then sniffed. "And what is that awful smell?" I put a hand over my nose to cover some of the worst of it.

He looked down at a large package next to the door. It was wrapped in brown paper, but there was no label on the packaging to indicate what was inside.

"I thought I aired most of the smell out," he said, running a hand through his hair.

"What are you talking about?" I asked, shaking my head.

"Grace, I messed up. I was self-centered and arrogant and thought everything was about me. I'm sorry. I wanted to do something for you. I wanted…"

His words trailed off and I was thankful. I felt a fog in my head as I tried to understand what he was saying.

He was apologizing. Was it for this past week at the office? Was it about Jared?

"Look. What's done is done. We can't change the past. I appreciate you owning up to it but—"

"I fucked up, didn't I?" he said, staring at me. His eyes held mine and something in my chest thumped. It couldn't be my heart. It just couldn't. "I didn't know what I was thinking. I thought maybe I could erase everything with acetone, but I can't, can I?"

"Acetone? Luke, what the hell are you talking about?" My muscles ached and my head hurt, but I didn't think I was so tired that I couldn't follow a simple conversation. Yet here I was. Completely confused.

"I wanted to make it up to you. I thought if I could erase what Jared wrote..." He shook his head, frustration etched on his forehead. "If I could remake the past. Maybe it would... I don't know... It's silly. Forget I even came by." He picked up the package and moved toward the elevator.

Curiosity got the best of me and the mention of Jared sparked something in my brain that I didn't want to presume. My heart had leaped to a conclusion that was too impossible to even contemplate. But something told me I had to know what was inside that package.

"Wait," I said, placing my hand on his bicep. It flexed when he balled his fists.

"I'm sorry I bothered you, Grace. I'm sorry—"

"What's inside the package, Luke?"

"It's stupid. I didn't even do a great job of it. There are still some dark shadows, even though the words aren't legible anymore. It's not—"

My heart hammered in my chest.

*Oh, god! Please don't let me get my hopes up. Please don't let it be what I think it is. I don't know what I'd do…*

I crouched down beside the brown paper and hesitantly found the opening to the package. Luke sighed and stared up at the ceiling.

*It's like a bandage, Grace. Tear it off. No use imagining something that might not be there.*

So, in one swift motion, I tore off the wrapping paper. Staring back at me was a familiar gray oil paint, surrounded by the pewter brown paint my mother had purchased at the art supply store.

I sucked in a sharp breath and fought back the hot moisture gathering behind my eyes. My hand trembled as I ripped off the rest of the paper, determined, yet sick to my stomach to see the words that had made me cry years ago. But when the paper fell to the ground and I stared at the painting that had tormented me for years, they weren't there. There were dark shadows where the letters had been, but the name was no longer etched into the painting.

I dropped to my knees and cried.

Covering my face with my hands, I didn't even bother to wipe the tears away. All the emotions I'd closed off since high school came pouring out of my eyes and my chest loosened as I finally released them and let go of the girl I'd been ten years ago. I hadn't realized I'd kept her tucked away in a secret place, afraid to let anyone see her—see how hurt she was. Then, in one fell swoop, I set her free.

I exhaled loudly and my shoulders shook, so I grabbed my arms and hugged myself.

"Shit, Grace. What have I done? I hadn't considered your reaction to facing this painting again or that it might bring back bad memories. I'm such an asshole."

He grabbed the painting and pulled it away from me. The fog cleared and the pieces of the puzzle started clicking into place.

"You went back to our high school," I said more to myself, having already pieced it together. "You dug up my painting and sent it to be restored."

"No. I tried to do it myself. The guy I called said he couldn't do it and it would take weeks to send it to someone in New York City. I didn't think I had that long. I wasn't sure if I would see you again after this week."

"Why did you do this? Are you trying to make up for what happened in high school?"

"Yes. And no. All I could think about was turning back time. I wanted you to have your painting without someone else's stupidity on it."

I nodded.

"But I didn't think it through. I didn't realize how much it would affect you." He tucked the painting underneath his arm. "I'll just put it back at the school. You don't need to look at it again."

Then it hit me. "This must have taken you hours to do. You did it all yourself?"

"Yes."

An emotion I didn't recognize erupted in the pit of my stomach. It resembled anger, but the urgency to release the emotion was stronger than that. I wanted to scream at the top of my voice. I wanted to…

Something must have registered on my face because Luke's eyes narrowed as I approached him. He put his hands up, possibly sensing something dangerous burning inside of me. My breathing hitched at the intensity of it.

"Grace. I know I've said it before and I don't know what to do to prove it. But I really am—"

I didn't want him to apologize again, so I put my finger on his lips. I wanted to hear nothing more.

I pushed him up against the wall and opened my mouth to say something when his eyes fell to my lips. My gaze bounced from his eyes to his bottom lip, and I faltered. The words died on my tongue. Then I tilted my head and pressed my lips to his. I moved slowly, hesitantly, unsure how he would react. Unsure what was happening.

Luke held his body still. He didn't move his lips or push me away.

*Oh, god. Maybe he's being polite and waiting for me to stop kissing him. Then he'll clear his throat and wish me goodnight.*

The thought stilled my heart. Humiliation clogged my throat. I pulled away from him, clutching my neck.

"I'm sorry. That was completely out of line and if I made you feel uncomfortable, I—"

I couldn't complete that sentence because this time it was Luke who pushed his body against mine, pressing me against the hallway corridor. He inhaled the air that I breathed right before he pressed his lips harshly against mine. They felt punishing, as did his hands that grabbed my waist and squeezed. I could hardly breathe, gasping for breath between each kiss. When he moved his mouth to the skin beneath my ear, I sucked in a lungful of air and shivered when I exhaled.

"Grace," he whispered, his breath tickling my ear. "Jesus, Grace."

He nuzzled my jaw until his mouth found mine again, and I lost myself in a storm of hunger and wanting. I *wanted* Luke. I had wanted him since the first day of high school and maybe every day since. I had just never allowed myself to admit it. It would hurt too much thinking that he'd betrayed me. But I'd let him down, too.

But he had restored my painting and perhaps even a chance at—never mind. I didn't want to ruin it by overanalyzing this moment.

A vibration in my pocket distracted us both and I grabbed my phone from my back pocket. The daily reminder to give my mom her medication buzzed. "I've got to go," I said.

Luke's hand trailed against my jaw as he stared into my eyes. I felt lost in his gaze.

"I'll see you tomorrow," he said, his voice husky and raw. His Adam's apple dropped as he swallowed hard.

I nodded and pulled away from his arms. He watched me as I walked inside my apartment and shut the door. Leaning against the other side of the door, I closed my eyes and exhaled. A knock made me jump. I opened the door and found the painting on my doorstep and Luke stepping into the elevator. He waved, then the doors closed. I picked up the painting and brought it inside.

Back in my apartment, I assessed my trembling legs and racing heart and giggled.

I may have been twenty-eight years old, but suddenly, I felt like a teenager again.

"What's so funny, Grace?" asked my mom when I walked back into the living room, the smile still on my face.

"I always thought I'd never want to feel fourteen again. But then life shows you—never say never!"

# 14

## Luke

She kissed me. Grace Sweeney kissed me. And I lost my mind. I replayed the moment over and over in my head last night and again this morning on the way to work. The feel of her body pressed up against mine, the way my fingers splayed her waist, and the possessiveness that grew within me. I'd never felt that before. She smelled like coffee and vanilla, strong and sweet.

As I walked down the marble floors of Crawford Corporation, my heart hammered in my chest. I wondered how she would react today.

*Would she ignore what happened at her apartment? Would I let it go and not press her on it?*

I had no idea what I would do if she pretended as though nothing had happened. Because I couldn't stop thinking about it.

"Luke," Colton's voice cut through my thoughts. "Can I see you for a minute?"

I stepped into his office. "What's up?"

"I spoke to Grace," he said, rubbing the back of his neck. He did that when he was nervous. Did Grace say something to him this morning? Was he about to lecture me about fraternizing with people at work? Ha! He should be the last person to do so!

"Listen, Colton. This isn't any of your business."

"Not my business? Crawford Corporation is my business, Luke! It's exactly my business," he shouted back.

"This isn't about Crawford Corp and you know it. It's about you wanting to control me."

"Control you? Is that what you think?"

"I know you took on a parenting role when I was young, but I'm not a kid anymore. I can date whoever I want. I don't need your permission."

He pressed both palms down on his desk and shook his head. "What *the fuck* are you talking about?"

*Huh?*

"You said you spoke to Grace?"

"Yes. And she informed me she'll be done with the audit by the end of the day. Which means you will be done, too. But I wanted to speak to you about other opportunities at Crawford Corp for you. Remember the operations manager role I mentioned earlier? I think that could really work. Wait…" His eyes grew bigger. "What did you think I meant?"

"Ah. Nothing. Forget it."

"Is something going on between you and Grace?"

"No. Yes. I don't know."

A hand grasped my shoulder and another voice jolted me. "You sound nervous, little brother. What's going on? Did you steal Colton's hair products again?" It was Ryan.

"I don't use—" began Colton but stopped himself. "Something is going on between Luke and the auditor, and I'm trying to get to the bottom of it."

"Are you really going to give him a hard time about dating an external auditor when you slept with your assistant?"

"Shh!" Colton stood from his desk and closed his door. "I don't want people to think I'm sleeping with my current assistant," he said, then shuddered. "And this isn't about me, it's about Luke."

"I'm not sleeping with Grace," I said.

"But you want to?" Ryan asked. When I didn't respond fast enough, he patted my shoulder again. "Why don't you bring her around for dinner, and we can all get to know—"

"No!" Both Colton and I shouted at the same time.

Raising both his hands, Ryan stepped back. "What?"

"We both remember what happened the last time one of us invited a girl for a family dinner. It didn't end well," I said.

Ryan pointed his finger at me. "Frances forgave me for that."

Colton sighed. "My wife is too good for me."

"I'm not inviting Grace to meet you two. I don't even know what's going on. So, I'd appreciate it if you two would stay out of my business."

I walked past Ryan as Colton muttered. "Yup. He's done for."

"Yep. I bet you he doesn't make it through the end of the day without—"

I didn't hear the rest of Ryan's wager as I ignored them both.

I needed to find Grace, and if Colton had spoken to her, then she must be in the boardroom.

She sat at the head of the table with James by her side. He looked up when I entered the room, but Grace kept her gaze on her laptop.

"Hey! Luke! How's it going?" asked James.

"Good. Good. How are you?" I asked, staring at Grace the entire time.

"You know, finishing up here, then thinking of heading to watch the game at the bar. Want to come?"

"Uh, I don't think I can make it, James. I think I have plans."

"You think?"

"Yeah."

"Oh, okay. Well, if anything changes, you know where to find me."

When Grace still didn't acknowledge me, I sat down at the desk on the other side of her. I cleared my throat, but she still didn't look up. James stared at her, then at me, and shrugged his shoulders as though telling me he didn't know what was wrong with her, either.

"Good morning, Grace," I said.

"Morning," she said, tucking one side of her hair behind her ear. I followed her finger as it ran down her neck and envisioned my tongue marking the same path.

"Did you sleep well?"

Her head snapped up and she stared at me with wide eyes. "How did you? I mean. Yes. Fine, thank you."

Her reaction made me wonder if she had tossed and turned as much as I had last night. "Can I get you anything?"

"Um, Daniel gave us the last of the files. So, we're good and should be done by the end of the day." She seemed nervous and I couldn't figure out why.

"Can I get you a coffee? With some vanilla flavor, perhaps?"

That caught her attention again. "How did you know?"

I leaned in closer and whispered, "I smelled it on your lips last night."

She gasped and turned to look at James. His head shot up. "What? What's wrong?"

I smiled.

Grace didn't.

"Sorry, I just had a thought. James, why don't you ask Daniel for the bank balances? I think I want to go over those again."

"But we already checked it."

"That's why I said I want to check them—again," said Grace, raising her eyebrow at James. I loosened my tie. Something about her taking control made her even hotter.

"Fine," James muttered and stood from the table.

As soon as he left, Grace turned to me. "You can't whisper stuff like that in my ear," she hissed.

"Why not?"

"Because James could have heard you."

"And?"

She exhaled. "And I take my job very seriously. I don't want him to think I mess around with people at work."

"So, are you saying you want to mess around with me outside of work?"

"No. Yes. I don't know."

I smiled. "Okay. I'll keep my thoughts to myself," I said. "But we need to talk about what happened last night."

"I know," she muttered.

"You don't seem happy about it." I ran my thumb over hers on the desk.

"I'm a little happy." She smiled.

That smile made my whole world light up. I wanted to pick her up and swing her around the room. But I stopped myself. "After work, I'll take you to my favorite place to eat. You up for that?"

"I just have to make arrangements for my mom."

"She can come with us."

Her smile disappeared. "She's in no condition to travel."

"It's just up the street," I explained, but she shook her head. "Okay. Let me know."

She nodded just as James walked back into the room.

"I'm going to grab a couple of coffees. You want anything, James?"

"Sure, I take mine black."

I left the boardroom and made my way to the kitchen. I found Erika stirring her mug of coffee.

"Good morning, Erika," I said. "Lovely day, isn't it?"

"Morning." She sipped her coffee and smiled. "Aren't you chipper this morning? What happened? Did Colton fire you?"

I barked out a laugh. "No. But that was a good guess."

She tilted her head and narrowed her eyes. "You met someone, didn't you?"

Her quick perception caught me off guard, and I may have stuttered. "Ah. No."

"You did," she said with a laugh and shoved my arm. "You met someone. Tell me all about her."

I smiled. I couldn't help it. Thinking about getting together with Grace seemed so natural and exciting. "She's smart. Gorgeous. And snarky. You'd love her."

She laughed and covered her mouth with her hand. "You nearly made me spit out my coffee. I will take that as a compliment."

"You should."

"Well, when do I get to meet her?"

As if on cue, Grace walked into the room. She stopped when she saw Erika and me laughing. "Sorry to interrupt," she said.

"You aren't interrupting," I assured her. "Is there something you need?" I knew my voice gave away my need as I felt Erika's eyes on me.

Grace ran a hand through her hair and walked past me. "No. Just came to grab some fruit I left in the fridge."

I nodded and watched her as she bent down to grab a container from the bottom of the fridge. Her skirt stretched over a beautifully rounded ass.

*Wait. Did she bend her knee just to tease me?*

I held my breath to prevent a moan from escaping my lips. Erika smacked my arm with the back of her hand. I turned to look at her and she narrowed her eyes.

"Okay, well, I'll see you," said Grace.

I watched her as she walked away. "I'll see you soon."

"Well, well, well. Sleeping with the accountant, huh?"

"We aren't sleeping together," I said. "Why does everyone keep saying that?"

"Maybe because the two of you together need to come with a 'highly flammable' warning. Geez, that was intense." She fanned herself. "I think I need to reevaluate my relationship. Because I want that!"

When she left the staffroom, I splashed some water on the back of my neck.

Erika was right. My body kicked into high heat when Grace stood near me and it wanted her badly. I couldn't wait for tonight.

I kept my distance for the rest of the day. I popped in and out of the boardroom to check if she needed anything. When she asked for a report, I got Daniel on it right away. It was kind of nice working together. Around three in the afternoon, I sat inside the office Colton had assigned to me, organizing a marketing plan for Mario's restaurant, when Grace walked in.

"Hey," she said, her hands clasped in front of her.

I smiled. "Hey. Do you need something? I can stop what I'm doing."

"No, no," she said, waving for me to sit back down. "I just came in here to tell you I can't go to dinner tonight."

"Oh," my heart deflated. "Why not?"

"Lorna has this thing tonight and can't stay late to keep an eye on my mom. I'm really sorry, Luke. I wanted to go."

"So, the only reason you're saying no is that there's no one to take care of your mother. Is that right?"

"Yes. I swear."

She nodded emphatically, and I believed her. "Okay. Leave it with me."

"Pardon?"

"I'll find someone to take care of your mom so you can have dinner with me."

"Luke, it's not like there's a queue of people available to fill the position. It needs to be someone with some medical knowledge of her condition."

"I understand. She has a kidney disease, you said?"

"Yeah, but—"

"I'll take care of it. Is six o'clock, okay?"

"For what?"

I wondered if she was deliberately being obtuse or if she wasn't getting that I would do anything to make this date happen tonight. Even if I had to fly some doctor in from New York City to stay with her mother.

"Dinner. With me. Six o'clock. I'll take care of your mom. Okay?"

"Ah... Oh... Okay," she stammered and turned to walk away. She looked over her shoulder as she walked back to her office, as though waiting to see if this was some sort of prank.

I didn't like to show off how much money I had because most of it came from the investments I'd made through the dividends of Crawford Corporation. But tonight wouldn't just take money to happen. I would need to call in some favors, too. I picked up the phone and started dialing.

# 15

## Grace

For the first time in my life, since I was a child, I was putting my trust in another's hands. I didn't know how Luke would do it, but I would trust him to find someone to take care of my mom tonight.

When I mentioned the date to her, she threatened to never speak to me again if I didn't go. I believed her, too. So, here I was, standing in front of my bedroom closet, trying to decide what to wear.

I had plenty of work clothes, but I wanted something that made me feel sexy. I had nothing like that. So, I pulled out the tight black dress I usually wore with a blazer but paired it with the highest heels I owned.

*Not bad,* I thought when I saw myself in the mirror. I grabbed the large hoop earrings I'd purchased last month but hadn't worn yet and put those on. Slipping on a couple of bangles, I assessed the final look.

*That'll work.*

"Grace!" my mother called from the living room. "There's someone at the door."

I hadn't heard the door, but the music was pretty loud. *Huh*. I hadn't played music while getting ready in forever.

"Coming!" I shouted.

"Honey, you look beautiful," she said when I walked into the living room.

"Thank you." I pulled down the dress. "Do you think it's too much? I don't know where we're going, but I didn't have many options."

"No. It's perfect."

A soft knock sounded at the door. "You better get that, honey."

I walked the short distance to the front door and opened it. Luke wore gray pants and a black dress shirt that seemed sized to fit the contours of his chest and arms perfectly. He had styled his brown hair so that the tousled locks all stood firmly in place. He looked every bit a Crawford right now and less like the teenager I remembered.

When my assessing gaze caught his eyes, I felt held in place by some invisible hands. He bit his bottom lip and swallowed. "You look incredible." His husky voice sent chills down my spine.

When someone behind him shifted, I realized two other people were standing there.

"Grace, this is Theo and Laura. They're both nurses at Mount Sinai Hospital with previous experience working with kidney disease patients and come highly recommended by two surgeons at the hospital. They've explained that your mother may tire easily, so I purchased a wheelchair for her should she wish to leave the apartment with their supervision."

Laura stepped forward first. "Pleased to meet you, Ms. Sweeney."

I shook Laura's hand, still trying to process everything Luke had just told me.

"Your mother is in great hands. You don't need to worry about a thing," Theo said. Then he turned and pulled a wheelchair from the hallway. I moved out of the way so he could push it inside.

"Hello there!" my mother called from the living room.

"Hello, Ms. Sweeney. My name's Theo and I'm pleased to meet you. Would you be interested in going for a walk this evening?"

From the couch, my mother looked at me, and her eyes welled up. Then so did mine. My mother hadn't been able to do much more than walk to the balcony for some fresh air in nearly a year. She hadn't been further than the front entrance of the building to step into my car for her appointments in that long, too. A walk. Well, I couldn't remember the last time she did that.

She straightened her spine. "I'd love to," she said. "Let me just grab my sweater."

"I'll get that Mom," I said.

"Let me," said Laura. "Is it this one here by the door?"

"Yes," I stammered. "Yes. That one's fine."

"Perfect. Well, you both should be on your way." Laura, not so subtly, tried to kick us out.

Luke stuck out his elbow. "Are you ready, Grace?"

Sneaking a glance at my mother, I watched as Laura helped my mom put on her sweater as gently as Lorna would have. I nodded, feeling safe, leaving her in their hands.

"Yeah. I'm ready," I said. "Bye, Mom. I won't be too late."

"Well, don't be back too early," she said, sitting in the wheelchair. "I've got places to go."

The smile on my mother's face was so beautiful that I had to look away or risk ruining my makeup. So, I simply nodded again and said, "All right."

I grabbed Luke's arm and left my apartment guilt-free for the first time in five years.

Once inside the elevator, Luke turned to me, his eyes searching mine. "Are you all right?"

I filled my lungs with a large inhale and smiled. "Yes," I whispered. "I'm happy. Thank you."

He reached for my hand and squeezed it. Whiffing his cologne and perhaps a hint of cinnamon, I closed my eyes and leaned against his arm.

We walked hand in hand through the beige hallway. They hadn't renovated this apartment building since the eighties and I suddenly became very self-conscious about it, with Luke by my side. I had a well-paid job, but with all the medical expenses, I hadn't been able to move us out of this place.

The feeling of comparison intensified when I saw the sleek yellow sports car in front of my building. "Aren't you worried someone would steal this parked out front?"

He shrugged. "Not really."

He probably could buy five of them without batting an eye.

But then he continued. "Most stolen cars in North America are automatic. Not many thieves can drive a manual car these days. I read someplace that only eighteen percent of American drivers can drive stick."

"Really? Well, don't tell many thieves that."

Luke came around and opened the car door for me. The interior of the car was all black and the leather seats were soft against my legs when I sat inside. Definitely not the plastic stuff. "Where are we going?" I asked when he started the engine.

"There's this little place with the best food in town." He pressed his foot on the gas and the engine roared. My body hummed and I fell back against the seat. I tried to hide a wide grin, not wanting to be impressed by a sports car, but I couldn't help it, it felt exhilarating.

Closing my eyes, I enjoyed the moment. Alone in a fast car with Luke on a date. I never—ever—thought this would happen. I didn't even want to hear his name for about ten years, but now here I was. Smiling and happy.

He hadn't been driving for more than fifteen minutes when Luke pulled up against the curb. "This is it," he said.

I leaned forward to look out the window. It was dark and many of the businesses were closed at this hour, but I could make out several clothing stores, a coffee shop, and a bakery, but no restaurant. Luke opened my car door and reached for my hand. We walked only a few feet, then he led me down a concrete flight of steps. That was when I saw the sign: *Mario's Restaurant*.

A bell chimed when Luke opened the door. It was dark inside, with only a few dim wall sconces. The furniture consisted of dark brown leather chairs and burgundy tablecloths. There wasn't any dust on the surfaces, nor any spots on the linens. Everything looked clean. The warm and doughy aroma from the kitchen called out to my stomach. It growled back in reply.

"Mr. Crawford," said the hostess. "Nice to see you again. Let me check if your table is ready."

There was just one other couple in the restaurant besides us. Unless a busload of people showed up, I was pretty sure a table would be available.

"Ah, here we go. Right, this way." She picked up two menus and led us to a secluded spot at the back.

I sat on the bench since the pillow top looked more comfortable than the wooden-backed chair. Luke hesitated for only a moment before taking a seat beside me. "I want to be near you. Is that all right?"

I smiled. It reminded me of when Luke had kicked Allen Parker out of the seat next to me in homeroom on the first day of school. I'd thought it was a bully move at first, but after speaking to Parker about it after class, he'd said Luke had slipped him a ten.

Luke rubbed his hands together after opening the menu and I glanced down as well. "So, what's good here?" I asked.

"Everything."

I snorted. "Well, it'll be hard to choose."

"Then don't. Order whatever you want. If you don't finish it, just take it home. I insist you bring something back to your mother."

I looked up at Luke, wondering if he'd always been this considerate or if it was a new quality. My emotions were so mixed up that I was having a hard time recalling the past. I just wanted to get to know the man in front of me better.

By the time the hostess turned server arrived, I had about six dishes I wanted to order but limited it to three.

"I'll have the grilled calamari to start, please. Then, I'd like to try your homemade gnocchi and the Caprese salad."

Luke watched me for a moment, pursed his lips, and said, "I'll have the fried calamari. The eggplant parmesan and your stuffed chicken, please."

My eyes shot up. He somehow chose the other three dishes that I'd wanted.

"I don't mind sharing if you'd like to try any of mine," he said, his eyes dancing.

I normally hated sharing food, but I couldn't resist the offer to try some of his dishes. "Sure. I wouldn't mind."

With his elbows on the table, Luke hid his smile behind his clasped hands. Did he really know me that well or did we have similar tastes? I was afraid either answer would confuse me. Could this be a thing—me and Luke?

*Don't overanalyze this, Grace. It's just one date. Slow down.*

"So, I have to admit. This isn't the sort of place I would have pictured you taking me," I said.

"Really? What did you picture?"

I laughed. "Well, it was a toss-up between a sports bar or some fancy French restaurant. Something that serves only tiny portions. Not because I think you eat tiny portions, but because you'd want to show off."

"If you haven't noticed, Grace. I'm not that different from the high school guy you knew."

I shook my head. "No, Luke. You're wrong. You're very different from the boy I knew." Or perhaps I was wrong about him.

Our dishes came out soon after and we shared all six dishes. Luke would moan and insist I try something and I didn't hesitate to dig in. I never enjoyed sharing a meal so much in my whole life.

"This place is amazing. Why isn't it packed?"

Luke folded his arms and looked around the room. "I think this place could be something. I have some ideas to market and publicize—"

"So, why don't you buy it from the owner?"

"Because this place is his life. And I don't see myself running a restaurant."

I bit into the crispy calamari. "What do you see yourself doing?"

He shrugged. "I wish I knew. I have all these ideas for different places but can't settle on just one."

"Sometimes I wish I still had choices. To just wake up and start over again."

His eyes searched mine. "What would you do if you could do it all over again?"

Thoughts raced through my mind, but I couldn't settle on any. "I don't know. But I wouldn't take everything so seriously again."

"Well, why don't we start tonight?"

Narrowing my eyes, I asked, "What do you mean?"

He pulled back his chair and offered me his hand. "I've got an idea."

A rush of adrenaline surged through me as I stood from the table. I didn't know where we were going, but I was excited to find out.

# 16

## Grace

As Luke opened the front door and I stepped out, a bright flash startled me. Then another, followed by five or six more. Luke grabbed my hand and rushed me to his car as footsteps trailed behind us.

"Luke! Is this your new girlfriend?" someone shouted.

Then everyone else chimed in: *What's her name? Where's she from? Are you two getting married?*

Luke opened my door and I dove into the passenger seat. I was still staring at the bodies standing in front, snapping pictures, as Luke started the car.

"What the hell was that?" I asked.

"I didn't think anyone followed us here. I'm sorry about that."

I was about to repeat myself when it hit me. I was on a date with one of the most eligible and richest bachelors in the city. Luke and his brother's exploits were often in the tabloids. Of course, the paparazzi followed him around. Heck, Omar even showed me a story only a week ago. I just couldn't believe I was now the one sitting here with him in his car. I shook my head.

"Are you all right?" he asked. "I know it can be unsettling the first time. But you get used to it."

My heart raced in my chest, and I tried to steady my breathing to slow it down. "What do we do now?" I asked as he pulled out of the street.

"Nothing. Ryan scared them with some legal threats a few years back. They can photograph us in public places but not on private property. Also, they can only photograph us at one place per evening, otherwise, he threatened them with harassment and stalking. No one's sure if he could win the case, but fortunately, in a smaller city, no company's willing to take it to court. It's easier to just comply."

"That's pretty smart," I said.

Luke groaned. "Please don't tell Ryan that. He already thinks he's the smart one in the family. He doesn't need anyone else to confirm it."

"So, if Ryan is the smart one and Colton is the responsible one. What are you?"

"Wait! Are you saying I'm not smart or responsible?" He smiled, but there were hard lines around his eyes and I wondered if he was serious.

"Of course not. But what do they call you?"

"Well, I've been told I'm the charmer."

I snorted and he looked at me with a side-glance. "Oh, you don't believe it?"

I shrugged simply to egg him on.

"You just haven't seen my charming side yet."

"Yes, I have. You used it on James and most of the people in the office. Except for me. I think I'm immune to your charm."

"That's because I haven't directed it at you yet," he murmured and turned toward me. In the dark car, his green eyes held mine until he dropped his stare to my lips. I shivered. It felt as though he'd licked them with just his gaze.

*That's impressive*!

I cleared my throat and turned to look out my window. We passed a familiar sign and I barked out a laugh. "You took me back to our old high school?"

"Well, you said something about starting over again. I think we should start fresh. Right from where things went sour."

I didn't think that was a half-bad idea. In fact, I was getting excited about it.

He pulled into the parking lot, and I jumped out of the car. Looking around, I was drawn by the scenery around us. The lights were on at the baseball diamond, making the sky pitch black on the horizon. There were trees surrounding the field, blocking any other building in the distance. It felt as secluded as the first day I'd walked this path. The steel bleachers shone white under the fluorescent lights. As I stared out into the horizon, a flood of memories rushed through me.

Luke's gentle touch on my arm gave me goosebumps. "Are you cold?" he asked.

I shook my head. "No. I'm… I don't know. Nostalgic? Pensive? Wondering why I cared so much about what others thought of me instead of just enjoying myself? I lost so much time."

He pulled me next to him and rubbed my arm as we both looked out onto the field. "I sometimes wished I had focused more," he said. "Then I'd know what I want to do with my life instead of just avoiding the decision."

My shoulders shook with amusement.

"What's so funny?" he asked.

"Us. The baseball star and the book nerd. We both wished we'd been the other. I guess that's the way life goes."

"I guess. But you know what else? We can still change it. Nothing is set in stone. Tell me one thing you'd do differently if given the chance?"

Exhilarated by the idea, I spun out of his arm and twirled in the middle of the field. "I would have tried out for the band."

He laughed. "Not exactly what I was thinking, but okay. What else?"

Walking toward the bleachers, I rose on my tiptoes. "Um... I would have... ditched studying to come to one of these games."

He stalked toward me. "That's better. What else?"

A thought popped into my head, and I bit my bottom lip. Luke raised his eyebrow, waiting for my response, but I shook my head. "It's embarrassing."

"Come on now. Don't hold back. What else?" He stepped forward to grab my waist, but I stepped to the side, out of his reach, and laughed. "I would have made out with a player behind these bleachers."

His mouth curved slowly into a roguish smile. Then he reached for my waist once more. This time, he didn't miss. Running his thumbs up and down my sides, he said. "Now that's something I can help you with."

Walking backward toward the bleachers, I nearly stumbled. But his grip on my waist steadied me. His eyes bore into mine and I felt his hand cradle the back of my head just before he pressed me against the metal steps.

I gasped and so did he, right before his lips came crashing onto mine. He kissed me relentlessly until I had to pull away and catch my breath. His other hand moved to my face and he hovered his lips over mine. Slowly, he licked my bottom lip and I shivered. When I slipped my tongue to meet his, he groaned and pressed his body to mine. I felt how badly he wanted me. His hard ridge pressed against my hip.

He moved his lips down my neck and sucked. The pull excited me, and I wanted him to do it again. But he raked his mouth over my shoulder, instead, pushing the fabric away until my dress began to sag. I caught it at my chest. "Whoa. That was close. I almost lost it," I said.

"Why did you stop?" he whispered in my ear, and I shivered.

"Because…," I stammered. "Because we're in a public place."

"No one's watching and you wanted to make out with a player. Well, as the former MVP of the team, I'm at your service." He curled his fingers over my hand to pull the dress down again, but I stopped him. He stepped back an inch to watch me, then nodded.

"All right. Keep the dress on," he said, as though he had just decided on something.

He lifted me from the waist and lowered me onto the side of the bleacher. My legs dangled as I tried to hold on to the seats on either side of me. I couldn't get a good grip. Afraid I would fall and break my neck, I reached for Luke's shoulders, which were just at my knees.

Finally, feeling secure, I laughed at our position. "How am I supposed to kiss you now?" I teased, lowering my face to his.

"You're not. But I'm going to kiss you." He licked his lips and spread my legs apart.

"Luke!" I admonished.

He looked up. His nostrils flared. "Tell me to stop only if it's what you truly want and not because it's what you think you should do. Tonight's about reliving the past—carefree and no regrets."

Oh, he knew me so well. I would regret saying no as soon as he put me down. So, I widened my legs and pulled him toward me.

"That's my girl," he growled and nuzzled his nose to my panties. I could barely feel him, but my heart raced from the excitement of it all. I looked out into the dark sky, blinded by the lights on the field, and burrowed my fingers into his hair.

He pushed my panties to the side and swiped his tongue along my entrance. I shivered from the first touch.

Slowly, he licked my inner thighs, inhaling my scent as he moved from one to the other. With his teeth, he pulled off my underwear and tucked them into his back pocket. Pushing both hands underneath my dress, he pulled my legs further apart and lowered his face again. The warmth of his breath on my sensitive clit gave me goosebumps and I knew he could feel the raised flesh on my bare thighs. He chuckled and I wanted to growl.

"Do you like that?" he whispered, his breath causing havoc on my hormones.

"You know I do, you bastard," I growled back.

He chuckled and placed his mouth right over me and hummed. The sensation rippled through my body and I groaned aloud.

I pulled on his hair, and the humming stopped.

"Don't tease me, Luke," I warned. "I haven't had sex in a really long time. I don't think I could take much more of this."

"Ah, Grace. Teasing is the best part."

With only the tip of his tongue, he tickled the top of my clit and I bucked beneath him. "Fuck you, Luke," I said and his laughter only made the humming worse.

I pulled his hair harder and this time, his growl caught me off guard. It sounded animalistic and raw. His fingers pressed into my flesh and he jammed his tongue into me and curled it inside, hitting my sensitive spot. "Yes," I cried out.

He pulled me closer to his mouth and lashed his tongue over me, this time with no hesitation. He didn't slow down or pause but thrashed and sucked until I could hardly breathe.

"Oh, god," I whispered, trying to hold on, grasping clumsily at metal pieces around me. I dropped my back onto the cold steel bleacher and held onto the seats beside me. "Oh, god," I cried louder this time as the climax roared in my ears.

"Luke!" I cried when the wave overtook me and hit me square in my core, taking my breath away. I panted as my body spasmed. I felt like one of those arcade games, my climax lighting up every nerve ending in my body that had laid dormant for what felt like years.

"Stop," I whispered when he continued to swipe his tongue over me. "I came." I felt the release, but my body was still buzzing. It was as though my body knew there was still more to give.

With his face between my thighs, Luke's hand caressed my breast. When his thumb brushed against my nipple, I felt another wave rush over me and I laid back down.

"That's it," he whispered. He lifted my legs onto his shoulders to free up his hands so that both hands now stimulated my breasts.

I arched my back for relief, but this only brought me closer to Luke. My heart pounded, the rhythm matching the pulse at my entrance. My skin burned with desire despite the cool air. "Please," I begged. Not sure what I was asking for but knew that only he could give it to me.

Loud moans crashed through the quiet night, and I didn't even recognize my voice. I'd never heard myself like this before. I gasped when he quickened his pace. Knowing I was close, but having already orgasmed, I didn't know if another was possible. But then a sharp pinch at my nipple stoked the fire inside me and everything that'd been simmering exploded and I screamed his name.

Lowering my hips onto the steel floor, I stared up at the dark sky. My ragged breath was the only sound in my ears. Even his soft kisses on my inner thigh made me squirm as my sensitive skin recovered from the best damn orgasm of my life.

"So, how was that for recreating new memories?"

It wasn't the first time a man had asked for validation after sex, but it would be the first time I'd told the truth. "That was the best sex I've ever had."

His face lit up brighter than the lights behind him. His boyish grin made me feel like we were teenagers again. I laughed and smacked his shoulder. "Don't look so proud of yourself."

He wiped his grin with his hand but still couldn't mask the amusement on his face. I bet if he could high-five me right now he would.

"Come here," I said and traced my finger along his smiling lips. I had looked at his face before, but I'd never wanted to memorize the angle of his jaw or the arch of his brow until now. *Pull yourself together, Grace. Don't start falling in love with the guy just because he gave you one great orgasm. Okay. Two.*

But my fingers continued to caress his face and his eyes softened.

"Come to Paris with me?"

"What?"

I wasn't sure if he was serious or not. *Besides, who said something like that?*

"You've always wanted to go to Paris and see The Mona Lisa. Let's go tomorrow."

"Tomorrow! Now I know you're joking."

He clutched my waist and lifted me off the bleachers. "I'm not," he said when I had both feet firmly on the ground.

"Luke, I can't just leave for Paris tomorrow. We don't have tickets and I have a job and my mother. I have responsibilities!"

"I have a private plane and I will pay Theo and Laura triple their day rate to stay with your mother for the week."

My head spun. I couldn't go to Paris and definitely not for a week.

"I have a meeting Monday afternoon. I can't miss it. It's for the new position I've been working so hard for."

"I promise we'll be back Monday morning."

I shook my head and my hands.

*Ah! What should I do? I've never done anything like this before. I'm not the type of person who picks up and leaves for vacation in a few hours.*

Luke clutched both of my hands together in his and waited until I looked up at him. "You can do this. You don't have to be the responsible one right now. Do something crazy for once in your life, Grace. Come to Paris with me."

Standing on my high school field with the guy I thought hated me but now wanted me to fly away to Paris with him, well, I got caught up in the moment and said the only answer that sounded right in my head. "Yes."

Luke pulled me into his arms, and I wrapped myself around his middle. I felt like I was at the edge of the earth about to fall over. He clutched me tighter, as though sensing my unsteadiness.

Water filled my eyes and I squeezed them shut. I'd just let go of a little part of myself. The part that had always held me back, afraid to step out of line. I was scared, but I was going to Paris.

# 17

## Grace

Luke walked me to my apartment door and, as promised, spoke to Theo and Laura in the hallway as I stepped inside. They had told me that my mother was asleep, but I couldn't leave for Paris tomorrow without speaking to her.

A soft creak sounded as I opened her door, but she didn't wake up. The wheelchair sat empty beside her bed and it made me sad as I'd never thought of getting one for her. I just kept believing she would get better soon and wouldn't need it.

Sitting on the bed, I ran my hand up her white cotton sleeve. Her frail arm was thinner than ever. She didn't stir. She must have had a very tiring night.

"Mom," I whispered. A soft murmur escaped her lips as though she had heard me, but her eyes remained closed.

"Mom," I said louder and closer to her ear.

Her eyes fluttered and she looked straight ahead before fixing her gaze on me.

"Grace? What's the matter, honey?"

"Nothing. How did it go tonight?"

"Wonderful. But can we talk about this in the morning?" she said, closing her eyes again. "I'm a little tired."

I hated disrupting her sleep, but I couldn't leave without telling her.

"Mom?"

"Yes," she slurred.

"I'm leaving for Paris tomorrow."

Her eyes opened wide. "What?"

I giggled. "I thought that would wake you up."

She blinked twice. "Are you serious?"

"I am. But if you're not comfortable staying with Theo and Laura, just say so. I haven't bought tickets or anything. Luke is taking us on his private plane so I can always say no."

"If you say no, I'll never speak to you again."

My heart ached at the command in her voice. My mother hadn't ordered me to do anything since… Well, I couldn't remember the last time.

"Okay, Mom. I'll go. But I'll be back on Monday after work."

"Don't rush on my account," she said and closed her eyes again. I knew her exhaustion was too deep to stay awake. I was glad I spoke to her, though.

"I love you, Mom," I said, but she didn't respond. She had fallen back asleep.

I ran my fingers along her salt and pepper hair, then bent down and kissed her cool cheek.

I closed her door softly behind me and found Luke waiting in the foyer.

"Is she all right?" he asked.

"Yeah. Just tired. She gave me her blessing to leave for Paris."

He smiled. "Great. Theo and Laura will be here by six tomorrow morning."

I shook my head. "I can't believe I'm doing this."

He reached me in two strides in my small hallway and grasped my cheek in the palm of his hand. "You can do anything, Grace. Always could. I'm just excited to be there along for the ride."

He leaned down and kissed my lips, slowly, purposefully. I closed my eyes and inhaled deeply. "I'll see you in the morning," he said. I nodded but kept my eyes closed, wanting to hold every second of this feeling inside my head.

The click of the door closing forced me to open my eyes. I walked back to the kitchen and checked my phone. I had a text from Omar only ten minutes ago, so I dialed his number.

"Well, if you're calling me back so soon, I guess the date didn't go so well?"

"We leave for Paris tomorrow morning at six."

"Nooo," he gasped, then let out the shrillest scream I'd ever heard. "Are you fucking serious, Grace?!"

I started shaking, not sure if my tremors were from fear or excitement. I couldn't tell the difference. "Yes, I'm serious! Should I cancel? I should cancel. You're right. I have that meeting about my promotion on Monday and even though he promised to be back in the morning, I need time to prepare—"

"Grace—you've been preparing for that meeting for the last four years. You'll be fine. But I can't believe he's flying you to Paris for what? Your second date? Man, sometimes I wish Richard were a billionaire."

"This is crazy. This is something you fantasize about. It doesn't happen in real life. I shouldn't go. I will only be disappointed."

"You don't wanna go to Paris because you're afraid it won't live up to some fantasy in your head? Grace, I swear, if you talk yourself out of this one, I will come there right now, put on one of your dresses and fly to Paris with Luke myself. Understood?"

I would have laughed if I didn't believe that Omar would do just that without hesitation. I filled my lungs with a big gulp of air and slowly drew it out. My heartbeat calmed down and I could think again. "Okay, I can do this."

"Of course you can. Now, what are you going to wear?"

I groaned, thinking of all the blazers and pencil shirts in my closet. "That's it, I'm not going! I'm calling Luke."

"I'm coming over and helping you pack. Don't you move until I get there. Do you hear me?"

"I hear you. I think Mrs. Taylor down the hall heard you, too."

True to his word, Omar knocked on my door ten minutes later and he rifled through my closet like Doctor Strange flipping through possible saving the world scenarios. He rapidly threw pieces together and I pursed my lips or nodded at his suggestions. When we finally had three outfits prepared, he wiped his brow. "I think we're done."

I walked over to him and wrapped my arms around him. "Thank you, Omar. I would have talked myself out of this if it weren't for you."

"I know, sweetheart. And you would have regretted it for the rest of your life. Now get some sleep because I won't be able to help you with the bags under your eyes if you don't."

I wiped at the bottom of my eyes, then smacked his arm when he snickered. "Okay, okay. I'm leaving. Have fun, Grace. And don't worry about what's-her-face."

"Faith Allens?"

"She doesn't stand a chance against you."

My lip quivered. What an emotional night. I walked into Omar's open arms and squeezed my friend as tight as I could. "Thank you," I whispered and realized I finally was allowing myself to open up again.

***

A car pulled up in front of my building at exactly six o'clock in the morning. Luke climbed out of the backseat and pulled me into his arms. "How did you sleep last night?"

"I don't think I slept at all," I said.

"Too excited to sleep?"

"Excited. Nervous. Still waiting for someone to pinch me."

I jumped at the sting on my rump, and Luke laughed into my neck. "You asked for it," he teased.

Never one to back down from a challenge, I cupped the front of his pants. "You wouldn't dare." His eyes rounded and he swallowed.

"Now, how do you like that?" I hissed between my teeth.

Bending his head forward, he whispered. "The thing is Grace," his breath tickled my ears and tiny goosebumps rose on my arms. "I like it rough."

*Oh my god!*

With my eyes still bugging out, he grabbed my arm and pulled me into the car.

I looked out the window, my hand still in Luke's, and tried to remember the last time I'd boarded a plane. My mom always made me renew my passport should I ever need to leave the country unexpectedly. I never understood her reasons, but she told me one could never be too prepared. *I guess I got my Type A personality from her.*

The car pulled up to the plane. The sun peeked through the early morning sky and the wind picked up as I climbed out of the car.

My short hair whipped around my face as Luke led me up the steps onto the private plane; I'd never been inside one. But not wanting to seem unsophisticated, I played it cool.

I tried not to let the white leather upholstery or spotless black furniture impress me. Nor the two flight attendants who promptly served me a glass of wine and two pillows as soon as I sat down.

Luke wiped a hand over his mouth, but he couldn't hide his eyes from the laughter he was suppressing.

"What's so funny?" I asked.

"Nothing," he said and cleared his throat.

"Obviously, something amuses you. What is it?"

"You can show some emotion, you know. I won't judge you for it."

My eyes widened and I quickly recovered.

He laughed out loud this time. "That's what I mean."

"What are you talking about?"

"Do you remember when we were twelve and we watched that scary movie in your apartment when your mom was at work? You always left to grab us something to eat or drink whenever the sinister music came on." He grabbed my hand and interlaced our fingers. "You don't have to hide your true feelings from me, Grace."

My heart jumped, and I couldn't look away from his gaze. It felt as though he saw behind the curtain I put up for the world.

I inhaled a deep breath and when I exhaled, I blurted out, "Your plane is fucking awesome."

Luke fell forward, chuckling.

After straightening in his chair, he wiped his eyes. He'd laughed so hard he had cried. "It is fucking awesome, isn't it?"

I nodded and sipped my wine.

"Do you want to watch a movie?" he asked.

"Sounds good."

After pressing a button on a remote, two panels slid away from each other, revealing a television screen. The movie *Scream* came on and I smiled into Luke's shoulder. He put his arm over me and I snuggled into his embrace.

***

"Grace, it's time to get up." Luke's voice sounded far away, yet I could feel him gently shake me. I opened my eyes and saw a flight attendant in front of me.

"Ma'am, please buckle your seatbelt. The pilot is about to start our descent."

I straightened in my chair and buckled my belt. As I looked out the window, the French Alps caught my eye. My goodness, I was in France.

As the plane made its descent, my stomach turned in anticipation.

# 18

## Grace

After freshening up at one of the nicest hotels I'd ever seen, Luke's driver idled outside the lobby waiting to take us to The Louvre. Driving through the streets of Paris, my mind raced to catch up to my heart. All these years, I imagined this moment. I imagined taking a hot tour bus with twenty sweaty strangers wearing running shoes and a baseball cap. Instead, I sat in an air-conditioned Bentley, wearing a red summer dress, and nude heels. Life was perfect.

A short time later, the massive structure of The Louvre came into view. The rows and rows of windows and hallways that could surpass a city block befuddled me. How could one man—albeit a king—live in a palace like this for himself while his people went hungry? No wonder they started a revolution.

Crowds gathered both inside and outside of the museum, with people taking photographs of themselves while picnicking outside or simply waiting in line to get in. When Luke steered us toward the side of the building, I redirected him. "Oh, I think the line starts here," I said.

"I know," said Luke. "But we're not going that way."

He ushered me toward a smaller entrance with a red canopy above the door. A security guard stood at the entrance. Luke flashed his passport and a business card and the guard opened the door for him.

"*Bonjour*, Mr. Crawford," said a man on the other side of the door. "*Suivez-moi*. Follow me."

My heels clicked on the marble floors. More people gathered inside, and the tour guide's voices boomed over the chatter.

Luke and I followed the smaller man with black-rimmed glasses down a separate corridor, one closed to the public. He knocked on a door and when no one answered, he opened it with a three-pronged key.

"*Après-vous,*" he said. "After you, Madam."

"Thank you. *Merci,*" I stammered, using the only French word I knew.

Several pieces of art lined the walls and I wasn't sure where we were exactly. No one else stood in the room. It was just Luke and me. Even our guide had left. Spinning on my heels, my eyes landed on a familiar sight. I gasped.

Framed upon the wall, her smile taunted me.

*Mona Lisa.*

"Oh my gosh," I whispered, slowly walking closer to the painting. Two semi-circle stanchions guarded it, but no other obstacles or people blocked me from devouring every detail of the painting. "She's beautiful," I said.

"She is," Luke whispered beside me and splayed his hand across my lower back. He pushed my hair behind my ear and gently placed a kiss on my temple. "I didn't want anyone or anything in the way of you seeing her."

I pressed my lips together, overcome with emotion. He had planned this in so little time. He remembered how much I loved this painting and knew how happy seeing it would make me. Other than my mother, no one else had ever put my happiness first. I tried to thank him, but the words caught in my throat. So, I turned to face him, went onto my tiptoes, and gently pressed my lips to his. He caught them and kissed me back just as slowly.

"As much as I want to lay you down and make love to you in this room, there are still security cameras around."

I dropped my head onto his chest and laughed. "I don't want to be on some paparazzi YouTube page."

"Wait here," he said and stepped behind me. I continued to stare at the painting, knowing I would never get another opportunity like this one again. The brush strokes were indiscernible, and da Vinci's use of shadows to depict a smile that was barely there had always moved me in photos, but to see it in person was a completely surreal experience. I felt as though I was looking in a mirror. At someone who tried to appear calm to the outside world, but inside, she hid her raving emotions. But if you were patient enough, you could see them.

"Take a seat," Luke said, turning me around. Behind us, he'd thrown a plush blanket on the ground and laid out a tray with cheese and grapes. "They were very particular about what I could bring inside."

"I'm sure they were."

He opened a bottle of water for me and fed me some grapes. I giggled. "I feel like I'm in one of those paintings."

"I don't know. I'm pretty happy you're sitting right here next to me."

"You really are a charmer, aren't you?" I teased. Yet I couldn't stop my heart from beating faster.

"Now tell me, Grace. After all these years explain to me, how do you see a smile?"

I laughed out loud, recalling our conversation all those years ago in front of my locker. Pointing to her lips, I said, "Do you see the faint shadows at the end of her mouth and how they curve upwards?" He nodded. "Then there's the shadowing along her cheeks and eyes. Da Vinci was a scientist and an artist. He studied human muscles and how they worked in a smile. He also knew that receiving light from your periphery vision differed from staring at it straight on. So, his use of shadows gives a sort of optical illusion. So, if you stare at Mona Lisa's eyes, cheeks, or anywhere away from her lips, you get a stronger sense of her smile."

"Huh." He tilted his head to the left, then to the right. "That's creepy," he mused.

I chuckled. "Maybe. But it's also genius."

The museum's curator arrived a short while later, inspecting the room circumspectly. We walked through the rest of the rooms hand in hand, but nothing compared to The Mona Lisa and the thirty minutes of heaven with just her and Luke.

"Where would you like to go for dinner?" he asked when we stepped outside.

"Is there something close to the Eiffel Tower?"

"Leave it with me."

***

It shouldn't have surprised me when a table, a violinist, and a server awaited us at the base of the Eiffel Tower all inside a plastic bubble, so locals and tourists would not disturb us.

"This is unbelievable, Luke," I said, looking around our bubble.

He smiled and in the candlelight, his face beamed up at me as though I'd just been the one who had made all his dreams come true instead of the other way around.

We talked about everything and nothing over dinner. I told him about the promotion I was up for and he told me about some recipe he was tinkering with at home. We laughed when I told him about my first and only attempt at making homemade French fries. I nearly burned down the apartment when I poured frozen fries instead of fresh potatoes into a pan full of hot oil. He made me promise to stay away from the stove and stick to only French kissing with him in the future. I sealed that promise with a kiss.

"Do you mind if we walk back to the hotel instead of taking the car?" he asked when we finished dinner.

"Of course not."

He interlaced our fingers and we walked through the narrow cobblestone streets.

"So, how many times have you been to Paris?" I asked after he pointed out his favorite bakery.

"Two I think. I don't even remember most of the trip the second time, but the first time I came, I stayed for nearly six months."

"Six months!" I pulled his arm back to look him in the eye. "But didn't you—"

"Didn't I, what?"

"I was going to say get fired. But I guess not."

He straightened his shoulders and I felt a weird tension between us for the first time. "So, what did you do for six months?"

He stared out into the street and didn't answer at first. I thought I'd said something wrong but he continued. "I threw parties, dated several models, and oh yeah, I worked at that bakery." He pointed ahead of us.

My eyebrows shot up. "That one? With the blue canopy and blue patio umbrellas?"

He nodded. His fingers eased up on my hand and his shoulders relaxed. "It was great. I learned how to make croissants and baguettes. I was terrible at it, that's why I hardly bake now, but I learned a lot."

"Really?"

"When I first arrived, that bakery was the only thing open at six in the morning when my friends and I emerged from whatever party we were at. So, I got to know the owner. I would frequent the bakery each morning and bring my friends with me. My friends and I..."

He trailed off and rubbed the back of his neck. "I don't know how to say this without sounding like a dick, so I'll just say it. We were the it-boys. Sort of like celebrities at the time. We partied, hosted lavish events for French A-listers, and trashed many hotel rooms in several of our all-nighters. I'm not proud of that part of my life, but there was a silver lining, I guess," he grinned.

"One morning, after a long night, I sat at the bakery drinking espresso when the owner told me he had to shut down by the end of the month, lamenting about the rent and the high cost of living. So, I called up a reporter I knew and she took my photo in the bakery that afternoon, drinking my espresso and a croissant I had baked earlier on my plate. I told her it was the best place in town. The following morning, shortly after the picture was published, a crowd began to form outside. People lined up for hours that day just to say they visited the place or took a picture at the table I usually sat at and posted it on social media. The lineups continued for months and traffic remained steady for years. It turned the business around." His voice became more animated as he told the story.

"Have you always been the fixer in your family?" I asked.

He turned to look at me, his brow creasing. "No. What do you mean?"

"Well, it seems like that's exactly what you did with the bakery and this whole trip and... well, my painting. It feels like you're always trying to fix something."

He stopped walking and stared straight ahead. "I never... I never really thought about it."

The creases on his brow deepened and I worried I somehow made this night more serious than I intended to. I had a tendency to rip the fun out of things. I was determined not to be that person right now.

Slipping my arms around his neck, I flicked my tongue underneath his jaw. "Why don't you show me some of your French cooking?" I suggested.

He looked down at my face, trying to read my expression. "But we just ate," he said, oblivious.

My voice deepened and I whispered, "I wasn't talking about food."

The creases on Luke's forehead disappeared and he squeezed my hand. "Follow me."

I struggled to keep up with his pace in my high heels, but we were only a block from our hotel.

"Good evening," the concierge greeted us as we stormed through the front entrance.

"*Bonjour,*" I called out and waved at the man just as Luke pulled me into the elevator. "Or is it *bonsoir*? I keep forgetting—"

Luke's lips cut off my rant and I melted into his arms. My tongue swept the inside of his mouth, fulfilling my earlier promise, and he smiled.

"I have protection," he whispered.

I shook my head. "I'm on birth control."

He closed his eyes. "My tests are all clean."

I sighed. "I don't remember the last time I had sex."

He chuckled, but his amusement vanished when the elevator stopped at our floor and we both rushed inside our room. After unbuttoning his cufflink, he moved onto his shirt, starting from the top. He reminded me of a lion stalking his prey, taking his time. I was definitely the prey. I stood frozen, watching his every moment.

"Take off your dress," he said.

His command provoked me. I was usually the one giving direction, but somehow at this moment, I enjoyed not having to think at all. So I untied the straps behind my neck that held my dress together. With a flick of my wrist, the dress fell down my body and pooled on the floor. I stepped out, holding Luke's gaze the entire time. Standing in my strapless red tube top and red panties, I waited.

"Lay on the bed." His voice had become hoarse, as though each word scraped against his throat.

I lifted my leg to remove my heels. "No. Keep your shoes on."

Slowly, I climbed onto the king-sized bed. The satin bedspread felt soft against my knees as I crawled on all fours. I heard a soft moan behind me, and I turned to look over my shoulder.

"You know exactly what you're doing to me, don't you?"

I narrowed my eyes but didn't say a word. I didn't want to speak, I only wanted to feel. Power surged through me, and I knew that if I ended the night now, it would be torture for him. And it would destroy me. I need this. I needed *him*.

When I reached the top of the bed, I pulled the cover down and sprawled myself over the white sheets, my arms across the pillows, one leg bent. Then I raised my eyebrows. That was all the command Luke needed. He tore off his shirt and crawled onto the bed, positioning his body on top of mine. His sculpted chest hovered over mine, rising and falling with every harsh breath. He lowered his head and kissed me slowly, his tongue lazily exploring every inch of my mouth. When I tried to reciprocate, he bit down on my lower lip gently, sending a rush of adrenaline through me. I grabbed onto his arms, his muscles bunching up as he held himself on top of me.

He lowered his head and whispered in my ear, "Turn over."

I shifted in his arms and held my hair as I turned onto my stomach. Luke skirted his hand underneath me, cupping the outside of my panties. "I've wanted this pussy for so long. I'm going to fucking take my time tonight." I groaned into the pillow at his vulgar words. I didn't think they would turn me on like that. I hated that word, but coming out of Luke's mouth, I wanted him to sing it.

Unhooking my bra, he smoothed my back with his hand, massaging my shoulders and caressing the side of my breasts on his way down. The movements seduced my body to relax despite the growing tension in my core.

When his palm reached my backside, he smacked it gently. It shocked me more than hurt me, so I jumped up. He rubbed the spot and whispered in my ear, "Was that too much?"

I shook my head.

"I have to hear you say it, Grace. Do you want to go on?"

"Yes," I hissed.

"Good."

The smack was harder this time and I gasped again.

"You still good?"

"Yes," I said into the pillow, holding back my moan.

"I can't hear you, Grace." He palmed my ass and caressed the sore spot.

"Yes," I shouted.

He pulled down my panties and pushed up my hips until I was on all fours again. "You gave me all sorts of ideas when you crawled over this bed."

Expecting Luke to position himself behind me, I was surprised to find his face between my thighs.

"Sit."

"Wha—What?" I stammered, looking around, unsure where to lower myself.

"Sit on my face. And don't you dare hover."

Closing my eyes, I widened my knees and slowly lowered myself down. I held most of my weight in my arms, which were still planted on the bed.

Luke growled and pushed his arms above his head, capturing my hands. He lifted them off the bed so that I had no choice but to sit up. Then he brought them around to his stomach, arching my back forward. Completely at his mercy, I forgot about everything and just focused on the sensation of Luke's mouth caressing me.

He moved his lips slowly, his tongue teasing its way around me, flicking my clit. I moaned and shifted above him, but his taunt arms kept me from falling. When the flicking increased and I knew I was close to climax, a slow moan escaped from my lips. "Yes," I whispered.

Luke let go of my arms, and I fell to all fours onto the bed. Disoriented, I looked back and watched him pull his pants off. He held his erection as he kneeled on the bed.

"I want to feel you come this time," he said and lifted my hips with his other hand. Opening my stance wider with his hand, he nudged himself gently at my entrance. When he felt me opening up, he pushed himself deep inside.

We both groaned. The feeling of Luke filling me was exquisite. My entire body tingled. Holding my hips, he pulled out slowly and then slammed his hips back in.

*Ah!* The impact hit a spot deep inside of me and my knees felt weak. I lowered onto my forearms, unable to hold myself up any longer. Luke reached for my hands and pulled me up, raising my chest above the sheet. He held both of my wrists in his hand as he slammed into me again.

"*Fuck*," I screamed aloud when the impact shook my core.

"Stay with me, Grace." Luke panted, as though he too was on the edge.

I closed my eyes and relaxed my body as I gave way to Luke's hard and fast rhythm. Each thrust of his hips pounded against a drum in my lower belly until it quivered and my knees shook. I heard nothing, saw nothing, but felt everything inside of me tighten. His thrusts hit the same spot over and over again until my moans became louder and my ears burned from the filthy words escaping his mouth. Finally, his pounding broke through the tension and released an explosion of pleasure that thrashed through me and I screamed. Above me, Luke shouted my name and released my wrists. I fell onto the mattress, spent and replete. He panted next to me, then rolled over, pulling me into his arms.

"Don't ever leave me, Grace," he whispered, but my ears still rang from the explosion inside of me. My adrenaline fired at every nerve ending in my body. So instead, I pressed my lips to his neck and waited for my heartbeat to slow down.

# 19

## Luke

A soft rapping at the door echoed in my ear, interrupting my memories of last night with Grace. I tried to ignore it, but it wouldn't go away.

*Knock, knock.*

"I'm coming," I grumbled as I rose out of the bed. Looking down, I noticed my body was still thinking of Grace. I checked the peephole. A hotel staff member waited outside with a room service cart. I always prearranged breakfast as I found it freshest between seven-thirty and eight o'clock in the morning. "Just leave it outside. I'll be right out."

"*D'accord, Monseigneur,*" said the man and walked away. Pulling on a pair of pants to not shock any hallway stragglers, I opened the door and wheeled the cart in.

"Luke?" Grace's groggy voice called from the bed. She leaned forward with her forearms propping her chest up from behind her. Her dark hair was tousled and her eyes were still a little sleepy. My breath caught at the sight of her.

"Morning, beautiful," I said and crawled into bed beside her. "How did you sleep?"

"Pretty great, actually."

"Why do you sound so surprised? Should I be offended?" I laughed.

"No, of course not. I just can't remember the last time I slept in another bed. I thought I would toss and turn, but the last thing I remember…" Her cheeks flushed and she bit her lip.

"Go on," I teased, running a finger down her arm and along her side. She squirmed out of the way, but I caught her and kissed her neck. She giggled. Grace Sweeney actually giggled and the sound squeezed my chest and filled my lungs, making it difficult to breathe. I missed her giggle. I had missed her so much, but I hadn't allowed myself to feel it.

"Grace—" I began, but she groaned.

"Is that breakfast? I'm starving." She scooted out of my arms and over the bed. She wore nothing and my thoughts raced to everything I wanted to do to her.

"If you plan to eat a bite of breakfast without interruption, I suggest you throw on some clothes. Otherwise, you'll be breakfast."

She pursed her lips as though she considered the idea, and my cock twitched. "Don't tease me, Grace."

She continued to kneel on the bed, tapping a finger to her lips, and I couldn't help the rumble in my chest when I said, "Come here."

She screamed and laughed and was much quicker than I'd expected.

She hopped off the bed and picked up my white buttoned shirt from the floor. Easing one arm and then the other into the shirt, I sat speechless as I watched. I recalled her wearing a pale blue shirt back at the cabin.

"I'm going to buy you a closet full of shirts to wear to bed from now on. I never thought a man's shirt would look so sexy on a woman, but you fucking pull it off like lingerie, Grace."

She twisted the shirt back and forth, modeling it for me. Her smile was contagious and her joy palpable. She spotted the cart and ran toward it.

"Oh, are those crepes? And chocolate inside? God, I love French food."

We both laughed as she removed the last two silver domes from the plates. There was a plateful of eggs Florentine, fresh croissants, butter, and a bowl of fruit.

I lifted the plates and set them on the round table next to the balcony door. "Shall we eat indoors or *alfresco*?" I asked.

Grace held a newspaper in her hands, her eyebrows drawn together.

"What's the matter?" I asked.

She unfolded the paper and pulled it closer to her.

"What is it?"

"I… I can't read a word of this but, I'm pretty sure this is a picture of me and you at the Eiffel Tower."

I walked over and extended my hand. "May I?"

She passed me the paper and I saw the photo she had described. It was definitely us. I admired Grace's profile, but I didn't think she would be up for compliments at the moment. "Well, this is to be expected, I guess."

"What? You're not upset?"

"Of course not. My brothers and I are used to this sort of thing. You'll get used to it too."

"What does the caption say?"

"Oh, I never read the stuff. It's all made up, anyway. No one spoke to us, so there are no details."

She crossed her arms. "Humor me, Luke."

"Fine." I picked up the paper and read the caption. "American billionaire returns with mystery girl in his arms."

I dropped the paper onto the round table.

"What else? There were several lines of text under the photo."

Picking up the paper again, I found the caption. "Sources say this new woman…"

"Go on," she urged.

"I just need a second to translate this in my head, as some words don't translate well."

"Translate them badly. Don't worry about it."

"Sources say this new woman has appeared from thin air. No one knows who she is but she's been spotted with Mr. Crawford in America and now here in our very own city. We wish her well, but…" I cleared my throat. "As we recall of our handsome billionaire, this Crawford doesn't keep a woman around for very long."

Grace's face fell, her smile gone. "Don't listen to this trash. They don't know me. And they definitely don't know us. Those other women—"

"Luke, I don't care about those other women. Or what that newspaper says. What do they mean about spotted in America?"

I wasn't sure. Those weren't the words that had bothered me. I would call Ryan after this and ensure he called this tabloid and warned them about making disparaging comments about me or my relationships.

Looking up from the paper, I noticed Grace on her phone. She gasped and turned her screen toward me. "Omar sent me this last night."

It was a photo of us leaving Mario's restaurant, but then next to that photo was a grainy shot of us on the bleachers. It wasn't clear, but, it was obvious where my head was and that the girl with short black hair was the same one on my arm earlier. *Fuck.*

Grace's hand trembled and the screen shook. "Oh my god, Luke. Everyone is going to see this."

"No, they're not."

"If Omar sent it to me, it's already out there. I'm a senior accountant. People respect me at work. How can I face them on Monday after this?"

I rubbed her arms and pulled her closer, but she pulled away.

"This is a disaster. I'm up for a promotion and if they see this—"

"I'm going to handle it. I'm calling Ryan right now. We have agreements in place. I promise you they will take down that picture within the hour."

When she continued to stare at it, I rubbed her back until she relented and dropped her head to my chest. "I will take care of this."

She nodded, and my heart wanted to reach out and hold her from the inside, too. I fucked up, but I would fix this. Pulling my phone out of my pocket, I dialed Ryan's number.

"Ryan, you need to take care of this," I said as soon as he answered.

"What are you talking about, Luke?" he asked.

"I'm sending you a picture." Grace passed me her phone, and I forwarded the photo to Ryan.

"Shit," he said shortly after. "Those bastards."

"I want you to tell them I'll sue for every last dime they own if they do not take down those photos from their website. Do you hear me? I will fucking sue them and then I will hunt them down."

"Calm down, Luke. We have agreements in place. I don't know how this happened, but I'll get it taken down."

"Make sure that you do."

"Luke?"

"Yeah?"

"The next time you want to go down… um, memory lane. Do it behind closed doors, huh?" he chuckled and it was the laugh that got under my skin.

"Fuck off, Ryan. I don't need a lecture right now." I pressed the red button to end the call.

After throwing both of our phones onto the mattress, I squeezed Grace tighter in my arms. "That picture will go away. I promise. In the meantime, try to eat something."

She nodded, but her mood had changed from playful to worried.

"Would it be so bad if everyone saw those pictures? We're grown adults and there was nothing explicit there." I hoped to make her feel better, but she just shook her head.

"If a guy gets caught making out with someone, he gets high-fives from his friends. If a woman is caught, everyone raises their eyebrows. No one is going to high-five me when I walk back into the office on Monday. They're going to look at me differently and while I know that's unfair, I worked too damn hard to get where I am to be seen as the latest watercooler gossip."

"You're right. I probably would get high-fives for that picture instead of cruel gossip. The double standard is pathetic."

She exhaled loudly and I pulled her onto the sofa and held her in my arms as we waited. Ryan's call came an hour later. Grace had agreed to eat some fruit and was biting into a strawberry when Ryan told me he had taken care of it.

"The story and pictures are down. Gag orders are in place and if any other website or tabloid publishes it, I told them I was prepared to take this in front of a judge. And they know in court sometimes it isn't necessarily who's right but who's got more money to outlast the other. Either way, we win. The picture is gone. Tell Grace she can be easy now."

"Thanks, Ryan. I owe you one."

"Any time, little brother."

When I ended the call, Grace looked up at me. Her large brown eyes looked hopeful and I smiled. "Did you hear any of that?"

"All of it. Do you believe him?"

"Ryan? Shit, yes. He loves me and he still scares me. I could only imagine what he told those assholes."

Grace expelled a deep sigh of relief. "Thank god." But her mouth was still unsmiling.

"What's wrong?"

"I don't know if I can handle this. All the paparazzi and stuff. I live a low-key life, Luke. I hardly leave my apartment. I don't like many people and don't know how to be likable."

"I like you and that's all that matters."

"Does it? I don't know if my anxiety will get in the way of us."

My mind panicked and I turned to face her. Cupping her cheek, I searched her eyes. They looked sad and I wanted so much to make her happy. "Grace, I know it's a lot to ask of you, but I don't want this to end. We'll avoid the photographers and stay in if you'd like. I hear my cooking is pretty good."

She smiled. "If one can believe your office staff, I hear that too."

"I also promise to keep my hands in proper places when we're out in public."

"And your mouth?"

My lips twitched. "Fine. And my mouth."

Her eyes brightened and she even laughed. "I want this to work, too. That's why I'm trying to be honest with you about who I am. I don't want you to change for me, and I probably can't change for you. We have to make this work so that we're both happy."

"I've never been fucking happier in my whole life." The truth of my words made my hands tremble. I ran my fingers through her hair and opened myself to her. "Say you'll give this a shot. We'll talk through it and if you don't feel comfortable about something, we'll work it out. I know being with me won't be easy, but say you'll try, Grace."

Her eyes watered and she threw herself into my arms, jolting me to the back of the couch. "I'll do more than try, Luke. I'll give it my best."

Her beautiful smile returned and I kissed her mouth, wanting to share in its warmth. I was falling for this woman.

But if I were honest, I fell for Grace the first day I met her.

# 20

## Luke

*Sixteen years ago…*

I laced up my red Jordans as I waited for my uncle to drive me to my first day of the seventh grade. The school was only a few blocks away, but he had promised me he would drop me off on the first day. He promised me last year and the year before, but something had come up.

"Hey, ready to go?" Colton asked as he and Ryan approached the front foyer, where I sat with my backpack on. "You said you were leaving early to meet Marcus and play basketball."

"He said he would drive me today," I explained. We never called my uncle by his first name. Colton and Ryan stopped a few years ago and I sort of picked up on the habit, too.

"He's gone, Luke," said Ryan, his lips turning up into a sneer. "Colton's driving us now." Ryan attended middle school with me while Colton went to high school.

"Let's go, Luke," said Colton. "We're leaving now."

I looked down the hallway, past Colton, to my uncle's recliner. It sat empty and shame burned inside my gut.

*He had promised me*! He had looked me in the eye and told me he would take me today. Why would he do that to me again? Was I that unlovable? Maybe this was a test. Or maybe he ran an errand this morning and would be back to take me. "No, go ahead. I'll wait."

"Luke, don't be stupid. He's not coming. Let's just go."

My lower lip trembled, but I bit down on the inside of my cheek. The pain helped redirect my attention. I shook my head, and Colton sighed. "Suit yourself, kid. But don't say I didn't warn you."

Colton and Ryan strode out of the house, Ryan looking back one last time. His eyes pleaded with me and he mouthed, *Come on!* But I shook my head again. This time, my uncle would come through. He had promised me and I believed him.

Ryan slammed the door behind them, and I jumped from the sound. At twelve, I no longer slept with the nightlight on, but loud noises still bothered me. The night my parents died, the phone rang in the middle of the night, startling us, and now whenever I heard a loud noise I felt uneasy.

Thinking of my bedroom, I thought to check my uncle's room, in case he was still getting dressed. I climbed the staircase and knocked on the door. When there was no answer or sound from the other side, I turned the knob and stuck my head inside.

My aunt slept soundly, her snores reaching me across the large bedroom. She never woke before noon. Colton said it was because of all the drugs she took. But I only ever saw medicine bottles next to her bed. I checked the study next. Even though I'd never seen him with a book, he liked to read the newspaper and drink whiskey in that room. I knew it was too early for a drink, but perhaps he was reading the paper.

But he wasn't there either.

*Damn it. Ryan was right. I was stupid. Why did I think this time would be different? Why do I keep doing this over and over again?*

My throat tightened, but I wouldn't cry this time. I was done crying over him.

I grabbed my school bag and flung it over my shoulder. Slamming the door behind me, I picked up my pace and raced toward the school. After walking about a block, I spotted Ryan's black hair. He crossed his arms and turned toward me, narrowing his eyes.

"He didn't show, did he?" he asked.

I shook my head but kept my promise. I didn't cry.

Ryan put his arm over my shoulder and leaned his head against mine. "You don't need him, Luke. You don't need anyone. You got that?"

I nodded.

When we reached the school, Marcus was already playing three-on-three and I didn't feel like joining, so I walked in the opposite direction.

*Oof!*

"I'm sorry," I said, realizing I'd bumped into some girl. Her notebook fell to the floor and a dark photo of a woman lay open on the ground. Picking up the notebook, I examined the picture.

"This is that famous painting… What's her name?" I asked.

She rolled her eyes and sighed. "It's The Mona Lisa."

"That's it!" I looked closer at the picture. "Why do you carry this around with you?"

She snatched the notebook from my hand. "Because it's the greatest," she huffed, her breath tickling my forearm. Then she walked away.

I'd never seen this girl before. She must be new. "Hey, what's your name?" I asked.

She turned her head to look at me over her shoulder, her long black hair falling in front of her heart-shaped face. "Grace."

"I'm Luke."

"Watch where you're going next time, Luke." She snickered. Her large brown eyes crinkled at the sides and I found my lips slowly spreading into a big, toothy grin.

I jogged up next to her. "What's your homeroom?"

"Ms. Chin. English. You?"

"Same. Mind if I walk you?"

She shrugged. "Suit yourself."

I sat next to Grace that day and missed another basketball game with Marcus at lunch to sit with her. I liked her take on things. She had this way of making me laugh without trying. "Why do teachers make us do icebreakers?" Grace asked. "It's so awkward." She shivered. "Do they really think it's a good idea to make us stand up and have everyone stare at us?"

I shrugged. "It wasn't so bad. Now I know your favorite artist is Vinci."

"It's *da* Vinci, and everyone laughed when I said it."

"That's because no one's ever heard of him. Most of us chose our favorite band."

She groaned and threw her head back. "Why didn't I think of that?"

I laughed while we walked back to class.

Later that day, I offered to walk her home from school. Her mother worked long hours, she said, and her dad was "not around". I told her my parents were gone, too.

She looked at me, side-eye, her lips pursed. "That's okay. Adults are stupid anyway."

I laughed. I liked Grace Sweeney. She made me feel like I could tell her anything. "My uncle is pretty stupid."

"Like I said. And adult men are even worse than women."

"You realize I'm a boy and will one day be a man, right?"

"Yep. But you don't seem stupid. So, don't prove me wrong."

I laughed again. This girl said exactly what she felt and didn't hold back. I liked Grace Sweeney.

"I won't," I said, not knowing that I would break that promise two years later in high school.

***

I laced up my boots as I recalled that memory. I may have broken that promise, but I would not let her down again. Straightening out of the sofa in the hotel room, I walked toward the balcony facing the city of Paris.

The Eiffel Tower lit up the night sky and tourists swarmed around it like moths to a flame. A possessive feeling enveloped me, as though I didn't want to share Grace with anyone else this weekend. An idea shot to mind.

"Grace?" I called out.

She popped her head out of the bathroom. "Yes?"

"Have you ever been to the south of France?"

She rolled her eyes. "I've never left New York State, Luke. No, I've never been to the south of France."

She shook her head, but her eyes crinkled, and I smiled. "I'm taking you tomorrow. We'll fly there and hop on one of our boats docked in Saint-Tropez."

"You have a—never mind," she laughed. "I'm learning to not ask questions. You live a very different life than mine, Luke."

"It doesn't have to be so different anymore," I said, walking up to her. She wore just her panties and a bra. The little lace scrap hardly hid much.

"I recognize that look, Luke," she said, stepping back. "You said we have reservations at seven. We won't make it in time."

"It's a private room, sweetheart," I said, catching her as she tried to run into the bedroom. "We have all night."

I picked her up and carried her to the bed. "Tell me you don't want this and we'll leave now," I said, watching her eyes warm up to the idea.

"All night, did you say?"

"Mmm-mmm," I murmured, kissing just below her ear. I loved that spot because she moaned involuntarily each time I swiped my tongue across it.

"I guess a few minutes wouldn't hurt then," she whispered, her voice raspy.

"A few minutes?" I asked, pulling away from her. "Well, now you've gone and insulted me. Guess I'll have to prove you wrong."

I slipped my hand underneath her lace panties and palmed her left cheek. She laughed and cupped my backside. A jolt of desire rushed through me as she pushed me closer. "Bring it on, Crawford," she said, her eyes staring straight into mine.

Fisting my hands to control my need, I growled, "Yes, ma'am."

I rolled us until she landed on top of me and with one flick I unhooked her bra. The flimsy fabric fell from her shoulders, revealing her breasts. Leaning forward, I swept my tongue across her flesh, awakening goosebumps along the way.

Grace dropped her head forward and I pushed her hair back. Cupping her face, I stared into her brown eyes. So many times, when the world seemed so alone, this face reminded me that there was someone out there who cared. I never realized it, but seeing her every morning—whether we were friends or enemies—made me feel alive.

During the last ten years without her, I felt like I'd lost my tether; that I was drifting in whichever way the current steered me, not sure what I wanted or where I was going. But staring at her face, my body settled, no longer wanting to drift away.

Pulling her down toward me, I held her in my arms. I kissed her temple, her lips, her neck. I wanted to cherish every part of her. I would take my time with Grace because without even knowing it, I'd been waiting my whole life to be with this woman.

My heart raced and my breathing hitched. Grace's face grew somber, as though she had read something in my expression. Panicking, I grabbed her waist and tossed her onto the bed beside me. Her chest heaved as I hovered my body above hers. Our breaths mingled and something sparked between us.

A phone rang in the background, and Grace stuck out her hand to reach for it. "It might be my mom," she said. I closed my eyes and nodded while she checked the caller ID. "It's Omar."

"Leave it," I said, harsher than I'd meant it to sound.

She bit her lip. "It could be important."

Tilting my head, I stared at her.

She rolled her eyes. "All right. I'll just check the message later."

"Grace," I began. "I don't want to tell you how to do your job. But it's the weekend and you need to unplug. Leave your phone off until Monday morning. You can use my phone to call your mom and I'll instruct Laura and Theo to message me if anything comes up."

She wiggled her lips from side to side, considering my proposal. I'd seen how hard Grace worked. She deserved an uninterrupted vacation.

Her leg bounced as she gripped her phone. "I don't know…"

"What's the worst that'll happen?" I asked.

"I'll lose my job."

"For not answering the phone on the weekend?"

She tossed me the phone and shook her hands. "Okay, okay, okay. Take it."

I laughed and snatched up the phone. "I promise, you won't regret this."

# 21

## Grace

My eyes fluttered open as a firm hand caressed my thigh. It was Sunday morning and I was in a swanky hotel room in Paris. I would have thought this a dream if not for the shivers that ran down my spine when Luke's lips kissed the middle of my back.

We had barely made it to dinner last night, spending most of the evening in bed. My inner thigh muscles protested when I squeezed them, remembering the workout Luke put them through all night. I didn't think I could squat that low for that long.

A rush of arousal ran through my body as his hand inched higher up my thigh and I dropped my head back the moment his fingers skimmed my clit. I groaned.

"I wish I could finish what I've started, but we really must leave now if we're going to make it." His breath tickled my ear but I'd heard every word.

"Where are we going?" I asked, tossing an arm over my eyes as Luke crawled out of bed to open the long white drapes.

Someone knocked on the door.

"That must be breakfast. I'll get it."

Luke stepped out of the bedroom and I listened to muffled voices in the other room. Reaching for my blue shorts and a gray t-shirt, I changed and met Luke at the round breakfast table by the balcony. The savory aroma of something meaty and familiar made my stomach growl. "Is that bacon?"

"Yep. And scrambled eggs, just the way you like them."

I smiled, pleased that he'd remembered. "So, what's the rush this morning?" I asked, filling my plate. Luke poured me a cup of coffee.

"The pilot I hired to take us to Saint-Tropez leaves in an hour. I paid him well to work on a Sunday, but it's his daughter's birthday party this afternoon."

Both Luke and I didn't grow up with our dads so hearing a man rushing back home for his child's birthday struck a chord with both of us because we both nodded at the same time as though we agreed we'd not allow him to miss that.

The pilot turned out to be a jovial man, with a hearty laugh and a thick French accent. He was excited to see Luke again. I couldn't recall when Luke said he'd been to Paris last, but Luke had a way of making everyone feel special. After receiving a clap on the shoulder from Luke, the pilot put on his headphones and flew us down to the south of France.

It was difficult to describe the colors of the Mediterranean sea. Deep blue hues saturated the middle of the ocean, but there were also green patches in the deepest parts and light blue ones near the shore.

A black sedan waited for us on the tarmac and drove us to the marina. Luke held my hand the entire time and my chest puffed out as I inhaled and relaxed on the exhale. I had never been on holiday and this jet-setting weekend seemed more like a fantasy than a reality.

I leaned into Luke's side and slipped my arms around his stomach. He pulled me in closer and held me tight. Without saying a word, I felt his breathing hitch and he lowered his head to kiss the top of mine.

When we reached the dock, I stared at the enormous white yacht in front of me. There were three levels, with handrails around at least two of them. The floorboards looked like light brown wood but I guessed were most likely laminate for the water. The front of the yacht had a white sunbed while the second floor had an entire canopied lounging set.

"Are you ready to set sail, Ms. Sweeney?"

"Do you even know how to drive this thing?"

"Your lack of faith in me only makes me want to show off more, you know that, right?"

"I do now," I laughed and took his hand as he helped me step onto the boat.

Luke flipped some switches and turned a large wheel. My body lurched forward while Luke steered the yacht out of the marina.

It took only a few minutes to reach open waters and Luke pushed the boat faster. The wind whipped my hair and I tasted the salty breeze on my lips. My shoulders relaxed and I turned to look at the coast behind us. I could barely make out the figures anymore, their bodies tiny beings that moved back and forth. It was only eleven in the morning, but with no cloud in the sky to block the sun, the heat became unbearable. I removed my t-shirt, revealing a tiny red bikini, and caught Luke's gaze on my body. He didn't smile and I worried he would crash the boat with his focus on me. "Are you paying attention to where you're going?"

"Nope. My attention is all on you right now."

His words boosted my ego. I unbuttoned my jean shorts and dragged them down to my knees, where they fell onto the deck. Stepping out of my clothes, I walked up to the front of the boat and laid a towel on the sunbed. I crawled on top, my stomach on the towel, and watched Luke steer. Kicking my legs up in the air, I hid my smile. He shook his head but laughed.

The boat slowed down and then came to a halt in the middle of the ocean. I turned my head to look for the shore, but I couldn't see it. Luke vaulted over the top of the railing and reached me in two strides.

He picked up the bottle of sunscreen from my bag and squeezed a large amount into the palm of his hand. The cream felt cool on my shoulders and I closed my eyes as his hands rubbed the protection across my back and then down my legs.

"Thank you," I said as he wiped his hands on a towel. He dropped beside me, looking up at the sky. A smile played on his lips.

"What are you thinking about?" I asked.

"Me. You. The future."

A part of me wanted to high-five him while another worried we were moving too quickly. We'd only just started talking again and if we continued dating, would he want to move in together? What would that mean for my mother? Would he want to put her in a nursing home? I wouldn't accept that. No way.

Luke laughed. "I can feel you thinking from here." He grabbed my hand and rubbed his thumb along mine. "Relax, Grace. You don't have to overanalyze this one. We will take this slowly and at your pace."

I nodded and my throat tightened. Luke knew me better than anyone else. Better than Omar, perhaps even better than my mother. I hid a lot from her and while I tried to do the same with Luke, he saw it anyway.

We both stared up at the cerulean blue sky for a little while, when Luke broke the silence. "I was thinking about what you said about helping Mario."

"Are you thinking of working in the kitchen with him?"

"No. I was thinking about helping him take his restaurant to the next level. You were right. I enjoy fixing things and restoring them to what they're meant to be."

"What do you mean?"

"After my parents died, we lived in our home with my uncle until Colton could earn enough money to move us out."

I nodded, recalling Luke telling me this the summer before we started high school.

"Even when Colton inherited our family's money and kicked our uncle out of the house, he didn't want to return to our home. Colton wanted nothing to do with it anymore. Something had happened… but that's his story to tell."

"Yes, of course," I said, appreciating his discretion.

"I couldn't let the house my mother and father had built fall apart. So, a few years ago, I restored it. I put in new windows, ripped out the old carpet, and installed hardwood floors. My father's study remained the same. I didn't want to touch that one. I was afraid it would lose the cedar scent from the wood paneling on the wall. That smell still reminds me of him. But everything else, I changed. I wouldn't let the last memories of our home be about my uncle, so I fixed the house and started brand new. And that's what I want to do for Mario's restaurant. He's an incredible chef but the place needs some renovations and he doesn't have the budget for it. But I do. I think I'll put a proposal together on Monday."

"That sounds fantastic, Luke. You'd be really great at that. Look at how you fixed my painting in one night.

When you put your mind to something, you get it done."

He smiled, still staring up at the sky, but he pulled me to his side. "I already have some great ideas for the reopening." His voice lowered. "You'll come, won't you?"

I laughed at the hesitation in his voice. "Of course, I'll come. I wouldn't miss it for the world."

He turned to stare at me this time, joy shining in his eyes, and perhaps a bit of the ocean mist. He leaned forward and kissed me slowly, his tongue sweeping my bottom lip. "Grace," he whispered. "Grace, I—"

I cupped his face and pushed my lips against his. I wasn't sure if he was about to say those three little words that would change everything. I wasn't ready to hear them yet. So much in my life was still undetermined and I wanted to enjoy the here and now without thinking of the future. For once in my life, I would live in the moment.

I straddled his hips and untied the top of my bikini. Luke leaned forward and flicked my nipple with his tongue, then circled it in a slow, lapping motion. My skin tightened and I planted my hands on his hard chest to hold me up. He pulled down my bottoms and I nearly lost my balance, teetering to the side.

"I've got you," he said and pulled himself up, his back leaning against the white cushion of the daybed. Sitting on his lap, Luke brushed my hair off of my face and held it in between his hands. "I know you're not ready to hear it, but you're the most important person in my life right now, Grace. And I want you to know it. Never doubt it." He did it again. He saw through me, despite my attempts to distract him.

I nodded, and he kissed me. This time, he wasn't gentle. He nipped at my lips, then placed his mouth at the pulse on my neck and sucked hard. I felt the pull of his lips down to my core. I dropped my head and bit his shoulder, the salty water tingling on my tongue. He growled at my response and ground his hips against me. He was hard and ready for me and I mewed in reply.

The next thing I knew, Luke was inside me and I moved my body in rhythm with the rocking of the boat. I pushed forward and felt the world move. When I lifted my body, I grabbed onto the steel at the back of the bed and then pushed down harder against him. The movement hit a sensitive spot and I gasped.

"Fuck," Luke cursed, and that spurred me on. Holding onto the iron bar, I used the leverage to ride Luke harder and faster than I'd ever done before. He squeezed my hips, his fingers trying to control me, but I was stronger than him in this position. He dropped his head as though defeated and relented to my control.

I rode harder and quicker. Panting, I asked, "Are you sure you want this?" I knew I wasn't just talking about sex.

"Yes, I can fucking take it," he shouted.

His confident words turned me on, and I wanted to praise him. I knew I was close, but Luke still held out. I felt my power surge and knew I would not last. "Luke," I shouted, and he sucked my nipple. My orgasm slammed into me and while I opened my mouth, I could hardly breathe.

Flipping me onto my back, Luke pounded his hips into mine and I shuddered at the pleasure of being filled while still riding the wave of my orgasm. The boat rocked and the waves crashed onto the side, but all I could see was Luke's face. His eyebrows were in a straight line, his forehead creased and his mouth slightly open. I knew when he quickened his pace that he was almost there and so I ran my hands up his chest and flicked his nipple with the nail of my thumb. He jerked and shouted, his voice hoarse.

"Shit," he panted. "I couldn't hold back after you did that."

I smiled. "I don't want you to hold back, Luke. Ever."

He curled his body over mine, and we watched the seagulls fly past us.

After returning to shore, we spent the rest of the afternoon walking along the streets of Saint-Tropez. The homes were not very large, but they were beautiful, with their terracotta roofs and yellow stucco walls. A woman watered the flower pots on her stone porch as we strolled through the neighborhood.

By evening, I was so exhausted that I convinced Luke to stay in. He ordered groceries and made Chicken Cordon Bleu. The white wine sauce hit my tastebuds without being salty and the asparagus crunched in my mouth just the way I liked it.

"We have to get some rest before our flight in a few hours," said Luke. "We can sleep on the plane, too, and when we land, it will be early Monday morning New York time."

"I can't believe this getaway was only two days. It feels like a week."

"Is that your way of saying you're sick of me?" he teased.

I pushed his shoulder. "You know what I mean."

He kissed my lips. "I do."

As Luke had expected, we both slept through take-off and most of the landing in New York.

"Here you go," Luke said, handing me my phone. "Monday morning, as promised."

"Thanks," I said, turning the device on. A bunch of text messages and phone calls from Omar pinged through and I couldn't read any of them as they just kept on coming. I knew my mother was okay. I'd just spoken to her a few hours ago and these messages were more than a day old.

Impatient to hear what was happening, I dialed Omar's number.

"I'm sure everything's fine," Luke said, placing his hand on my collarbone. "I can hear your heart beating from here."

"You're right. He's probably worried about what I'm going to wear for my interview this afternoon."

"Grace?" Omar's voice sounded panicked on the other end and my heart stopped.

"Omar, what's wrong?"

"Oh my god, Grace. Did you get any of my messages?" he shouted. "Are you at the office? Where are you?"

"Slow down, Omar," I said, trying to calm him and me down at the same time. "We just landed and I should be back home in about an hour."

"Oh no," said Omar, his voice dropping.

"What's going on?"

"Grace, you'll be fine. I'm sure they'll give you another chance."

"What the hell are you talking about?" His words stopped me; my legs froze.

"They moved your interview to this morning, Grace. It starts in five minutes."

"What?" I screamed in the middle of the tarmac. "They can't do that."

"I heard it was something about a big budget meeting getting moved to tomorrow and so Faith suggested they hold the interviews this morning."

"She knew I had taken Monday morning off. She must have seen the schedule. I can't believe—"

"Maybe you can still make it," Omar said, but the hesitation in his voice told me he didn't think that was possible.

"I'll make it, Omar. I've got to. See you soon," I said and ended the call.

"Did I hear that right? Did your interview get changed to this morning?" Luke asked. "They can't do that."

"They can and they did. I have to get there. I have to go."

"All right. Eric, can you take us to this address ASAP? If you get any speeding tickets on the way there, I'll pay for them. Just go!" he shouted.

Eric nodded and slammed his foot on the gas pedal. Luke and I both lurched back, but the rush felt good on my nerves. I would make it. I had to; the alternative was not possible. I needed this raise. My mother's health depended on it.

# 22

## Grace

Eric sped down the freeway and my body crashed into Luke's at every turn, but we somehow made it to my office in just under an hour without being pulled over.

But when I stood on the sidewalk about to go in, I looked down at my jean shorts and t-shirt and groaned. "I can't walk into the meeting like this," I said aloud.

Turning his head, Luke scanned the street. Then he grabbed my hand. "Come with me."

He raced us toward a store whose sign read closed, but a woman stood at the register staring at the computer. Luke pounded the glass door with his fist so hard I thought it would break. The woman pointed to her empty wrist and then the sign at the door. The store didn't open for another half hour. Luke pounded harder, and the sign at the door crashed down onto the floor.

The woman rushed over and shouted through the glass door, "We're closed! And if you break my window, I will sue you."

"I'm Luke Crawford. I will pay you for your time. I just need you to open your store for us right now."

"Crawford, did you say? As in Crawford Corp?" she asked, her eyes widening.

"Yes," Luke shouted.

"Well, why didn't you start with that?" She picked up the sign and unlocked the door. "Welcome to Charmed. How can I help you?"

Luke looked at me.

"Uh, do you have something I could wear for an interview? Something professional?"

"Yes, of course. Follow me."

The woman took her time looking through racks of clothing when I said, "Honestly, anything will do. I just need to wear something other than this."

She pursed her lips and stared at my waist. "Okay, I got you."

In the change room, I zipped up a white fitted dress that hit just at the knees and sighed in relief when it fit.

"Thank you. I'll take it," I said to the woman.

"Go!" Luke said. "I'll take care of everything here."

I nodded and ran out of the shop.

Pushing through the glass front door, I raced to the elevators. Someone had already pressed the button, so I stood back and waited impatiently. I tapped my brown leather sandal on the marble tile, watching the digital numbers above the elevator descend.

*No, no, no. Why are you going to the basement?*

I pushed the button repeatedly, knowing it was useless, but it made me feel better. Finally, the elevator pinged and the doors opened.

When they opened again, Omar stood waiting for me in the foyer.

"Many of the partners have left the boardroom, but I think Damon is still there," he said.

I nodded and rushed down the narrow hallway. Slowing my steps as I got nearer, I saw Faith's head pop up from behind her computer. She stood with a hand on her hip and a smirk on her face, but I ignored her and knocked on the boardroom door.

"Mr. Fromer, sir. I'm sorry I'm late." I held in a breath, giving my heart time to slow down and my voice to steady.

He checked his watch. "More than an hour after the scheduled time isn't late, it's disrespectful," he said and shut his laptop.

"Mr. Fromer, wait!" I called after him before he could leave the boardroom. "I didn't know the meeting time had changed. I was in Paris and I didn't have my phone."

He pursed his lips and nodded. "I understand."

Relief washed over me. "Thank you."

"But if you want to be a senior audit manager at Delmar & Tuch, you'll need to make some sacrifices. The person we're looking for has to understand that while you may not work weekends, you're expected to check your phone for any changes to meetings and such. I'm sorry, Grace. I know you're a hard worker. Perhaps the next time a position comes up, you'll be ready."

This position hadn't come up since I started with the company, so who knew when the next one would be available.

"Mr. Fromer, have you made your decision, then?"

He tucked the laptop under his arm and checked his watch again. "We haven't made a formal announcement, but we think we have a candidate in mind." His gaze shifted to Faith and she smiled.

"And there's nothing I can do to change your mind? I've put together a portfolio of my work and achievements I can share with the team via email. I have it ready to send now." I pulled out my phone and opened the app to my cloud.

"It's too late, Grace. You had your opportunity and you missed it. I've got to go. Excuse me." He stepped out of the boardroom and the moment he turned the corner, I lost my composure. My legs wobbled and I sat down at the mahogany desk, dropping my head in my hands.

*What am I going to do now? I needed this promotion… I couldn't afford the new medication without it, and definitely not transplant surgery.*

I raised my head at the soft knock on the door. Omar pressed down on his lips. "I take it the meeting didn't go well."

"Well, apparently I completely missed the meeting and no, Mr. Fromer wouldn't allow me to reschedule or send my portfolio to the team."

"Asshole," he whispered under his breath.

"Maybe. Or maybe he's right. I messed up and people who mess up don't get second chances at work."

"You know that's not true, Grace."

"Do I? I work harder than anyone here, Omar. I should have known better, but…"

"But what?"

"Never mind. That's not the issue right now. Right now, I have to figure this situation out for my mom's sake."

"Have you tried contacting human resources, putting your mother under your insurance plan? We have decent benefits."

"They won't consider her a dependent. I've tried to argue this many times, but they keep finding loopholes that deny her. It's so damn frustrating!" I smacked the table, then dropped my head again.

I'd never lost my composure at work. Never. But I felt lost and broken. All those late nights working until midnight, only to wake up early the next morning and start all over again. All those weekends I spent reviewing accounts instead of binge-watching TV shows, all because I thought it would pay off. In the end, meant nothing.

*Absolutely fucking nothing.*

Tears welled up in my eyes, but I was too angry to let them fall. I knew Faith could see me now and while she was probably enjoying my anger, I wouldn't let her see me cry. Balling my fists, I stood from the boardroom chair.

"I'm heading back to my desk," I said. "I need to figure out what happens next."

"I believe in you, Grace. And sometimes everything works out for a reason."

"Too soon," I said, fighting my bottom lip not to quiver. "But thank you."

I walked to my desk and closed my eyes.

"Good morning, Grace." Jackson stood by my cubicle, his eyes searching mine. "Are you all right?"

I cleared my throat and put on a smile. "Yes, perfectly fine. How can I help you?"

"I emailed you last night about tomorrow's audit location."

I groaned inwardly. "I haven't had a chance to open it yet. I—"

"That's perfect. The location has changed and I wanted to tell you in person before you wrote it in your calendar."

"Thank you, Jackson. I appreciate it."

"You're welcome." Then he tilted his head and said, "I heard about the meeting this morning and I just want you to know that I think you're very professional and deserve that position, regardless of what anyone else says."

"Anyone else? Who is saying otherwise?"

"Oh, uh, no one." He jerked back and looked around the office. "Just Faith… and maybe a few other people."

"What?" Why would anyone be calling me unprofessional just because I missed one meeting? I knew plenty of people in this office who routinely showed up late to work. "They're calling me unprofessional because of one meeting? That's absurd." But it still bothered me. I couldn't deny it.

"Well," Jackson rubbed his bottom lip and looked around again. "It's not just about the meeting."

"What else could anyone have to say about me?"

"It's nothing. Forget I mentioned it."

"Jackson, you're not leaving until—"

"Faith told everyone that you got the Crawford account because you're sleeping with one of the brothers. She said it was unethical and they should demote you, maybe even fire you, for ethical reasons." He clapped a hand over his mouth. "I'm sorry. I don't believe any of that, but—"

"But?"

"But she had proof."

My head spun and my heart knew what he was about to say next, but my mind wouldn't piece it together yet. "What kind of proof?" I asked slowly.

"She took a screenshot of a man and a woman… well… he was…"

I put my hand up to cut him off.

"Anyway, the caption said it was Luke Crawford, and Faith insisted the woman was you. She even referred to another newspaper article. She said something about a friend she follows on Instagram from Paris… I don't know."

I rubbed my temples as the fog in my head cleared. The partners didn't want any scandal within their company. They changed the meeting time knowing I was in Paris and probably wouldn't see the email. If this was true and they were concerned about how the story would reflect on Delmar & Tuch, I could be at risk of losing more than just a promotion. I could lose my job.

My cell phone rang and I jumped in my seat.

"I'll let you take that," said Jackson, looking relieved that he had an excuse to leave me.

Luke's face popped up on my screen. He must have set that up while he had my phone. When he *took* my phone from me.

I tapped on the screen to silence the call. I wasn't ready to speak to him right now. I might say something I would regret later.

Turning on my laptop, I opened my email and focused on work.

I didn't lift my head until noon when Omar tapped on my cubicle. "Want to grab something to eat? My treat."

"Thanks, but I have a lot to catch up on. I'm going to skip lunch." Keeping my head down, I didn't look Omar in the eye. I was ashamed about that picture and wondered if he thought less of me because of it. I knew he didn't think I did anything unethical, but it was enough that he saw me in such a vulnerable position that no one else was meant to see.

"Are you sure?" he asked, his voice soft.

"Yep. Thanks for asking." I began typing gibberish on my laptop, hoping that would send Omar on his way. It did, but my chest still tightened when he left. For the first time in a long time, I felt like I had no one I could turn to. But I'd been here before, fourteen years ago. I survived that and I would survive this, too.

Luke called six more times that day. Every time my finger itched to answer it, I told myself not to. The same feelings of isolation and shame from being ridiculed in high school had now resurfaced, and I knew that if I spoke to him, I would say something in anger. I needed to calm down first.

I didn't speak to anyone else that day. After finishing the Crawford account, I began researching for tomorrow's audit. I would complete that one sooner than anyone else had before and I would do it better than them, too. I would prove to these assholes that I wasn't reflective of one night because I was so much more than that.

By the time I climbed into my car, I was exhausted. My shoulders and neck ached from typing on my laptop all day. My back hurt from sitting down and only allowing myself bathroom breaks. I knew I was punishing myself, but I couldn't stop it.

As I rode the elevator up to my apartment, my eyes shut and my body swayed. The jet lag was killing me and I just wanted to sleep this day away. After making dinner, I planned to tuck myself in and not get up until morning.

But when the elevator doors opened, my heart stopped. Luke was there. He was leaning with his back and head against my door and pushed off when he saw me. My face must have shown my exhaustion, because his brow creased and he asked, "Grace, are you all right?"

"I'm fine," I said.

"I called you six times, but you didn't answer. I was ready to rush security to get to your desk, but I didn't think you'd appreciate that."

"No, I wouldn't have." I fumbled to get my key out of my purse.

"What's the matter? Did the interview not go well? I'm sure you're just being hard on—"

"I didn't get an interview."

"Well, I'm sure they'll reschedule one."

I balled my fist around my key. "No. They won't."

"Well, that's ridiculous. I'll just call them and explain."

"No!" I said. "Don't do anything else."

He closed his mouth and cocked his head. "What do you mean by anything *else*?"

I shut my eyes and breathed through the pounding of my head. "Look, Luke. I'm tired and—"

"I get it. I'll call you in the morning and we can go for lunch and talk about everything."

"There's nothing to talk about. Everyone thinks I got the Crawford account not because I work hard but because I slept with one of the Crawford brothers." I was still so angry about the vile rumors.

"What?"

"Yes. So, I didn't get the promotion and I won't make partner anytime soon, but most importantly, I can't pay for my mother's medical bills."

He shook his head and rubbed his forehead. "But we took down the picture."

"Faith had screenshotted it."

"That little—"

"I've got to go."

"I don't want you to leave upset. Let's talk about this."

"I don't want to talk right now, Luke."

"Everything will be all right."

I don't know why his placating tone irritated me, but I snapped.

"No. It won't be all right. Everything is not fine. I don't have a cushy trust fund I can fall back on. I have serious bills to pay and it's all my responsibility. Not all of us are lucky to be born rich, you know!"

"Hey that's not fair," he said, crossing his arms over his chest.

"No. Do you know what's not fair? That you take nothing seriously. You float about your day—your biggest decision is deciding what you want for lunch and never having to worry about someone else that depends on you. You have no responsibilities and no care in the world while the rest of us live paycheck to paycheck and fight for every dollar we earn. And yet you are the billionaire. You are the one the tabloids follow around and people fawn over."

He stepped back as though I'd slapped him. And perhaps I had with my words. I immediately regretted them and knew I should never have had this conversation jet-lagged and angry. "Luke, look—"

He raised his hands. "No. I think you've said enough."

He turned and walked away.

"Luke?" I cried. But he didn't turn back.

"Grace?" my mother called from the other side of the door. "Is everything okay?"

I wanted to run after Luke, but I'd hesitated too long. The elevator doors closed and Luke was gone. But I wondered if my mother hadn't called me, would I have run after him? I wanted to say yes, but my tired mind and body betrayed me.

# 23

## Grace

It was Friday and I still hadn't spoken to Luke. Every time I thought of calling him, my righteous anger would protest, remind me I'd lost a promotion because I was so distracted by him, and I would put the phone down. I asked James to call Crawford Corporation and speak to Luke and see if the company had questions about the audit. I'd planned to casually ask James if Luke sounded okay. But the receptionist had told James that Luke no longer worked at Crawford Corporation. I wondered what happened. Did Luke quit? Did Colton fire him? What was Luke doing now? So many questions whirled around in my head, but the one that kept me up at night was always the same. Was it over?

Not ready to answer that question, I kept busy with work as I always did. I finished the last audit in only four days. And scheduled a personal day today. I didn't tell anyone, not even Omar, but I was heading to an interview with Charters, another accounting firm. The company was small but growing and it recently acquired some big clients, so its prospects looked good.

I pulled open the brown aluminum handle of the front door and walked inside. There was a brown carpet on the floor and the reception desk was dark wood. At least I suspected it was wood at first until I felt the film at the edges of the desk.

"Can I help you?" the receptionist asked. He wore a blue blazer with a light blue shirt and khaki pants.

"Yes, I'm here for the eleven o'clock interview."

"Ms. Sweeney?" His voice was soothing.

"Yes, that's me."

"Perfect. Right this way."

I followed him down a narrow, carpeted hallway. Not the same dark brown carpet as the one in the hallway. This one was a lighter.

As we turned the corner, I spotted five people, three men, and two women, seated at a large boardroom desk. The brown high-gloss desk reminded me of something I'd seen in a movie from the eighties.

"Ms. Sweeney, thank you for meeting with us."

"Thank you. I appreciate the opportunity."

Sitting in a bulky black leather chair, I pulled myself to the table and clasped my hands together.

"Your resume is very impressive. You've only been at Delmar & Tuch for five years and you've completed an impressive amount of audits. How did you accomplish that?"

I explained my method and the system I put into place for all my audits, and they all nodded and took notes. I bit down on a smile that tugged on my lips.

After a few more questions that resulted in more nodding and note-taking, one of the men asked, "Do you have a salary expectation?"

I remember someone telling me not to answer this question, to leave it open-ended, but I wasn't here to be coy. I needed the money and I wouldn't leave my current employment without it or the title that I'd lost at Delmar & Tuch.

"This is a list of the average salaries for senior audit managers. With my experience and reputation with clients, I believe this number right here is what I'd be looking for." I circled one of the higher salaries and passed the paper to the man who'd asked the question. He shared it with his colleagues, and they nodded once more.

After answering a few more questions, a woman in a black suit said, "I think that was the last one. Do you have any questions for us?"

I asked about the hours and the company culture and the type of insurance they offered. It sounded similar to the one I had now and worried I still wouldn't be able to claim my mother as a dependent. But with the raise, that shouldn't be a problem.

The same woman walked me to the reception desk and shook my hand. "Thank you for coming today, Ms. Sweeney. It was a pleasure to meet you."

"Thank you. You as well." Before I left, I turned to ask her one more question. "When do you think you'll make a decision?"

She checked her notebook. "We have a few more people to interview today and next week. We hope to have our final decision in a couple of weeks or so."

"Thanks again," I said and shook her hand.

It wasn't a far drive back to my apartment, another thing I liked about this company. The people seemed nice and even the humble office was more to my liking than the intimidating and cold boardrooms at Delmar & Tuch.

I was feeling better for the first time since my argument with Luke. What did my mom always say? *Don't worry so much, honey. Things always have a way of working out in the end.* Maybe she was right.

I stopped by a bakery before heading home and picked up an apple pie, my mom's favorite. I would celebrate the small wins for a change.

As I stepped off the elevator, I noticed my apartment door was wide open.

My heart stopped, but I forced myself to breathe.

*Don't panic. Maybe Lorna just stepped out to grab something and forgot to shut the door.*

While that was completely plausible, the tiny hairs on the back of my neck stiffened.

"Mom?" I called when I stepped inside.

The apartment was empty. The only sound was the clicking of my heels on the laminate floor. "Mom, where are you?" I shouted, running to her room. She wasn't there.

I checked my room next and the bathroom, but those were empty as well. The wheelchair stood in the foyer, so they hadn't gone far. I spun around in the living room.

*Think! Where would they go?*

Pulling out my phone, I tried calling Lorna, but the call went straight to voicemail.

*Shit! Maybe the reception is bad here.*

I raced toward my balcony, and that's when I saw her. My mother was on the concrete floor, curled up on her side.

"Oh, my god. Mom?" I kneeled beside her. "Mom?"

She didn't open her eyes when I called her name. Nor did she wake when I shook her shoulders. But when I tried to lift her head, I noticed a pool of blood on the ground, matting her hair to the side of her face. Remembering the last time I'd found my mother on the floor, my stomach dropped. Instinctively, I put two fingers to her neck and checked for a pulse. It was faint, but she was still alive.

I ran inside to grab my phone but turned when I heard footsteps racing down the hallway. Lorna appeared at my doorway, her face sweating. Or was she crying? I couldn't tell because she wiped at it before I could ask.

"Thank goodness you're here," she said.

"I have to call 911. My mother's hurt."

"I called them," she said, gasping for air and holding her side. "When my phone didn't work, I ran downstairs and across the street to the dental office to use their phone. The ambulance is on its way."

I ran back to my mother to check on her. Her breathing was shallow and her face was pale.

"What happened?" I asked Lorna, smoothing my mother's dark hair away from her face.

"She wanted to go outside for some fresh air, but she wasn't having a good day today, so I suggested the balcony. We sat outside for a bit when I noticed goosebumps on her arm. I told her I'd go in and get her a sweater. I was in her bedroom when I heard her shouting something about a green sweater, so I went back into her closet to look for a green one when I heard the crash."

Lorna rubbed her face and sobbed into her hands. "I don't know what happened, but when I ran to the balcony, her chair had fallen over and your mother was unconscious on the ground."

She started shaking, so I pulled her into my arms and squeezed her tight. "It's okay," I murmured.

"I'm so sorry," she cried. "I'm so sorry, Grace."

"This could have happened to anyone," I said.

We both turned toward the entrance when a knock sounded on the door.

"Did someone call an ambulance?" a deep voice asked from the living room.

"Out here!" I called. "On the balcony."

Two paramedics rushed toward us. "Ma'am, please step aside," the burlier one said.

Standing on our narrow balcony, I flattened myself against the wall to make room for both of them. They checked my mother's limbs before strapping a brace on her neck. Slowly, they lifted her onto the gurney.

"Which hospital are you taking her to?" I asked.

"St. Joseph's. It's the nearest one."

I nodded. "I'll be right behind you."

"Can I come with you?" Lorna asked.

"Yes. Definitely." I grabbed her hand and we followed the paramedics out the front door.

I broke several traffic rules on my way to the hospital but fortunately, there weren't many cars on the road. But I still didn't make it in time to see the paramedics bring my mother in, so I had to ask a nurse at the front desk.

"Yes. I saw them bring her in, but I don't have any information yet. Please take a seat in the waiting room and I'll let the doctors know you're here."

"Thank you," I said, and sat next to Lorna.

A few hours later, Lorna got up. "Can I get you a coffee?" she asked, stretching her arms.

"No, thanks. I'm not hungry."

"Me neither," she said. "I just need to get up and move around. Sitting and waiting is making me anxious."

"You don't have to stay, Lorna. Really. I'll keep you posted."

"I can't leave you here alone."

*Alone.*

She was right. If something happened to my mother, I was truly alone. My face crumbled and Lorna pulled me into her arms.

"I won't leave you, Grace. I'll stay here all night."

I hugged her tight, finally releasing all the pent-up fear I'd held in until now. I cried until I could hardly breathe and Lorna just squeezed me tighter.

"Thank you, Lorna." I pulled away and wiped the tears from my face. "I really needed that. But I'll be okay now. You have a family waiting at home for you. I'll just curl up on one of these couches."

"I—I can't leave you like this," she said, looking around the waiting room. The brightly colored furniture had some dark spots, but it didn't look all that bad.

"I'll just sleep, anyway. I promise I'll text you as soon as I hear anything. Go."

"I'm just going to tuck my kids in and then I'll come right back here."

"Don't. I'll be fine. Go." This time I pushed her toward the exit and nodded my head when she turned to look over her shoulder. I waved my hands, shooing her away.

I kept the pasted smile on my face until Lorna exited the automatic glass doors and walked out of sight. Then my face crumbled, and I fell into one of the large armchairs and let the tears fall.

I checked my watch and realized two hours had passed and still nothing from the doctors. I walked over to the nurse's desk.

"Excuse me, are there any updates for me?"

"And you are?"

I realized this was a new nurse. The other shift had ended about an hour ago. "My name's Grace Sweeney. The ambulance brought my mother in earlier."

"Let me check." She got up and went into a private hallway. A few minutes later, she returned. "The doctor said she'll be out shortly to speak with you."

"Thank you," I said, breathing a sigh of relief. I wasn't sure if the delay was good news, that she was all right and they hadn't wanted to wake me or something else. I couldn't imagine the other options.

"Grace Sweeney?" a voice called from the end of the hallway.

I shot up and rushed toward the woman in blue scrubs and a white coat. "I'm doctor Nadine Johnson."

"Hi. How's my mother? Does she have a concussion?"

She pursed her lips. "A mild one and she doesn't have any broken bones. The way the paramedics described it, they suspected her chair broke most of her fall."

"Thank god." I breathed a deep sigh of relief and wiped the sweat that had formed on my brow. "Can I take her home tonight?"

She pursed her lips. "I'm afraid not."

"Do you need to watch her overnight?"

"Yes, but that's not all."

"What do you mean?"

"I'm afraid your mother's kidneys are severely damaged. We're hoping she will make it through the night…" She continued speaking, but I had a hard time following the rest. *Hoping she'll make it through the night*. What was she saying?

"I don't understand. Is my mother not going to make it?"

"We don't know for sure. There are some tests we can run and perhaps some medication we could try, but it would just be for the short term. Your mother needs a transplant immediately."

The world fell from underneath my feet and I stumbled forward. I had no way of getting the money for a transplant immediately. I thought I had a couple of years before that was necessary. My insurance would cover her hospital stay for now. I would worry about the money for the transplant later. "Please. Do what you have to do to keep her alive."

She nodded. "We'll keep you posted." Then returned to the automated doors behind her.

I somehow reached the armchair in the waiting room, not remembering the steps I took to get there. I felt as though I were watching a movie or living in a dream. This couldn't be happening to my mother. I couldn't lose her.

I gasped at the pain in my chest and clutched the top of my sweater.

*What am I going to do?*

# 24

## Luke

It'd been nearly a week since I'd last spoken to Grace. But not an hour went by without
thinking about her. One minute I hoped she'd call, the next I debated whether to call her. She had said things that had really stung. The truth in her words hurt. She was right. I didn't have any serious responsibilities or career goals like her. Maybe I wasn't good enough for her. Maybe I should stay away before I fucked something else up. She deserved a better version of me. I wouldn't call her until I got my shit together.

Later that night, I went to Mario's Restaurant for dinner. Looking around the dark empty room, I realized I could help him if I committed to it. I proposed a remodeling and rebranding plan to him. He'd shied away at first, explaining he didn't have the funds to do that.

"Do you like the ideas?" I asked him, sitting at one of the brown leather booths.

He smoothed down his mustache. "Of course, I do. I just can't afford them."

"Sell a portion of the business to me and I'll provide the capital."

His gaze shot to mine, his eyes searching for any joke. But I wasn't kidding. I had a new business venture in mind and Mario's Restaurant would be the first project.

Five days later, the plan was coming together. The company that helped remodel my home jumped on board with my plan and ripped out all the old dark wood furniture and carpet.

As I circled the room, I took in the new white paint on the walls, the new patio doors that used to be small windows at the front, and even a new wall, closing the kitchen off from the dining room. Mario's daughter Victoria helped me choose the fresh new fabrics for the benches and chairs, which were to arrive soon. It felt like one of those remodeling TV shows where everything changed in a week. With the capital and the Crawford name, it wasn't surprising how quickly this all came about.

"I can't believe this is the same place I stood in only a week ago," said Mario, surveying the room. "I can't believe this is Mario's Restaurant."

"Well, about that," I said. "Remember our rebranding conversation? I think we should change the name, too."

"Oh."

His face blank, I explained my reasons. "I understand your family is from Naples. You speak so proudly of it when talking about growing up there. So, what do you think of the name Taste of Naples?"

He raised his eyebrows and rubbed his lips. Then he smiled. "I love it!" He reached for both my shoulders and pulled me in for a hug. Well, that went better than I'd expected. I chuckled when he slapped my back. He pulled me away and wiped a tear from his eyes.

"Thank you," he said.

"Well, don't thank me yet. Our grand opening is next week and that will be the real test."

# 25

## Luke

Saturday morning, I rolled out of my king-size bed and poured myself a bowl of cereal. I didn't have the energy to even fry an egg. I sat at the center of the kitchen island, two stools on either side of me, and stared at the solid oak table.

I'd sanded it down myself and varnished it after renovating the house. I'd bought twelve new chairs—big, upholstered ones, imagining my brothers and our families sitting all together.

The chairs all sat empty. My chest tightened, longing for the image of a full table. Pushing back my stool, I left the kitchen and went to the study to pour myself a drink. I didn't care that it was only ten o'clock in the morning. If I didn't drown this feeling out, I would be miserable all day.

I retreated to the study. Leather-bound books lined two of the four walls, floor to ceiling, and a dark wood ladder stood against one wall. A large maple desk sat in front of the window; a glass bar right next to it. I poured two fingers of scotch into a glass and swirled it around.

I often drank here when I felt down. It didn't necessarily make me feel better. Something was always missing. Yet, the scent of the wood and old books was familiar and comforting.

Just as I brought the glass to my lips, I surveyed the room again and acknowledged what was missing. People.

Whenever I came to this room as a child, I found my father at his desk. Sometimes, my mother would be here too, or one of my father's business associates. Often, I would hide under my father's desk while Ryan tried to find me. My father would cover for me every time, saying he hadn't seen me, and I would cover my mouth with both hands to muffle my laughter at having outsmarted Ryan. Even though I knew it had been dad, I couldn't help feeling we'd done it together.

*That's what's been missing. That feeling of togetherness.*

For most of my teenage years and all of my adult life, I felt like I needed to prove to myself that I could do it on my own. That I didn't need anyone else because people eventually abandoned me in the end. My parents. My uncle, and even Grace.

At least I'd thought she had abandoned me, just like everyone else had. I'd thought I wasn't worth someone's time. I'd shut her out, not wanting to get hurt again, and ran away. I had done it to protect myself.

*Shit! I've done it again.*

I dropped my glass on the desk, not having taken a sip, and nearly stumbled with the realization. I had pushed her away again, afraid that I would get hurt. But what about her?

*Fuck!*

*I'm a stupid, selfish asshole.*

I reached into my back pocket for my phone and dialed her number. After the third ring, I dropped my head into my hands. She wouldn't pick up. I knew after a week of not speaking, she probably didn't want to talk now.

*Dammit!*

I pushed off the bed and paced the room. A million different words raced through my mind. Explanations, excuses, either way, they were just words and words weren't good enough right now. I needed to go to her.

Grabbing the keys to the fastest car I owned, I ran to the garage and started the engine. It roared to life and lifted my spirits. I would beg her to take me back. If I had to, I would grovel on my hands and knees. I would not lose her for another ten years. I didn't want to waste another ten seconds.

Grace's apartment building was across town. I screeched to a halt at the yellow light, realizing I had to control my emotions before I scared her. I felt like some raging bull who'd finally glimpsed the red cape. Only in this case, the red cape was my stupidity.

In the foyer of her building, I cursed the slow elevator and promised myself I would buy her a new apartment, *hell,* a new house, to avoid these damn slow elevators.

Finally, the doors opened and I ran inside.

"Can you hold the doors?" a man called behind me. I was about to shout no but gritted my teeth instead. I pressed the button and waited an agonizing two minutes while he strolled to the elevator. No wonder most women I knew complained about self-centered men. Tonight was a revelation of dumb things guys do.

"Can you press eight, dude?" I was about to comply when I realized that was the floor below Grace's apartment. My finger hesitated above the button. That would just slow me down.

I looked him straight in the eye. "I'll give you a hundred bucks to get off on the ninth floor and take the stairs down?"

The bastard pursed his lips and shook his head as though turning the offer down was a possibility. He reached across me to press the button himself.

"Touch that button and it'll be the last thing you do," I said, my voice low but clear.

He dragged his arm back and straightened his ball cap twice.

I crossed my arms and waited for the doors to open.

When I finally stood in front of Grace's door, I inhaled deeply and relaxed my shoulders. It would not be a good idea to approach her as this fuming bull right now. I curled my fist and knocked lightly on her door.

I checked the buttons on my shirt in case I'd missed any in my rush to get here.

I tried the doorbell.

When no one opened the door, I pressed my ear to it and listened. It felt creepy at first, but I told myself I was just listening for the TV.

Nothing but silence. These were either thick doors or Grace was ignoring me. I knew she loved to sleep in and watch movie marathons with her mother on Saturdays, so I was pretty sure she was home.

Was it possible that she saw my car parked in front of her building and was ignoring me now? Yes, that was a real possibility.

I didn't begrudge her for it. I considered leaving and coming back whenever she'd pick up her phone, but that could be never, and I wasn't walking away again.

I banged harder on the door this time. "Grace?" I called. "I know you're there. Please. I just want to talk. Open the door."

I thought I'd heard a sound, so I pressed my forehead to the door.

"Grace?" I called, a little softer this time. "Please."

After a few minutes, I finally said, "I just want to apologize. I've been an idiot. I'm so sorry. I—" I wanted to say this all to her face, but I wasn't sure if she would ever open the door.

Someone cleared their throat behind me, and I stiffened.

"Excuse me," an older woman wearing a floral dress with white pearls and holding a straw purse stared at me. "I was about to call the police when I heard all the banging."

“I apologize, ma’am,” I said. “I’m just trying to speak to someone inside. But she’s not answering.”

“Of course not,” she said.

Feeling defeated that even the little old lady had no hope for me, I leaned my head back against Grace’s door and slumped my shoulders.

“Grace isn’t there,” she said.

“Are you sure?” I asked. She was wearing glasses, but the prescription could be old.

“I know everything that happens on this floor, young man,” she said with a proud shrug of her shoulders. She stepped closer to look at me. “How do you know, Grace?”

Grace and I hadn’t labeled our relationship yet but I knew this woman wouldn’t tell me anything if I didn’t give her a straight answer. “I’m her boyfriend.”

She waved me off. “Grace doesn’t have a boyfriend.” She turned to leave, but I stopped her.

“Please. It’s very new but I’ve known her for a long time. How do you know Grace isn’t here?”

“Well, I heard your little speech a few minutes ago, and it sounded sincere.”

I groaned inwardly.

"Grace hasn't been back since the ambulance came to her door."

"The ambulance?" I asked, panic rising in my chest. "Is Grace all right?"

"She looked fine to me." Pursing her lips, she added, "Her mother, though."

She shook her head and cast her eyes down.

"Which hospital did they take her to?"

"How the heck should I know? Do you think I know everything around here?"

Yes, I did think that.

"Did they take her to Mount Sinai?" I asked.

"No, St. Joseph's would be closer," she said, then snapped her finger at me. "Oh, I see what you did there."

"Thank you, ma'am." I ran past her and the elevator, knowing it would take me less time to run down the stairs than wait for that blasted thing.

Hoping in my car, I typed the hospital's address on my phone and found the shortest route there. I made it in less than fifteen minutes.

"I'm looking for a patient with the last name Sweeney?" I asked the receptionist. Clicking her tongue, she searched for the name on her computer.

"Room 1204," she said.

"Thank you."

Another elevator and another heap of patience as I waited in the crowded space for visitors to exit on every floor. By the time I reached the twelfth floor, my hands shook and the back of my neck burned from rubbing it so hard.

But everything came to a standstill when I turned the corner and saw her. She had pulled her black hair into a ponytail, but several pieces fell through. She wore black tights and an oversized red sweater, her arms crossed against her chest.

She gasped when she saw me and my heart leaped when she dropped her arms and ran toward me. She was only a few feet away, yet it felt like an eternity until she reached me.

As she neared, I noticed her eyes were as red as her sweater and swollen, too. Seeing her in distress, pain shot through my chest. She slammed her body against mine and I pulled her into my arms. I held her against me until her heartbeat synced with mine.

Running my hands over her hair, I lifted her head to look at me. Her eyes were bloodshot and sunken as though she hadn't slept in days. "What happened?" I asked.

"My mom," she cried. "She's in an induced coma. Her left kidney is not functioning at all and her right one is failing hourly. Her meds haven't been working for a while, but I thought I still had time." She let out a sob that ripped my chest open. "It's really bad, Luke. I don't know if she'll make it through the night."

"Shh," I tried to calm her down, but her shoulders shook violently.

"She took care of me my whole life. She never missed a day of work to raise me on her own, and still she made time for me. I wanted to pay back everything she'd done, but I couldn't do it. I messed up. I worked hard and I still didn't get the promotion. I couldn't pay for what she needed. I failed her. I failed my mother." Her voice bounced off the walls in the empty, sterile hallways, and her sobs echoed in my ears as though they were gunshots firing at me. I felt every inch of her pain and wanted to carry it myself.

As I held her, my eyes searched for a nurse, or a doctor, anyone that could explain to me exactly what was going on. I didn't want to put Grace through repeating all the details to me.

A woman walked up to the nurse's station, wearing a white lab coat. There was no one else at the desk as she wrote inside a white file folder. I felt conflicted, as I didn't want to let Grace go, but I wanted to help her. When Grace's arms tightened around my waist, I knew I couldn't let her go.

"You did everything you could, Grace. You didn't give up on her. This isn't on you." I couldn't help thinking that perhaps it was on me. If I hadn't walked away from Grace all those years ago, I could have done something to help her mother these past ten years. Maybe her illness wouldn't have gotten this far along.

"Have you had anything to eat?" I asked, rubbing her back.

She moved her head back and forth across my chest. I took that as a no. "What about sleep? When was the last time you slept, Grace?"

"I closed my eyes last night on this chair. I'm okay."

"I'm calling Laura and Theo. One of them will stay here and relay any information to you regarding your mother as you get something to eat and a few hours of sleep."

"I can't," she said, shaking her head.

I lifted her chin with my finger and stared into her brown eyes. They were drowning in tears and I could hardly breathe.

"You don't have to be a martyr, Grace. I will make sure your mom receives the best care possible. I promise you."

The words rumbled in my chest; the promise hung between us. I waited to see if she would trust me. "I know your mom is the most important person in your life. I will take care of her as I will you."

"I—" she opened her mouth and I knew from the glint in her eyes she was going to tell me she didn't need anyone to take care of her.

"I know," I said. "Just let me take care of you. Not because you can't, but because I want to."

She nodded and closed her eyes. A tear fell down her cheek and I wiped it away with my thumb. Lowering my head, I gently pressed my lips to her cheek and tasted the saltiness of her sadness. It broke my heart. I wanted to take it all away, so I kissed her, hoping that I could show her how much I cared.

When she raised her head, I moved my mouth to her neck and below her ear. I couldn't stop. I missed her so much and wanted to apologize, but knew now was not the time for my absolution. Right now, it was all about her.

I slipped my hand over hers and drew her toward the elevators. "I'm going to take you to my house where you can rest."

I should have been relieved that she didn't argue with me. Instead, her lack of fight frightened me more.

## Grace

The white walls in the hospital hallway blurred into one and I stumbled, thinking I would crash into it. Luke held my hand and put his arm around me when I faltered the second time.

I closed my eyes and let him lead me. I was no use on my own anyhow.

The cool night breeze whipped my hair while the humid summer air warmed my skin from the cold, sterile temperature inside the hospital.

"Wait here," Luke said and leaned me up against the hospital wall. I closed my eyes and didn't open them, not even when the engine of a car rumbled in front of me.

Cupping my shoulder, Luke walked me to his car, and I dropped inside like a sack of potatoes, smacking the back of my head against the headrest. I groaned inwardly, having barely enough energy to muster up any sound.

The next thing I knew, the cool night breeze spilled into the car and Luke's arms snaked their way underneath my thighs and back. He carried me up a few steps and inside. I made out only the fact that we were inside a home, then I immediately closed my eyes again.

Luke's biceps bunched underneath my arm and his heart hammered next to my cheek. I felt safe, warm, and cared for. The latter was a feeling I hadn't felt since I was a child.

He laid me on a soft bed and removed my sneakers. He peeled my black socks off of me, one at a time, then ran his hands up my sweater to unhook my bra. His strong fingers on my bareback made my eyes flutter for a moment, but then his hands were gone and my eyes closed.

I heard some rustling and Luke's voice, but I couldn't make out the words. My world had turned black, and I felt as though I were falling into an abyss.

# 26

## Grace

The scent of bacon pulled me from my sleep. I turned my face into my pillow and felt wetness next to my mouth.

*I looked around the room, disoriented. Where am I? What happened?*

I couldn't recall anything.

I patted down the spot, and when that was useless, I simply turned the pillow over.

Spotting myself in the mirror, I combed through my hair, hoping to smooth out most of the wayward strands. I walked over to an open door, looking for the bathroom, and was relieved to see a tiled floor. When I lifted my eyes, my mouth fell open.

*Holy Shit.*

The bathroom was the size of my entire apartment, maybe bigger. There were two sinks, two shower heads, and two toilets. No, wait, that one didn't have a toilet seat. As I got closer, I realized it was a bidet. My foggy brain started piecing it together. This was Luke's bathroom.

Turning back to the white marble countertop, I turned on the faucet and splashed cold water on my face. I found a fluffy white towel on a shelf to my left. Five more were underneath it.

Spotting some blue liquid inside a plain glass bottle, I unscrewed the cap and smelled it. Definitely mouthwash. I swished some in my mouth, gurgled for a few minutes, and spit it out. Some blue spots splashed onto the countertop, and I wiped them up with the towel.

Padding across the bedroom, I opened the door to the hallway and immediately wished I had my phone. I should call Luke and ask for directions to his kitchen.

A sizzling sound made its way upstairs and I followed it. The light gray staircase with the black iron railing led to an even bigger foyer than the hallway upstairs. Soaring ceilings and tall windows made me feel like some princess locked up in a castle. I couldn't believe this was Luke's home.

More sizzling caught my ear, and I turned to the left toward another hallway. Turning the corner, I squinted as the floor-to-ceiling windows welcomed the rising sun outside. I couldn't decide which was more breathtaking. The view of the sunrise behind the trees or Luke standing shirtless in front of the stove. His muscled shoulders bunched as he flipped a pancake on the skillet, and his triceps flexed when he shook the pan to his left.

"Morning," I said, walking up to the stove.

Luke turned toward me and my eyes fell to his contoured chest. I'd seen his bare chest before, but it was like gazing at The Mona Lisa. It impressed me every time.

His lips turned up into a smile, and his eyes softened when they rested on my face. "Morning. How did you sleep?"

"Pretty good." Then, recalling my wet pillow, I asked. "Did we sleep together?"

"I'd like to think if we did, you'd remember it." He waggled his eyebrows. "But to answer your question, no. I slept in the guest room."

"Oh," I said, unsure if I was relieved or disappointed. Why would he sleep in the guest room? Maybe he was still upset with me. We hadn't talked about what happened, but when memories started flooding in, an image of my mother lying in a hospital bed, deathly pale with tubes coming out of her nose, hit me and I stepped back.

"What's wrong?" Luke asked, dropping the spatula and rushing toward me. I held up my hand. "My mother. I have to go to the hospital."

For a moment, I prayed it had all been a terrible nightmare and my mother was back at home with Lorna.

"I spoke to Theo and Laura this morning. She's stable now, which is great news."

I knew he meant to reassure me, but his words confirmed the nightmare, and I winced. "I need to go. Can you take me?"

"I will, I promise. I just need you to eat first."

I was just about to argue that I wasn't hungry when my stomach growled.

Luke filled my plate with pancakes, scrambled eggs, and bacon. I wish I could have been more delicate about it, but I sucked back my breakfast and scraped the last bits of eggs with the edge of my fork, and ate the crumbs, too.

Luke leaned over the breakfast counter and smiled. "I love to watch you eat," he said.

I watched him skeptically, waiting for him to burst out laughing at his joke, but he just continued to stare at me with this strange look in his eye.

"Luke, we need to talk about what happened between us…" I started.

"I know," he said, straightening up from the counter, his smile disappearing.

"But I just can't right now," I said. "My head is overwhelmed with what's happening with my mother and wondering how the hell I'm going to pay for dialysis let alone transplant surgery and I just can't think of the right words for you right now. I need some time."

"I understand," he said, solemnly. "Your mother's health is what's important. There's time to talk about us later."

I nodded. "Thank you." Rising from the kitchen stool and placing my plate inside the dishwasher, I turned to Luke. "I'll be ready in five minutes."

"I'll meet you out front."

After figuring out how to turn on the shower system, I washed up quickly and met Luke in the driveway. He stood next to a red, shiny sports car checking his phone. He looked up, "Ready?"

"Yes."

He drove down his street, and for the first time, I noted the neighborhood. The other homes were as large as Luke's, but none had the charm of his home. The old, stoned walls, the manicured trees, and shrubs alternating in red leaves, orange and green. It was perfect.

It was another reminder of how different this Luke was from the boy I remembered. I looked down at my stained red sweater and black tights and winced. For a second, I wished I had worn something else, but then I shrugged it off. I wouldn't feel bad about who I was. I snuck a glance at what Luke wore and he was in a relaxed black t-shirt and blue jeans. I guess that was something else I loved about him. He never made me feel uncomfortable about who I was.

Luke made a right turn at the main intersection and I did a double take on the street name. "Luke, I think you made a wrong turn. The hospital is the other way."

Luke ran a hand through his hair and clutched the steering wheel with the other. "Don't get upset. I'm not trying to overstep you, but some decisions needed to be made last night, rather quickly, so I made them."

"You what?" I said, my eyes nearly bugging out of my face. "Why didn't you wake me? You had no right to make any decisions. How did the hospital even accept you as the decision-maker?"

"The hospital your mom was staying at gave me a hard time, but I transferred her to another hospital."

I shook my head and inhaled deeply. I didn't want to yell at him. He'd been so kind to me last night and this morning. "How did they allow you to take my mother without my permission?"

"Let's just say I made a sizable donation to the hospital."

I closed my eyes and kept calm. "Luke, where is my mother now?"

"She's at the Institute of Medicine and Health. It's a private hospital but it has the best technology and doctors on staff. I would trust them with my own life, I swear."

He turned to look at me, but I still didn't know how to process this information.

When he pulled into a private parking space at the hospital, I didn't even question it. I opened the passenger door and jumped out. I followed Luke through the automated doors and was stunned for a moment. For a hospital, this place was gorgeous. Soaring glass ceilings, clean white floors, and there were even green leafy plants scattered throughout. A few of the doctors lined up at the Starbucks in the lobby and nodded at Luke.

"Good morning, Mr. Crawford," the receptionist called as Luke and I walked past her. I think she may have sighed when Luke greeted her back. I lengthened my stride to keep up with Luke's pace.

We took the elevators up to the fifth floor. When the doors opened, the first thing I noticed was the smell. Not the usual stale, laundered scent but a fresh eucalyptus, as though we were inside a spa rather than a hospital.

"Your mother's in this room," he said and hung back as he let me walk through first.

It was a private room with a gorgeous view of the city below, but when I turned my head toward the bed, my eyes fixed on my mother. She had regained some color to her face and her eyes stared back at me.

"Grace?" she whispered. A tiny smile crept through her lips.

"Mom?" I fled to her bedside. "You're awake."

She nodded but closed her eyes again. I turned to Luke. "What happened?"

He tilted his head toward the hallway, as though he didn't want to wake my mother, and stepped out.

When I joined Luke outside the room, he explained. "The other hospital didn't have the medication needed to sustain your mother until surgery. They said she wouldn't make it through the night without them. So, I decided to transfer her here. They've already started her on a full round of the meds intravenously as well as dialysis. I'm still waiting to confirm the surgery date. I'll follow up this morning."

*New meds, dialysis, surgery.* I couldn't keep up with all the words Luke had thrown at me and I tried to make sense of it all. "Luke," I stammered. "I don't think my insurance will cover any of this." Then I balled my fists. "I'll go to the bank this morning and take out a loan. I know I'm good for it."

Luke grabbed my hand, then let my fingers slide against his skin, as though he regretted his action. "I'll take care of it, Grace. I told you I would."

"Luke, I can't ask you to do that."

"You didn't."

I shook my head and he placed his hand on my shoulder. "If it makes you feel better, you can pay me back."

I nodded. "Okay. I promise. I'll pay you back, every cent."

He frowned and swallowed, the working of his throat capturing my attention. He looked into my eyes and seemed to decide on something that he wasn't going to share with me. "All right." He checked his watch. "I have to be somewhere in a few minutes." He handed me a card. "Call Eric whenever you're ready to go home and he'll drive you."

I stared at the card in my hand and by the time I looked up, Luke was already halfway down the hallway. His steps were quick, as though he were late. When he stepped into the elevator, I turned around and returned to my mother's room.

Pulled a chair to her bed, I sat down and covered her hand with mine. "I'm right here, Mom," I said and she smiled.

Her eyes fluttered until her gaze held mine. "You've always been, Grace. Thank you."

I couldn't hold back my tears any longer so I let go, and wiped my eyes with the sleeve of my red sweatshirt. "I don't know what I'd do without you, Mom. I couldn't even function thinking that I'd lose you. This is a very toxic relationship." I laughed and my mother tried to chuckle but ended up coughing. "Sorry. Don't laugh, okay? I'm not sure how to put these wires back if any of them get loose."

She patted my hand and closed her eyes. I watched her as she slept, content to have another day with her. Some days, I knew she felt like a burden on me. But I never saw it that way. She was everything good and I was lucky to be her daughter.

My phone buzzed and I pulled it from my pocket. It was a text from Omar.

Omar: I haven't heard from you in a while. Are you okay?

Me: I'm sorry, I've been MIA. So much to catch you up on. Are you free to chat?

Omar: Always free for you. Call whenever.

I dialed Omar's number and told him everything that had happened with my mother.

"Where is Luke now?" he asked.

"That's your question?"

"Well, your mom's in good hands, it sounds. You, I'm not too sure about."

"What do you mean?"

"So, you just let him go, with no apology, no kiss, no freaking make-up session. What is wrong with you,

Grace Sweeney? Are you trying to ruin this fantasy for all of us?"

"Omar, he made decisions about my mother's health without me."

"It sounds like you were in no condition to make good decisions. Can you fault him for trying to help?"

"I... I... it's just not the right time. I told him we'll talk later," I stammered.

"Oh, sweetheart. It's always the right time to tell someone that you love them."

*Love them?* Was Omar right? Did I love Luke? I cared for him and I thought about him all the time, and whenever he touched me, it felt like my entire body would implode. Was that love? I wasn't sure. I only knew love from my mother. But this was different. One minute, I wanted to kill him for making medical decisions without me. The second, I wanted to kiss him until I couldn't breathe for saving my mother's life.

*Is that love?*

# 27

## Luke

Victoria folded the last white napkin and placed it on the glossy white table. "What's next, Luke?" she asked.

I checked my itinerary. "Janet will be here shortly to set up the media tables. We're having a media luncheon before the party tonight. You didn't forget did you?"

"Are you kidding, daddy's been planning the menu all week."

"Good."

"Do you think people will come to the opening?"

I smiled. Of this, I was sure. "I haven't invited anyone to a party in forever. I've extended the invite to VIP guests only. They'll come. They're curious about what I'm up to and will show up. I've called the TV crews for the opening. Once everyone sees the city's biggest names here, you'll be booked solid for a month."

Mario clapped his hands behind us. "I can't believe it. I feel like Cinderella and you are the prince," he said.

"Um, I'm not too sure about that analogy," I laughed. "How about we just stick to business partners?" I stuck out my hand.

He shook it, then pulled me in for a hug. "No, Luke. We're family."

His words took me by surprise. At first, having Mario's arms around my waist felt awkward. But when he squeezed a little tighter, something in my chest loosened and I hugged him back. I wondered if this was what it was like to be hugged by a father.

Or an uncle.

I cleared my throat and patted Mario's shoulder. "This is going to work, Mario."

"I know. I have faith in you, Luke."

*Damn it!* Why was I having such a hard time swallowing? I cleared my throat and coughed. "Excuse me. I think I need a drink of water."

Victoria ran into Mario's arms and I left them proudly surveying the new dining room.

The next few hours flew by. The publicist I had hired to ensure the guests were happy and the media luncheon went smoothly was great. Janet even set up a couple of interviews with local papers and magazines. Mario was thrilled, and I was proud, too. We pulled off a renovation and a Grand Opening in less than three weeks.

*Not bad for someone who couldn't handle responsibility.*

"Luke!" someone shouted my name. Ryan walked into the restaurant, with Colton trailing behind him. "This place looks incredible," he said, and nudged Colton with his elbow. Colton grunted, "Yeah. Great."

I laughed. I knew Colton was disappointed I hadn't joined Crawford Corporation. "Look Colton, I know you wanted me to be operations manager. But I would have been terrible at it and you know it."

He shrugged his shoulders. "You were a pretty shitty lead on the audit."

I laughed. "Thanks."

"But you want to get into the restaurant business now?" Ryan asked, looking around.

"Not exactly," I explained. "I have this idea of a company that flips restaurants kind of like flipping homes. But better. I want to start a subsidiary of Crawford Corp., an affiliate company. I want to research restaurants that have growth potential but just need the capital to do it. I would provide the capital and the strategy and become a partner for a set number of years. We can negotiate the timeline."

"And you think this will make money?"

"I do. But more importantly, it'll make me happy."

When Colton's frown didn't change, I added, "And teach me responsibility?" I raised my eyebrows, waiting for his response. It wasn't exactly a smile, but his face softened. "That sounds promising," he said.

I laughed. I didn't know how Frannie put up with him. "I've put together a business plan for two more restaurants I have in mind."

"Two more, did you say?" He crossed his arms over his chest. "Let's meet in my office tomorrow at noon."

I put out my hand, and Colton stared at it. Finally, a smile crept on his lips. "Pleasure doing business with you, little brother."

Ryan looked around the room again. "So, who's coming tonight?"

"Oh, the usual. The Hendersons, the Friedmans, the Jacksons, the Persauds."

"Wow, you stacked this place," said Colton, with a glint in his eye. For the first time, it felt as though he saw me for who I was, not just his little brother.

"I can finally use my powers for good," I chuckled.

"What about Grace? Is she coming?"

I froze. I didn't mean to. I texted her to see how she was doing and got daily updates about her mother from Theo and Laura, but after being so overbearing about the hospital transfer, I'd tried to keep my distance until she was ready.

Janet had mailed her an invitation, but according to Eric, she hadn't requested a ride home in days. Eric simply picked up the clothes that Omar had left on her doorstep and brought them to Grace at the hospital. She hadn't been back to her apartment at all. I knew her mother's room had great bathroom facilities, but I was hoping she'd go home to rest. But that was Grace. She did nothing halfway.

*I should text her tomorrow and ask if she'll go out to dinner with me.*

I didn't want to put any more thought into her coming tonight. She hadn't seen the invitation, so there was no way she'd be here. I wouldn't let myself be disappointed because she wasn't rejecting me this time.

I had to grow up and not get my feelings hurt when someone didn't show up for me. I was a grown man, and having Colton and Ryan here was enough.

*It had to be.*

***

"Luke, the food is to die for," said a guest with black-rimmed glasses. I couldn't remember her name, but Janet had introduced me earlier, so I knew she was important. I hadn't kept up with the who's who in the media in a while.

"It's the best pasta in town," I said. "That's why I backed it up."

"Well, if you're putting your name behind this, I know it will be successful."

Funny how people put so much weight on a name.

"Excuse me," I said. "I just need to check on the kitchen."

She bit her bottom lip and placed her skinny hand on my forearm. I stared at the large rocks on her fingers before looking back up. "Don't be long. I'd like to get to know you better." She popped an olive in her mouth and dragged her tongue around it. The act distracted me momentarily, but nothing about it or her aroused me. She reminded me of every other woman I'd dated. She only wanted me for my name. I'd be just another wealthy family she could add to her list of influential friends.

"Sorry, but I'll be busy tonight," I said and when she opened her mouth to protest, I added, "Maybe you should try my brother, Ryan. He's always up for a good time." Her eyes lit up and I wondered if Ryan would thank me or kill me later.

I pushed through the stacked bodies, excusing myself and shaking some hands as I made my way to the kitchen. Mario stood at the stove, tasting sauce from a wooden spoon. "This needs a pinch more salt," he said to his sous chef. I hired one for Mario last week and told him he would need him with all the people in the restaurant. Mario was skeptical at first, having always worked alone, but he had grown to trust Louis this week.

"How's everything?" I asked when Mario turned toward me.

"Ah, Luke. It's wonderful. All of it. I can't believe how many people are here."

"There are even more people outside the restaurant than inside," I said. "This is good, Mario. This is really good. We'll be booked for two months."

When Mario took a step forward, I knew what he was about to do. "We can hug later. Now, we have to get these plates out there."

"Fine, fine. Always work with you."

I laughed because no one had ever said that to me. Maybe I did have a bit of Colton's work ethic in me. I shuddered at the thought and rushed over to Mario to hug him. The burly man slapped my back and kissed me on the cheek. A big wet one, too. I groaned. "Don't make me regret this, Mario," I laughed and wiped my face with the handkerchief from my new suit. Janet had insisted on me wearing one.

I checked my watch. "There's only a half-hour left before the end of the event. Are the deserts ready?"

"Yes. Just five more minutes."

"Great. I'll go check in with Janet and see if anything is outstanding on her end before closing."

When I returned to the dining room, the space seemed even more crowded than before. My friends showed up late for events, so it didn't surprise me. I searched the room for Janet. Her high black bun was pretty easy to spot. I spotted her near the entrance. She was arguing with someone at the door.

"Excuse me," I said, trying to make my way to her. If someone was giving Janet a hard time, I would take care of it. But I'd only gotten a few steps into the crowd when Janet turned around and the person she was arguing with came into view.

My heart stopped, and the loud laughter of the people around me quieted to a hum. I wanted to run but my feet were stuck in place, as though my mind didn't want to confirm if this was a dream because I was happy to live in a dream where she showed up. Where she showed up *for me*.

I closed my eyes, inhaled sharply through my nose, and let it out swiftly through my mouth.

*Please… let this be real.*

When I opened my eyes, Grace was still there. She had her arms crossed, but when she saw me, they fell to her sides. Her eyebrows softened while her eyes pleaded with me.

My body kicked into gear. "Out of the way," I said as I pushed past the crammed bodies. "Hey, watch it," some guy called behind me, but I didn't care. Grace was here and I couldn't get to her fast enough.

"Grace!" I shouted above the crowd.

"Luke," she called back, waving her hand.

Janet stared between me and Grace. "Do you know her?" she asked. "She says she's invited, but I don't see her name on the list."

"What are you talking about? I know I put her name on there." I looked at Grace and added, "Just in case you saw the invite."

"Well, I don't know what to tell you. But I don't see a Meany Sweeney on here."

"What?" I turned to Grace and she shrugged her shoulders. "I thought that'd be the name you'd use after the way I spoke to you." She watched me carefully, her gaze searching mine. "I'm so sorry, Luke."

I shook my head, emotion burning at the back of my eyes. "I'm the one who's sorry, Grace. I walked away again."

"No!" She placed her hand on my arm. "I was upset and I said some things I didn't mean. I thought I needed to do things on my own, that I didn't need anyone. But I need you, Luke. I want to be with you."

I couldn't explain how much I needed to hear those words from her. I'd always believed I wasn't good enough for Grace and she didn't need me. But to hear her say it, to see the emotion play across her face, wrecked me.

I grabbed her waist and lifted her off the ground, smothering my face into her shoulder. She laughed this time and wrapped her arms around my neck.

Turning with Grace still in my arms, I said to Janet, "You've got it from here?"

"Most definitely," she said.

"Good. Cause we have a lot of catching up to do."

I didn't catch Janet's face because Grace squirmed in my arms. "Luke, put me down."

I bent to set her on her feet and she straightened her black tight-fitting top and smoothed down her hair. Her eyes shot me a glare, but she sucked in both lips to hide her smile.

*God, how I missed her.*

I grabbed my phone and sent a text. Then, holding onto Grace's hand, I pulled her toward the door. "Where are we going? I just got here," she protested.

"We need to talk, and I need to kiss you. I can't do either of those things here, so we're leaving."

Just as we exited the restaurant and climbed up the steps to street level, a black limo pulled up. I opened the back door and waved Grace inside. She hesitated at first, looking behind us to see if the car was meant for someone else perhaps, but then she recognized the driver. "Oh, hi, Eric," she said and slid across the black leather seats.

I caught Eric's gaze in the rearview mirror, and he nodded. Seconds later, the tinted window behind him came up and I was alone in the back seat with Grace.

"I'm sorry that you lost your promotion," I said, turning to her.

She shook her head and swept the fallen strands behind her ear. "It's okay, Luke," she started, but I needed to say the rest.

"I respect who you are and that you take your work seriously. You've built a career for yourself and you've done it while supporting your sick mother."

"Luke, stop," she said, covering my mouth with her hands. "I'm not mad anymore. I was upset in the moment and I said things I didn't mean and regretted them the next day. But I was stubborn and confused. I'm not used to anyone taking care of me. I thought it made me weak instead of stronger."

"You're the strongest person I know, Grace. I thought I was giving you space, but I was just scared."

She placed her hand gently on my cheek. "I know."

I looked up and saw in her eyes that she knew. She had figured out my survival tactic. I'd done it to her before.

"You can't walk away whenever you're angry or disappointed in me," she said. "I know there'll be many times in the future. And there will be times when I'm so angry with you I just want to scream and rail, but I won't. If we're going to make this work, we have to acknowledge what we do to ruin relationships and work on those habits. If we don't…" She shrugged her shoulders. "I don't know if this will work."

*No! I will not lose her. It's time I'm honest with her and myself. Say out loud what I've known for so long in my heart.*

Holding her shoulders, I held her gaze. "I realized looking back on so many pivotal points in my life that I had walked away from commitment and responsibility because I didn't want to form an attachment to people only for them to abandon me. I wanted to walk away before they could hurt me. I get that, and I know I won't change overnight, but I'm willing to try."

My heart ached at the look in her eyes. She believed me, but the words weren't enough.

My thumb caressed the familiar roundness of her cheek, the smooth curve of her lips, and I knew I wanted to wake up to her face for the rest of my life. "I love you, Grace. I always have. I was just too afraid to admit it—afraid you'd leave me."

"I'm not going anywhere," she said, grasping my forearms. "I'm sorry I didn't realize the reasons why you had walked away. I promise to give you space if you need it. But I want you to come back to me and hold me and tell me everything will be okay. I will never abandon you, Luke. I've loved you since I was a girl. I loved you through the worst times in my life. But you've seen me at my worst and you're still here. I want to know your worst, Luke. Tell me what happened in your past. I promise you I'll still be here. I'll always be here."

I felt something inside my chest crumble. A wall, an invisible fortress that I had built to protect me from getting hurt, fell to the pit of my stomach and I could finally breathe. I never realized how much of myself I held back—how much I allowed fear to stop me from loving. With her words, she climbed my walls and crushed them. She forced herself inside my heart and detonated an explosion of emotion that ran through every vein in my body. I was throbbing and breathless for her.

I kissed her mouth and whispered between breaths. "I will tell you everything about my past, I promise. But not tonight. Tonight is about the future, and I want to spend every moment of it with you."

# 28

## Grace

Luke ran his fingers along the top of my leg and I squeezed my thighs together when he slid his fingers inside my panties. "What about Eric?" I asked.

"I didn't think you were into threesomes, but I could ask."

I smacked his shoulder. "You know what I mean."

"He won't hear a thing." His stealthy fingers pushed past my thighs and when he brushed my clit, I knew I'd lost the battle. I moaned in his arms and fell back along the long stretch of seating in the back of the limo.

I unknotted Luke's tie and smirked when he sighed in relief. Staring at him I realized, this certainly was the start of new beginnings. I meant what I'd said. I knew we both had flaws and we would have to work hard not to fall into the same patterned behaviors, but I also knew how much we both wanted to be together.

"How did you know about the party?" he panted into my mouth as he unhooked my bra.

It took me a moment to gather my wits to understand his question. "Oh, I found the invitation tonight when I got home. I barely had time to change and was out the door."

He stopped unbuttoning his shirt and stared at me. "You dropped everything and came to this? For me?"

"Of course," I said, caressing his cheek. His jaw flexed and he threw his shirt onto the limousine floor. He unbuttoned his pants without once breaking eye contact with me. "I love you," he said.

"I love you, too," I whispered, and in one swift movement, he was inside of me.

We both groaned, and I squeezed my thighs to ease the pressure.

"Don't," he gritted between clenched teeth. "Or I won't last."

"That'll be a first," I said.

He laughed and pulled my head up to him and kissed me. When he broke free, he sat himself down and pulled me on top. I straddled him, prepared to give him all that I had, but he shook his head.

He lifted me from his lap and turned me around in reverse cowgirl. "Do you like it like this?" he whispered, his breath caressing my neck. He pushed my hair to the side and slid his tongue from my shoulder to my earlobe. I shivered in response.

When I didn't move, he urged me with his hips and I followed his rhythm, moving forward, then back. In my last thrust, I pushed back into his groin and wiggled my bottom, and he dropped his head back with a moan.

Then his hands snaked to my front and cupped my breasts and the sensation that ran straight down to my core surprised me. It was like a shock of electricity to my clit. He circled my nipples with his middle fingers and pushed me forward with his hips. Somehow, even in this dominant position, Luke still took control. I wanted to fight back, then lost this battle willingly. There would be others, of that, I was sure.

The limo hit a bump in the road and it nearly unseated me from Luke's lap, but we both panted from the impact it had on our bodies. I was so close—that elusive orgasm building in my belly. The rhythm felt so good, the angle perfect as Luke hit my spot with every deep thrust of his hips. My breasts tingled from his wicked fingers and my hot skin cooled with every panting breath on my flesh.

My legs shook and my head lolled as the orgasm built. I moaned his name, pleading for more. I needed just a little more. Luke circled fast and pushed his hips harder and I exploded with a shout. I flattened my hands across the roof of the limo as I tried to stay up.

Luke flattened his palms on my breasts as he rode me harder and harder. I felt a smaller orgasm run through me as he finally roared in pleasure.

I dropped my arms and leaned back against Luke, winding my hands behind his neck to hold him. His lips were on my jaw. I could not see him, but I could hear him… feel him… sense his smile.

"Let's go home," he said, and I nodded in agreement.

***

Something delicious was cooking in the distance, and I smiled. I could get used to waking up like this every morning. Rolling out of bed and putting on Luke's shirt from last night, I remembered how much he liked me in them. I would save money on new pajamas.

I found Luke sitting at the kitchen table with a tablet in his hands.

"What are you looking at?" I asked, grabbing a fork to fill my plate.

"Grace, look at this," he said and pulled me over to sit on his lap. He nestled his chin on my shoulder and scrolled through a newspaper article. There was a slideshow of last night's event, and the headline read, *The city's hottest new restaurant opened its doors last night.*

"And there's more." He opened several other browser windows, each one with pictures and tweets about the Taste of Naples and the must-have dishes to order.

"Janet says she's received several interview requests already and Mario is so excited because he's booked for the next three months."

I'd never seen Luke so happy, and I was glad to share this moment with him. "I'm so proud of you, Luke. You should try replicating this for another restaurant."

He grabbed my shoulders to face me. "That's exactly my business plan. I need to go over some numbers with an accountant. I was thinking of hiring a pretty brunette, but I'm not sure what she'd say."

"I don't know. I hear she's very good, but very particular." I pretended to frown.

"I will make it worth her while." He pressed his mouth to mine, and I inhaled the electricity between us.

"I'm serious, Grace. If this business idea of mine takes off, I will need to hire your company. I will insist you take the account as I only work with the best. Your company would love that."

"They would," I said, imagining Faith's face when I brought another Crawford company to the firm. They would reconsider me for the manager position, I was sure of it.

"Speaking of work," I said. "I better get going before I'm late. Do you think you can drop me off?"

He raised his eyebrow. "Of course not."

Confused, I stared at him, waiting for him to smile. He didn't. He walked over to a cabinet and grabbed a set of keys. Throwing them at me, he said. "Here. And if you don't like the Audi, let me know which one you'd prefer to take to work."

"Oh, I can't do that," I said, dropping the keys on the table as though they weighed a ton. And perhaps they did on my conscience. I'd always worked for everything I'd achieved. No one had ever handed anything to me. Well, not before Luke.

He walked up to me and placed his palm on my cheek. "I thought after our conversation last night that we were together. Officially."

"Oh, we are," I said, reassuring him.

"Then, take the car. What's mine is yours, Grace."

"You trust me with it?" I asked skeptically.

"I would trust you with much more."

I lifted onto my toes and kissed him. "Thank you," I said. And rushed to get ready for the day.

I spoke to Laura and Theo on my way to work. My mother was awake during the day now and they kept her company while I went to work.

I spoke to her doctor this morning. My mother's surgery was scheduled for next month, but they reassured me she would be stable until then. I didn't know how I was going to pay for the surgery. But when I called the hospital administrator on my way to work to inquire about payment plans, she told me a generous donor had taken care of the payment. Suspecting the name, but still wanting her to say it, I asked. She said the donor's name was Jeanie Sweeney. "Is she a relative of yours?" she asked with a southern accent.

I laughed aloud—snort and all. She must have thought I was crazy and maybe I was for letting Luke pay for the surgery. But I would pay him back somehow—with interest. I smiled at the thought.

Just as I was about to turn off the car, another call came through. The number was vaguely familiar, so I answered it. "Hello?"

"Grace Sweeney?"

"Yes?"

"This is Harriet from Charters. You interviewed with us last week."

"Yes, hi!"

"Is now a good time to chat?"

I looked at my watch, five minutes before I was supposed to start work. But I shook off my old habits and tried something new. "Yes, no problem. I have time now."

"Great. Well, after reviewing other candidates, we'd like to offer you the manager position at our firm. If you're still interested, the job is yours."

I was glad she couldn't see me because my mouth flapped open like a fish.

"Grace? Are you still there?"

I leaned forward and dropped my head onto the steering wheel.

*What should I do?*

This firm was much smaller than the one I was at now. But I wasn't looking for prestige anymore. I'd worked so hard at Delmar & Tuch, they knew me. Sure, I didn't get this promotion, but there would be others. And Delmar & Tuch was a bigger firm. I gave myself some time to think this over.

"Thank you, Harriet. I appreciate the offer. Can we schedule a time to discuss this further? I'm free at noon tomorrow."

"Sounds great," she said. "Chat soon."

"Goodbye," I said and sat in my car for a few minutes before rushing to work. Some habits were hard to kill.

As soon as I walked down the hallway, Omar stopped me. "How was the party last night?" he asked. Then, with a hand to his hip, he raised his hand. "Never mind. Judging by the two red spots on your cheeks, it went well. I want to hear all about it."

"Oh, look who strolled into work today," another voice called from behind me. I rolled my eyes before pasting a smile on my face.

"Good morning to you too, Faith," I said, then pivoted on my heel and walked toward my cubicle. "Let's chat at lunch," I called over my shoulder to Omar.

Unfortunately, Faith followed. "Quite the ride you took to work today. Guess you don't need that promotion anymore."

I wanted to tell her it was creepy that she looked for my car in the mornings, but instead, I smiled and said, "It doesn't matter if I need the promotion or not, Faith. I earned it. More than you did."

She sucked her teeth and pressed her tongue against her cheek. "I'm sure you earned that car, too." The irony of that statement made my blood boil, but I wouldn't shame another woman, not even Faith.

I took a step forward and raised my eyebrow. "Get out of my cubicle. You're not worth my time."

She shook her head and walked away.

I settled into my chair and stretched out my fingers. I enjoyed working, not all the time, but I liked delving into a new client's file and looking for someone else's errors. It pleased me, and I smirked at the pettiness of that thought.

A knock at the top of my cubicle startled me and I straightened when I saw Damon Fromer, the partner who refused to reschedule my interview, standing there.

"Do you have a minute to chat in the boardroom, Grace?"

"Of course," I said, and followed him down the hallway. He sat in one of the chairs and lifted his leg to rest his ankle on his knee. The casual gesture put me at ease, and I took the seat next to him. "How can I help you, Mr. Fromer?"

"Grace, you've been with us for many years and your work has not gone unnoticed."

I breathed a sigh of relief, and a smile tugged at my lips. Finally, some acknowledgment of everything I'd done for Delmar & Tuch.

"It's unfortunate that the promotion didn't work out, but there's a new role we've been thinking about that would work well with your skill set."

"New role?" Sometimes companies created job positions for people and perhaps this was one of those times. It wouldn't be crazy to open up two manager positions. "I'm open to new possibilities."

"That's great. We think you'll love working on the second floor, training new staff."

"Training? New staff? But that's not what I do."

"Think of it as a new opportunity for you." He looked around the room, avoiding my eyes momentarily. "Also, you won't be needing your cubicle, but you'll have until the end of the day to clear it out."

I felt as though the world tilted on its axis and everything in the room swayed to the right. My stomach turned and I felt nauseated. "Are you…" I couldn't get the words out. "Are you firing me?"

"No, no. Of course not. Just assigning you to a different role."

"I see," I said. The pieces clicked into place. "You're not firing me, but you're demoting me." My eyes held his, and he loosened his tie.

I couldn't believe it. After all these years. "Is this because I was late for one meeting? One meeting and I'm out?"

He put his hands up. "No, no. It's not that. It's…"

I raised my eyebrow, eager to hear his explanation. Well, not exactly eager, more like pissed off.

"Look, Grace. We just can't have that sort of reputation in our firm. Our clients are not looking for that kind of notoriety. We can't have you client-facing anymore. But there will always be a place for you at Delmar & Tuch."

*Reputation? Notoriety?* Oh, my gawd! This was still about that picture with Luke on the bleachers. I remembered my conversation with Faith, but that only ignited my fury. Then I recalled some past indiscretions and my indignation exploded.

"And what sort of reputation is that?" I asked, standing up. "Are our clients looking for the reputation of a man who cheats on his wife with the latest intern in the office? Is that it?" Fromer's face went paler than usual. "How about the sort who skims off the top of his expense account to pay for his weekend rounds of golf? Is that more a client's preference, Mr. Fromer?" I asked, my voice rising. "Because I'm pretty sure that if I weren't a woman, we wouldn't be having this conversation right now. Instead, you would ask if he had a sister. Am I wrong?"

"That's not true. This isn't because you're a woman. It has nothing to do with that."

I nodded my head. "Right. Because all the partners' indiscretions—and there are many more than the ones I've listed—occurred before they made partner. Those indiscretions were acceptable because?"

His cheeks flushed, but he maintained his composure. "Times are different now," he said. "We have to be more careful."

"You're right," I said, calmly. "Times are different. And for me, the time for making excuses for men's poor behavior is gone."

"What are you saying? Are you going to HR? I'll have my lawyer deny any wrongdoing."

"Save your money because you're not worth mine." I looked him straight in the eye. "I quit."

I walked out of the boardroom; my steps measured. I would not run from him. I was the one leaving this toxic place behind. They were happy when I was working my ass off, but not willing to pay me for it. I knew this was just an excuse to keep my salary down, with no chance of a promotion. I was done being walked on. I was done not knowing my worth. I was great at my job and I would take the position at Chatters.

Yes. This was the day of new beginnings, after all.

# 29

## Luke

*One year later…*

A bead of sweat broke onto my forehead, and my throat tightened. I undid the first button of my shirt, tempted to loosen my black tie, but left it in place. I still wasn't used to wearing these things.

"Nervous, brother?" Ryan asked beside me. He wore a gray suit and his black hair was perfectly styled while mine wouldn't cooperate today. Perhaps I should stop running my hand through it.

I shook my head and he chuckled. "Could have fooled me."

*Damn it! He's right. I'm freaking out.*

I knew in my heart she would show today, but old and stubborn thoughts in my head somehow popped up a few minutes ago. *Do you really think you're good enough for her? Why would she show up for you?*

I balled my fists and inhaled deeply, and counted to ten. I started doing that about a year ago whenever self-doubt gripped me. For the most part, it worked, but today was different. Today was the biggest day of my life.

This past year with Grace had changed me. I'd always presented confidently to the world, but inside, I'd been riddled with imposter syndrome. I hadn't understood that until recently. I only knew that I would run from commitment and responsibility because of it. Colton feared I'd run today, but there was no way that I would. Grace was the best thing that had ever happened to me.

She would show.

The murmurs from the guests rose when Grace's mother walked in and sat in the front row. She smiled at me—a brilliant, confident smile that settled my nerves. She wouldn't have smiled if her daughter had run.

The music started, and Ryan slapped my shoulder. "Show time."

I straightened my jacket and redid my shirt button. I'd just checked the cufflinks Colton had gifted to me this morning when a movement at the back of the room caught my attention.

There was a garland of red roses framed around the double doors and a white carpet set for the aisle. When the doors opened and she appeared behind them, I lost my breath.

Her black hair was styled into soft curls around her face. She wore no veil but a sleek white dress that fell along her body and shimmered under the light. She looked like a goddess from a painting or a dream.

"Breathe," Ryan whispered beside me, and I sucked in a sharp breath.

Omar stood beside her and walked her down the aisle. Her dress wrapped around her thighs with every step she took toward me.

As she approached, my eyes landed on her lips. She had painted them red, and they formed a smooth line. But when I looked at her eyes, I knew she was smiling. Mona Lisa's smile, that elusive, ambiguous smirk that if you looked too hard, you'd miss it.

She was my Mona Lisa. My elusive love. I thought love didn't exist, that I couldn't see it, but I now realized I was looking in the wrong places.

She showed up and made this the happiest day of my life, and I couldn't wait to make her smile every day for the rest of hers.

When she reached me, her cheeks twitched and I grinned. I extended my arm to her and she released her hold on Omar to interlace her fingers with mine. That's when she smiled broadly and my heart burst open.

"I love you," I whispered. "I promise to take care of you every day of our lives."

The minister in front of us leaned forward. "We're not at the vows yet, lad." Then he cleared his throat and began. "Dearly beloved..."

## Grace

I held Luke's face between the palm of my hands and he leaned down to kiss my lips. "Are you happy?" he asked.

"The happiest I've ever been." I smiled and kissed him back.

We were on the dance floor at our reception, and he pulled me closer to him. I rested my cheek on his chest and sighed in contentment. As I glanced across the room at the white linens and chairs, and the red roses that dripped from every corner of the room, I still couldn't believe this was real.

Shortly after getting together, I moved into Luke's home. It was a huge step, but both of us were tired of packing overnight bags.

Luke asked me if I wanted to use the study as my office but I told him I wasn't planning to work late anymore, but sometimes I would sit there and read if he had to work late with a new restaurant owner. His business took off this past year and he had to hire an entire team. He kept an office at Crawford Corporation so he saw his brothers often. Although he outwardly complained about it, I knew he wouldn't have it any other way.

As for me, my career at Chatters catapulted. Luke brought his company to our firm and a few months later, Colton did the same with Crawford Corporation. Harriet couldn't believe it and she quickly made me a partner after that. I was still trying to bring Omar over to us, but he said he was enjoying the drama at Delmar & Tuch right now. Maybe later.

Mr. Fromer tried to coax me back, saying he'd make me a partner, but there was no way I'd ever go back there. They didn't want me; they wanted my connections. But I knew my worth now. Good riddance.

Yet despite all these milestones, the most incredible, life-altering change in my life this past year was my mother's health.

She received her kidney transplant, and after a couple of months of rehab, she moved in with Luke and me. Although, 'moved in' was misleading because Luke had built her a guest house with a full-time nurse and housekeeper. She didn't even protest the extravagance. She was so happy and so was I.

I hadn't realized how much my mother's health had weighed on me. I'd been carrying the weight by myself for so long that I couldn't remember a time when I wasn't staring at her anxiously, wondering if she was overtiring herself or worrying if she could make it across our tiny apartment on her own.

Now, she laughed and swayed side to side with Omar on the dance floor. She wore a long red dress to match the roses in my bouquet and her hair was twisted up into a chignon. She laughed at something Omar said and threw her head back.

*She looks beautiful.*

Tears pooled in my eyes, and I stared at the ceiling, hoping they would go away.

As Luke rubbed my back, I thought about how I used to perceive the world, and in particular, Luke. When he had shut me out of his life, I'd thought of him as a spoiled boy who cared little for me or my feelings. I'd taken my pain and turned it into anger.

I didn't let others get close to me, telling myself I didn't have time because of my mother, but that wasn't the whole truth of it. The truth was that I'd been afraid to fall in love again and get hurt; afraid I would do something wrong and turn people away from me. So, I kept my distance.

Leonardo da Vinci once said, "All our knowledge has its origins in our perceptions."

I thought I knew the kind of person Luke was but I knew nothing. I thought working hard meant I deserved more than others. All of that was wrong. I wasn't happy about pushing people away. I was only happy when I understood where they came from.

Until I saw Luke, not only with my eyes but listened with my ears and heart, I never really understood him. If work hadn't forced us together and I hadn't learned of Luke's past, I would have only seen what my eyes wanted me to see and never the truth behind my perceptions.

I stared into his eyes, the same green eyes that had captured my attention all those years ago, and saw what

I'd always been too blind to see. My future, my strength, my love staring back at me.

# *EPILOGUE*

## Grace

Omar leaned over my shoulder, a bag of popcorn in his hand. The buttery smell made my stomach growl. "You're not working, are you?" he asked.

I smiled. "No. I'm just editing a picture I took of the baseball diamond." I showed him my phone. "What do you think?"

He sat down beside me and offered me some popcorn. I happily took a handful.

"Looks good. I like how you even got Luke and his brothers into the shot."

My smile widened as I took another look at the picture. I adjusted the lighting to bring out the pink hues of the setting sun in the background.

Turning my attention back onto the field, I looked for Luke again. He stood leaning on a bat outside of his team's bench, next to his brothers and Richard. He had convinced them to start a private men's league among their friends and business associates. They rented the field weekly for their games.

"Looks like Luke's up to the plate," said Omar, munching on his popcorn.

I clapped my hands and whooped in my seat, along with the other fifty or so spectators on the metal bleachers. The weather was cooling and a brisk wind whipped up my hair that had grown nearly to my shoulders.

At the first pitch, Luke pulled back his bat and swung across the plate. A loud crack echoed in the air as the ball sailed deep into the park. The outfielders ran toward the fence, but the ball landed in a corner. Luke ran to first base, passed second, and slid into third just as the umpire called him safe.

I jumped up, cupping my mouth, and cheered as loud as I could. "Yes! That's my husband!"

Shaking off the dirt from his uniform, Luke looked up to the stands and his eyes caught mine. A brilliant smile spread across his face, so bright that I couldn't look away. He stared at me, and an emotion I couldn't explain crossed his face. He reminded me of a little boy who'd won his first championship. With his eyes holding mine, he brought two fingers to his lips, then pointed them at me.

I giggled like a teenager, bouncing on the tip of my toes with my hands clasped in front of my chest.

Moved to touch him, I waved frantically, as though the distance meant nothing, and I could feel him across the field. This was the fifth game of the season, but he pointed to me every time he saw me in the stands. And each time, my heart soared higher than any home run.

*I love you,* I mouthed across the field.

He grinned and I read his lips: *I love you, too*

I wished there was a way I could take back the past and all those times he felt alone.

But I couldn't.

I could only promise that every day for the rest of our lives, I would always show up for him.

***

Thank you for reading THE REMAKE. If you enjoyed Grace and Luke's story, please consider leaving a rating or review. This really helps indie authors.

If you'd like to read France and Colton's story next, check out THE MIX-UP, available now. Here's a quick blurb:

When the grumpy CEO finds me in his office and mistakes me for someone else, I realize this could be the answer to my family's financial problems. I just didn't count on my heart to mess it up.

No one pays attention to me, the mailroom girl at Crawford Corporation, and I prefer it that way. Until Colton Crawford, the company's surly CEO, finds me in his office holding another woman's resume and offers me the Personal Assistant position on the spot so he can move on with his day. I try to correct him, only for him to increase the salary offer. It's not like I can't do the job, I'm more than qualified, and my family really needs the money. I vow to tell him everything… after payday.

Except, Colton makes me want things I haven't desired in a long time. I'm afraid that when I confess, I risk losing not only my job but the one person who sees the real me.

# ACKNOWLEDGMENT

I want to thank so many people who helped me finish this book.

To my readers, newsletter subscribers, and ARC team, you motivate me each day to write and create stories that I hope you'll love. Your comments and encouragement push me through my hardest days and I thank you for it.

To my Alpha and Beta readers, Gilda, Christine, and Karhyll, this book would not be what it is today without you. Your questions and reactions pushed me to dig deeper. Gilda and Christine, you supported me through some difficult times while writing and editing this book, I cannot thank you enough. Karhyll, I absolutely love the ending. You wanted one more scene, and I couldn't be happier with the final result. Thank you all so much!

To my family, my husband, and children, you are my rock. I cannot imagine my life without you and any inspiration of love and acceptance in my novels come from you.

# ABOUT THE AUTHOR

Eve Marian is a former journalist and public relations executive. She lives in a suburb of Toronto with her husband, two children, and a clever cat named Chase.

To receive the latest information on new releases, giveaways, promotions, and more, sign up for her newsletter at www.evemarian.com.

Made in United States
Troutdale, OR
03/01/2024

18101552R00228